SILENT RITUAL

ANDREW JAMES GREIG

Storm
PUBLISHING

This is a work of fiction. Names, characters, business, events and incidents are the products of the author's imagination. Any resemblance to actual persons, living or dead, or actual events is purely coincidental.

Ebook ISBN: 978-1-80508-479-2
Paperback ISBN: 978-1-80508-481-5

Cover design: Blacksheep
Cover images: Shutterstock

Published by Storm Publishing.
For further information, visit:
www.stormpublishing.co

ALSO BY ANDREW JAMES GREIG

The Girl in the Loch

A Song of Winter

The Devil's Cut

Whirligig

"Every Night & every Morn
Some to Misery are Born
Every Morn and every Night
Some are Born to sweet delight
Some are Born to sweet delight
Some are Born to Endless Night"
Auguries of Innocence, by William Blake 1803

PROLOGUE

When Lauren Martin eventually managed to open the front door, hands encumbered by the weight of two full carrier bags, her screams drew back the curtains.

Seaview Drive is an unremarkable street in a quiet and forgotten backwater in Northwest Glasgow. Twelve-storey apartments pack families close like battery hens and loom over a squat row of terrace houses huddled on the other side of the street. Built in the 1960s to house families from condemned inner-city slums, the buildings now protest their age like geriatrics. The terrace houses are numbered one to twenty and are eagerly sought after by those cloud-dwellers who yearn for the luxury of a patch of garden and front door at ground level. They nestle at the foot of their towering neighbours, stunted in the perpetual shade these gargantuans cast over an urban concrete jungle.

Number seventeen was unique only due to the shaft of sunlight that threaded between two adjacent tower blocks every midday, throwing a golden beam of light for almost an hour upon its bricks and rough mortar, windows and red rooftiles. Anyone of a religious persuasion might imagine some holy miracle occurred here – a virgin birth or other celestial sleight of hand captured in heaven's spotlight.

Inside, there are signs that differentiate this house from its seemingly identical neighbours. The pentagram etched onto a bedroom floor; the body weeping blood from a hundred deep wounds; the young man frozen into inaction with a knife still held in his hand.

ONE
AQUA

Julie Simpson's Monday shift finished at 7 p.m. By the time she left the hospital, it was nearer eight – emergencies stretched staff so thinly Julie could swear she was in danger of becoming transparent. She threw a light jacket over her nurse's uniform and joined the pedestrians thronging the pavement. Home was only a thirty-minute walk away, but she felt tired to her bones. When she saw the taxi, Julie raised her arm with relief, reassured to see a woman driver. She collapsed into the back seat with a heartfelt sigh. Sod the expense, she needed to be home. The anticipation of a long soak in the bath filled her thoughts as the taxi pulled away. Within minutes, she'd fallen asleep.

* * *

The taxi didn't stop at Julie's address. Instead, it continued driving to the city outskirts, turning into a quiet industrial estate all but deserted at this hour. The driver pulled open a warehouse door, drove the taxi inside and shut the door against prying eyes. Inside, the unit, industrial lighting illuminated a rack of garage tools, workbench and coils of rope. Incongruous in the setting, a hazmat suit hung on the wall.

The taxi driver switched on overhead extractors and donned the hazmat suit with some difficulty as she waited for the fans to reach full speed. She left the headpiece for later. On the floor, a pentagram had been drawn with precision. She walked the outline, head bowed in deference to the true gods, repeating a phrase in Latin.

'Aquam vitae aeternae offero.'

The Latin was badly mispronounced, spoken in a deeper voice than may have been expected, but there were no onlookers there to comment.

She stopped at the one point marked with an inverted triangle. There could be no doubt the sign for water was feminine. She raised both hands heavenwards in supplication.

From a pocket in the NBC suit she drew a flask, holding it up with the reverence of a priest officiating at a mass.

'Take this, all of you, and drink from it. This is the cup of My Blood, the Blood of the new and everlasting covenant. It will be shed for you and for all so that sins may be forgiven.'

She lowered the flask to her lips. Sipped, then let the rest of the flask's contents pour onto the symbol at her feet before delicately setting it onto the workbench. That had been done well, she thought. Water was the most important, that's why she had to start with that element first. The moon goddess, Clota – the goddess of the Clyde. She had to be paid her tribute first, and it had to be right.

Taking the NBC mask, she settled it over her blond hair and face and switched on the air valve. The ropes awaited, and it was going to be a long night.

In the back of the taxi, Julie slept through the entire ritual. She would never awaken again.

TWO
PINCUSHION

'I did it. I killed my dad.'

The camera must have been positioned high up on the wall, angled down on the gangly, adolescent youth folded in on himself at an interview table. He nervously swept lank hair away from his angular face with an automatic gesture, gaze lifting from contemplation of the bare table surface to stare straight into the camera lens. Teàrlach paused the video and studied the boy's expression, frozen in the moment when he confessed to the murder of his father. There was no anger, exultation or guilt evident – merely the empty features of a young man devoid of hope and accepting of his fate. Even through the low-quality rendering offered by the police recording, he could see intelligence in the boy's eyes, resignation rather than insolence in his slumped stance.

Man, not boy, Teàrlach corrected himself. Logan Martin was seventeen when sentenced two months ago and lucky to be handed the minimum twelve years for murder by the judge. Now he was eighteen and residing at His Majesty's expense in Barlinnie Prison where he was likely to remain until he reached thirty. Twelve years that should have been the best of his life constrained behind concrete and barbed wire.

The file open on his desk merely confirmed the court's findings. Logan had been discovered by the police at the murder scene, his father's blood on the knife he still held in one hand. Keith Martin's wife had arrived home with bags of shopping and opened the front door onto a bloodbath, letting loose a scream loud enough to attract their neighbours' attention. They'd called the police, providing a running commentary with the fever pitch excitement of sport commentators.

Chloe, Teàrlach's young office manager, had the emergency call audio on file. She pressed play with a manicured finger, and recordings from multiple phones sequentially narrated a domestic tragedy in breathless voices on an otherwise quiet Sunday in June.

'There's a man with a knife.'

'Someone's been stabbed – it's the dad I think.'

'She's gone inside. There – can ye no hear her screaming? You'd better come quick before she gets it an' all!'

'The boy's got a blade. He's just standing there covered in blood.'

An ice-cream van had played 'Greensleeves' in the background, supplying a surrealist soundtrack to the calls. The van stayed there all the way through, from the first arrival of the police until a body bag signalled the end of the act. Catering to rubber-necking locals with 99's, ice lollies and sweets as the crowd grew ever larger. Thanks to the ubiquitous mobile phone, high-definition photographs catalogued each moment. The view from front door into the hall, various shades of red caught by the noon sun as it shone a beam as accurate as a stone-age megalithic monument aligned to the summer solstice. Logan standing unnaturally frozen in place like an actor who'd forgotten his lines. The mother, Lauren Martin, dragging her catatonic daughter out of the house, eyes wild with fear and legs stepping high and awkwardly over tins and bottles newly spilt from shopping bags. Jade Martin, sixteen years old, extending one arm out to her brother inviting him to run away with her, the other held fast in her mother's fiercely protective grip. The police, approaching Logan with caution, shouting at him to *DROP THE WEAPON, DROP THE WEAPON*. Guns, black and sinister, pointing at his body, at his head until he lay prostrate on the ground before them, arms stretched out like a supplicant begging for mercy. Mercy he hadn't shown to his father, collapsed on the hallway floor like a pile of discarded clothes soaked in blood. Logan bundled roughly into the back of a police car, head forced down, wrists secured.

Teàrlach had the photographs spread over his desk, timestamps visible on each one. There were even a handful of videos Dee had scraped from the internet, but they all played the same feature, just from differing angles and with varying quality of camerawork. She'd wryly commented they should reassemble the videos, call it the director's cut.

The three of them gathered in his office. Teàrlach with his back to the window, summer sun catching the River Clyde and somehow managing to even turn that pharmaceutical drain into a jewelled ribbon. Skyscrapers shimmered like mirages in the heat; a fine dust covered everything and everyone. An air of lethargy pervaded the small office, the task they had been given appeared meaningless. He'd written *Project Sisyphus* on the box file cover.

The private investigator's two other members of staff were similarly affected by the heat. Chloe, having worked for him for two years, took the only other available chair, establishing seniority over the new hire. She idly handled one of the photographs, unperturbed by the content and turning it a full 180 degrees until the dead father's head pointed upwards. Teàrlach could still see the scar on her neck where makeup had run in the heat. A band of white refusing to tan even in this weather. A permanent reminder of the time she had tried to end it all and how close he'd been to finding her dead.

'Looks guilty to me,' Chloe stated. She replaced the photograph so it joined the others, swept long, black braids away from her forehead and sighed heavily.

'Why are we even looking at this?' Dee chipped in as she leaned against the doorway, catching what little breeze struggled through the open window. The air smelled of city – an aromatic blend of traffic, people and tar as roads had begun to melt under the fierce onslaught of an unnaturally hot sun. He caught her eyes on his, grey-green and curious. Her freckles had come out in force – the redhead's standard startled response to even faint sunshine.

It was a good question. The murder had been two months ago, midday on midsummer, and described by the police as an 'open and shut case'. One suspect and one confession. Logan's father's body was described by the prosecution as looking like a pincushion. Forensics had struggled to count the wounds inflicted by the knife. Had Logan been a few months older, he'd have been facing life instead of a meagre twelve years. But now he was yesterday's news, and everyone had moved on. Everyone except his aunt.

She'd arrived unannounced yesterday, introduced herself as Nicole Martin – Keith Martin's only sibling. The resemblance was there in her overlarge round head, stout body, sensible round glasses perched on a snubby nose. Teàrlach's first impression was of a cartoon character or Lego figure brought to life. She'd been accompanied by a tall, willowy woman with a Scandinavian accent who she'd introduced as her wife. Apart from a heavily accented 'pleased to meet you' the wife remained silent, allowing Nicole to do all the talking.

'I want you to find out how my brother, Keith, really died,' she'd opened. 'I don't believe for one second that Logan killed him.' She had fixed him with a look that dared him to contradict her.

'The evidence was fairly clear...'

She had cut Teàrlach off with her fist slamming down on the table.

'NO! I'll not have it! Whatever happened in that house, it's not what we've been told. I know the boy, he's a gentle soul.' She had momentarily run out of steam, facing him with cheeks inflated and red with anger. 'It's the others you need to look at. Lauren and Jade.' She had exchanged a troubled look with her Scandinavian partner, their hands sought contact, held each other for support. 'Monsters!'

Teàrlach had filed the description away for consideration. It was clear there was little love lost between Nicole and the two women in her brother's life. He dug deeper.

'Why do you say that?'

Nicole turned towards her partner, received a nod of encouragement.

'Lauren took an instant dislike to me from the moment we met. Then she poisoned her daughter against me as well. The things they called me to my face!'

'But you kept a good relationship with your nephew, Logan?'

Her expression had softened at his name. 'Logan was always a sweet boy, kind and attentive. Lauren and Jade treated Keith like dirt – always complaining there was never enough money. I had to help him out sometimes. God knows what they spent the money on. It wasn't on decent furniture or clothes, that's for sure!'

'Do you have any evidence? Is there an alibi or any mitigating factors that could help Logan?' He had asked more from politeness than from any expectation of the woman producing anything that the police hadn't already heard, considered, then rejected.

She had shaken her head. 'I don't have any evidence, but I know he couldn't have killed his father. He loved Keith – more than that woman.' She'd spat the last words out with undisguised vehemence.

'Lauren?'

She had nodded, then produced a handkerchief from inside her sleeve and dabbed at her eyes, glasses pushed up onto her forehead to allow access. The women linked hands, her partner's anxious gaze alighting on Teàrlach, followed by a tight smile.

'I don't know what I can do for you. The evidence is stacked against your nephew. He pleaded guilty.' Teàrlach had pronounced these words with an air of finality. Whatever the woman thought about her nephew's supposed innocence – the bloodied knife still in his hand when the police arrived said otherwise.

'You *must* investigate! That boy will spend the best years of his life locked away with awful men and he didn't do it. Something made him confess. He's protecting them – Lauren and Jade – he's giving his life for them, and they don't deserve it.'

'What makes you think Logan made a false confession?' He had watched her face carefully as she wrestled for an answer.

'I've known him since he was a baby. Logan was the sweetest child...' She had stopped to dab at her eyes again, breathing deeply. 'He wouldn't hurt a fly. I just know he couldn't have done this to his own father.'

'You don't feel the same way about Lauren or Jade?'

She had sniffed. 'I'm not the parent, Mr Paterson. I'm allowed to have favourites. Jade is a nice enough girl, but she's only ever been interested in herself, never a thought for anyone else. As for Lauren, well. He could have done better!' Nicole had glared at them, searching for anyone brave enough to contradict her.

'I still don't know how I can help.' Teàrlach had responded.

She'd opened her clutch bag at that point and slammed a packet down as a challenge.

'There's ten thousand pounds. I've more if you need it. How much of your time will that buy?'

Teàrlach had been nonplussed, unsure that this woman in front of him was entirely sane and even more unsure how to approach a case like this.

'A week, more or less,' he'd answered.

She'd peered intently into his face with eyes magnified by the round lenses.

'Then see what you can find. In a week. More or less. You can contact me at any time.' She had handed over a business card, gold scalloped edge and the words Martin Kennels with an address in Thornliebank, Glasgow. A gold paw print aligned with an email, another paw print next to her mobile number. With that, she had turned and marched out of the office before he could refuse such an open-ended and hopeless task, her mismatched willowy shadow keeping close company.

Now the three of them stared at the evidence they'd been able to pull from social media and the press. The interview recording had already been retrieved, then saved where a police search wouldn't find it. Dee covered her tracks with the care of a professional hacker, which – considering the illegality of how she'd been able to pull the recording from a supposedly secure police server – was just as well.

'What do you want us to do?' Dee enquired.

Teàrlach turned away to look out over the city, baking in a late August heatwave. Even the traffic sounded sluggish, engines labouring up hills, airliners dragging vapour trails behind them as they headed for the shelter of rare clouds. The city air felt heavy, starved of oxygen. He failed to find any inspiration outside the window, took a deep breath in an attempt to dispel the lethargy laying claim to his body. He thought of Sisyphus pushing that boulder up the hill.

'We investigate. Like it says on the door.' He picked up his car keys and notebook. 'Chloe, see what you can find out about the Martins. Call around the local shops; see if they used to have arguments, what were people's impressions of the family dynamics? Did the boy and his dad get along? Dee, see if any of the family had previous: assaults; drug use; even parking tickets. Is there anything the police tried to conceal? Financial problems. Who benefits from his death?'

'Where are you going? Are we actually taking this case on?' Chloe asked in incredulous tones.

'There's nothing else on the books and she's paid for a week,' Teàrlach replied. 'I'm going to have a look at the scene, talk to the next-door neighbours. It's worth a try.' He made it as far as the door before calling back to them. 'See if Logan is accepting visitors. If he *is* innocent, then he'll want to talk.'

'It's up for sale, the Martin house – with Pritchard's Estate Agency. Want me to make an appointment for three?' Chloe shouted after him. Teàrlach raised a thumb in response.

THREE
PENTAGRAM

Seaview Drive was nowhere near the coast. Even with powerful binoculars, all you'd be able to see were the multiple blocks of flats opposite: twelve identical levels of stacked humanity. They shared the same desultory patch of grass optimistically seeded with young trees, desperately clinging to stakes for survival. The nearest waterway was the Forth and Clyde Canal somewhere nearby, offering nature a perilous foothold in a region town planners termed high urban density. Teàrlach parked outside number seventeen, made obvious by the For Sale sign which sagged on its temporary wooden pole as if it, too, was exhausted by the heat.

The Martin house was no different to all the others, a long line of two-storey terraced buildings dwarfed by the high-rises all around them. They mostly shared the same joke – model boats or china lighthouses in the windows, anchor-shaped door knockers. Number seventeen had none of that but then it had been stripped bare – even the curtains were gone. Teàrlach peered through the front windows, holding a hand against the glass to reduce the glare of the sun. The room was open-plan, kitchen units at the back and another window opening out to a small patch of garden. It was an altogether unremarkable house, only differentiated from its neighbours by facing a gap between the high-rises.

A car drew up with Pritchard's Estate Agency branding. The young driver parked behind Teàrlach's vehicle and climbed out, full of false bonhomie and desperate to clinch a sale.

'Mr Paterson?' He eagerly extended a hand.

'Yes. Thanks for arranging a viewing so quickly.'

'Not at all. Pleasure. I'm Simon, Simon Pritchard. Here's my card. Let me just find the... there we are.' He produced a key and opened the front door, inviting Teàrlach in with a flourish of his arm.

Teàrlach paused in the doorway. 'Do you mind if I look around on my own? I like to imagine myself moving in, decide where I'm putting the furniture. That sort of thing.'

He saw Simon's face fall, saw the excuse beginning to form that clients must be accompanied.

'I'll be sure to ask you any questions when I've had a quick look around, show me where the meters are and all those practical things. I just want a few minutes to decide whether it's right for me.' Teàrlach added his most winning smile, unused muscles protesting at being so abused.

The salesman was already mentally counting his commission. 'Sure. I understand – I'll just be in my car catching up on paperwork.'

Teàrlach waited until he'd closed his car door, heard the engine start up and the whine from an air-conditioning unit join the mechanical chorus, then entered the hallway. He had no trouble in overlaying the scene from the photographs. A new hall carpet had been fitted. Beige wool and nylon mix replaced bloodstains and death. The walls sported a new coat of magnolia emulsion, but in the daylight, he could see the outline of blood spatter showing through like an imperfect memory.

The house retained a miasma of death even over the sweet chemical tang of new carpet and paint. He couldn't put a finger on it – a sense of danger, a place to be avoided. An ability handed down from unknown generations of ancestors, locked away as genetic memory to enhance his own chance of survival. Maybe such an ability would die out with modern life with its well-lit streets and civilisation. Then again, Teàrlach reconsidered, maybe a sixth sense was needed today more than ever.

The hallway told him nothing, merely confirming this was where the murder had happened. Teàrlach imagined the father standing there, arms attempting to block the knife as it plunged repeatedly into his torso. Sliding between ribs, thudding against bone. He took a photo, an angle that showed up the remnant stains which two coats of cheap magnolia were unable to disguise. Struck by a thought, he wrote *arms* in his notebook. There hadn't been a mention of hand cuts or arm wounds in the forensics summary, and Keith Martin would have instinctively tried to defend himself. A cursory inspection of the ground floor provided no additional insights. The Martins had all but been swept clean from the property, eradicated down even to the missing lampshades and bulbs. He could have believed nothing had happened here at all except for the stubborn stains on the hallway wall. Standing at the front room window, Teàrlach gazed out at the tower blocks, balconies sporting sun loungers and deck chairs despite the north facing aspect. It takes a certain kind of misplaced optimism to sunbathe in permanent shadow. Perhaps you needed that positivity when life has dealt you an unplayable hand. He caught the estate agent watching him, gave a palm-up salute and headed for the stairs.

As a child, he'd run upstairs as fast as he could to escape the nameless terror that pursued him; then, counter to any logic, he'd run just as quickly back down again once his mission had been accomplished. There was a sense of that now as he ascended, slow foot after slow foot until he arrived at the landing with his head as dizzy as a mountaineer requiring oxygen. Teàrlach set his mind to the job, brushing off childish fears with irritation. At least the temperature was cooler inside. The sun would only hit the house in the middle of the day. Even in high summer, tower blocks lay in wait to catch the sun and throw the building back into shadow.

Upstairs held no architectural surprises – a shared bathroom lay in front of him, his face staring back from a mirror over the sink. Shower over the bath, toilet with black plastic seat. A smell of damp pervaded, almost certainly emanating from underneath loose tiling by the bath where years of showering had soaked and swollen floor timbers. The master bedroom lay at the front of the house, built-in wardrobes leaving a double bed sized rectangular gap where the carpet retained an original hue of darker green. The cupboards were all empty, waiting patiently for the next influx of human detritus. There were no memories here, apart from patches on the walls where paintings or photographs once held meaning. The boy's bedroom was situated at the back of the house, window facing out towards an identical row of terrace houses like a mirror image. A strip of dying grass filled the garden, yellowed with thirst. He could view other gardens from here, scattered snapshots of the residents' lives coloured with plants, vegetable patches and broken furniture.

Teàrlach spent as much time here as he dared, prising up the carpet in search of loose floorboards – places where Logan Martin might have concealed his hate and anger. The room was as empty as a nun's sex life and felt much the same way. Whatever energy or madness had driven Logan to stab his father to death had left no trace.

He entered the girl's room last, opening the door to an airless, windowless space. There would have been room for a single bed and a chest of drawers but not a lot else. Teàrlach tried to imagine Jade Martin cowering in here as her father was brutally slaughtered at the foot of the stairs. Had she tried to barricade herself in? Another note added to his notebook. The room held an oppressive air which he put down to the lack of any windows. This was more of a storage cupboard than a bedroom, repurposed to meet the needs of a growing family. He was glad to leave, then stopped as the carpet caught underneath the door. Teàrlach raised the offending section higher, peeling back from the corner of the room until half the floor was uncovered. There, outlined in precise geometric detail, lay a star pentagram with symbols carved above each apex. His phone clicked multiple times, committing the picture to digital memory, then he pulled the carpet back into place.

Teàrlach left the house, meeting Simon the estate agent as he headed towards the front door.

'Well, what do you think? It's a good size for the money, reduced for a quick sale.'

Two boys pulled to a stop, gravel spraying from bicycle tyres.

'Hey big man! You don't want to live there. It's a murderer's house.'

They pedalled away with gleeful laughter as Simon took a step towards them, features contorted with anger.

'I'm sorry, but I'm no longer interested,' Teàrlach informed him as he walked away, ignoring the estate agent's protestations and with his head full of questions. Once he'd parked up away from the house, he called Chloe.

'I'm sending you a picture of something I found under Jade Martin's bedroom carpet. It's a pentagram, so I need you to find out if Jade was simply a Goth or whether she was involved with a local coven or something.'

'Coven?' Chloe expressed incredulity in a single word.

'I don't know. Coven, witchcraft, black magic. Could be a teenage thing, but see what you can find out.'

'Will do.'

'Oh and ask Dee if she can access the full coroner's report. I don't remember seeing anything about knife injuries to Keith Martin's hands or arms. There should be a mention if he was defending himself. Also see if there's any mention of Jade trying to barricade her bedroom door. I don't know what furniture she had, but her room would be pretty much impregnable with something jammed against the door. If her brother had just gone completely insane, I would have expected her to try and do something. I'm going to try the neighbours each side – see if they heard anything.'

Simon drove past in his Pritchard's Estate Agency car with a face like thunder, too angry at losing a sale to notice his client parked up a street away.

'And send a note to Pritchard's Estate Agency thanking them for their time, but I've decided against moving to Glasgow.'

'It's a mean city,' Chloe countered.

'Aye, and don't we know it. See you guys later.' He cut the call and drove back to number seventeen.

Number sixteen favoured a china lighthouse on the windowsill, blue and white bands painted in horizontal stripes. Teàrlach rapped an anchor-shaped door knocker and waited. He didn't have to wait long. A woman, slightly stooped and with the friendliest smile, opened the door. Two bright eyes surveyed him from head to toe. The smell of lavender wafted out into the sun-baked air, hanging around her like a fragrant cloud.

'Yes dear, what can I do for you?' Her voice cracked with age. Classical music played quietly in the background.

'My name is Teàrlach Paterson, I'm a private investigator. I was wondering if I might ask you some questions.' He could see the smile evaporate as the shutters came down.

'I don't have time to talk to you newspaper people.' She

pushed the door only for Teàrlach's hand to interrupt, offering her a business card.

'Excuse me, young man, or I'll have to call the police.' She squinted at the card, pulling on glasses that hung on a cord around her neck. 'What's this? Private investigator.' She continued reading. 'Teàrlach – I've not heard that name since I was a girl.' She looked at him more closely, analysing his features in the hope of finding a resemblance to someone long gone.

'I'm named after my grandfather. He was from Harris.'

'Well, why didn't you say so, come in and have a cup of tea. I've made cake, would you like some?'

He followed her into the front room, separated from the kitchen by a wall with a serving hatch.

'You sit here,' – she pointed at an armchair covered in a floral print – 'I'll get us tea and cake. Do you take sugar?' Her voice faded, coming back with the question as she peered at him through the hatch.

'No, thanks. As it comes, please.'

There followed the sound of a kettle being filled and saucers being retrieved from cupboards.

'Where on Harris?' She appeared birdlike in the opening once more, head tilted sideways in an effort to hear more clearly.

'Losgaintir, opposite Taransay.'

'Well, there's a thing.' She returned, carrying a tray set with teapot, cups and saucers, which she proceeded to unload onto a table beside him.

'I'll get the cake.' She returned to the kitchen, leaving time for him to continue looking around. The room hadn't been redecorated since the terrace was built in the 1960s or '70s. The wallpaper had a large block pattern in random sizes, orange and purple predominated the palette making Teàrlach's eyes hurt. He had a concern that the design could set off a migraine attack. A painting of a young Asian woman with a blue skin tone took central place on the opposing wall – he'd seen similar prints as a child. Beside them were old sepia photographs of a fisherman involved in mending creels or putting out to sea. He moved closer for a better look.

'Ah! Thought you might recognise the view.'

'Where is it?'

'Looking across to Taransay. They're taken from Luskentyre Beach – your grandad may be in one of the photos.'

He shook his head. 'I never met him, and I've not seen any photographs. Wouldn't be able to recognise him if he was there.'

She looked scandalised for a moment, then sighed heavily.

'I don't know. Everybody rushes about these days, but are they going anywhere?'

The question remained unanswered.

'Sit down, sit down,' she commanded. 'Have some of my Victoria sponge.' A plate appeared in front of his face, and he thanked her, taking a bite and trying not to look at the garish wallpaper.

'So, what are you *investigating*?' she added impishly, sitting opposite him with beady eyes and a smile on her lips.

Teàrlach imagined she'd make a good fox if reincarnation lay in wait for her.

'It's to do with the murder of Keith Martin.'

'Yes, I rather thought it might be.'

'I'm trying to find out why he was killed. By all accounts the son, Logan, was a quiet, gentle boy.' Teàrlach lifted a bone china cup, attempted to fit a finger through the handle and when that proved impossible, lifted it like a mug. The tea was so hot it scalded his lips, then his fingertips started to send urgent signals to let go. The cup returned to the saucer faster than he intended, but the bone china survived the impact.

She studied him impassively. 'The Martins were a lovely family. It's terrible what happened. Terrible.' She took a sip from her own cup, seemingly impervious to the heat and smacking her lips in appreciation. 'As for the boy being gentle – well, I could mention a few things.'

Teàrlach waited in vain a few long seconds, then asked encouragingly, 'How do you mean?'

Her lips drew tightly together. 'I'd rather not say.'

He took another bite of cake whilst they remained in stalemate.

'Lovely cake.' Teàrlach held it up in confirmation before taking another bite. He had missed lunch altogether, so it was a welcome snack. 'Did they fight at all? Did you hear arguments or were you aware of any underlying tensions that might explain the events of that day?'

She thoughtfully considered before answering, returning her cup to its saucer prior to making judgement.

'These walls are thin, Mr Paterson. Not like the stone cottage I grew up in. Sometimes, I hear things I'd rather not – if you ken my meaning?'

Teàrlach nodded wisely, the cake adhering to the roof of his mouth and necessitating more saliva to process than he had available at that instant. He eyed his tea as backup.

'Well, Keith wasn't a drinking man, but he'd had a skinful that morning. Shouting and crashing into the furniture. It sounded like an earthquake was happening next door!'

She leaned in closer, eyes widening. Teàrlach stopped chewing under such intense scrutiny.

'I think he was possessed!' Her gaze automatically locked onto a crucifix hanging on the wall.

Teàrlach managed to swallow. He could feel his eyebrows raise.

'Possessed?'

She nodded. 'Keith didn't sound like himself – and he dabbled in things he shouldn't.'

She made the sign of the cross to ward off evil. Teàrlach thought of the pentagram in the daughter's bedroom.

'What things were those? Were they satanists or something?' He felt that he was finally getting somewhere.

Her scandalised expression told him he'd missed the mark. The teacup went back to her lips, and she observed him shrewdly as she sipped hot tea.

'Gambling, Mr Paterson – *When they had nailed him to the stake, they distributed his outer garments by casting lots.* Matthew 27:35,' she added as way of confirmation.

He nodded wisely, searching the room for inspiration before she started on a religious rant. His gaze came to rest on a stuffed toy cat, holding the living room door open.

'Unusual doorstop.'

She followed his gaze, twisting awkwardly in her chair to face backwards.

'That's my Poppy.' She spoke as if the creature was alive, turning back to Teàrlach with moisture in her eyes.

He looked again and realised the 'toy' was the work of a taxidermist. Now that he had a proper look, Teàrlach saw that the cat shared little of a stuffed toy's cuteness. This creature bulged in odd places as if ravaged by disease, its limbs held the pose of a torture victim which was only reinforced by the unfortunate expression frozen on the cat's face.

'How lovely.' His words fell far short of the compliment he'd aimed for.

She didn't appear to notice. 'He was such a comfort to me – and then I found him in the garden. Someone had killed him.' She produced an embroidered handkerchief, held to her nose for a wet blow. 'Doing that to a sweet, defenceless animal.'

'Who'd do such a thing?' Teàrlach cast the lure, waited for a bite.

Her lips clamped shut again as she dabbed at her eyes with the handkerchief.

'I have a good idea, but I couldn't prove anything. Poppy used to go in all the gardens – everyone loved him.'

Not everyone, Teàrlach thought.

'You think it was Logan, or one of the Martins?' he prompted.

Her eyes narrowed, letting him know this line of questioning was unwelcome.

'No one could wish for better neighbours. I was sad to see them go – of course, they couldn't stay. Not after that.'

'No, I suppose not.' Teàrlach wondered at her mental acuity following such a conflicting statement. He began to feel that his time was being wasted. Whatever the old lady knew – and she had hinted that she knew something – she was clammed up tighter than a banker's wallet. Teàrlach tried a last throw of the dice.

'Do you suppose the neighbour on the other side might be able to provide some insight about Keith Martin's murder?'

A soft smile played at the edge of her lips. 'Donald? No, he's hardly ever at home, not since his mother died. Such a shame, they were very close and such a lovely woman. He helps look after my garden you know.'

She nodded at the next house along, away from the Martins'.

'I meant their neighbours on the other side, at number eighteen?' Teàrlach clarified.

She laughed at this, putting her cup and saucer down in case she spilled scalding tea on her lap.

'Well, dear me. I shouldn't think so, dear.'

'Why is that?' Teàrlach asked.

'Because they're dead,' she answered matter-of-factly. 'Died a year ago and no one's been able to find out who their relatives are, so the house just sits empty.'

'I'm sorry to hear that.' He *was* sorry. That was the only other likely source of inside information into the Martin family dynamics taken away. The tea had cooled sufficiently for him to hold the cup, and he blew across the surface before risking another sip.

'Course, the police should have investigated their deaths if you ask me.' Her gaze fixed on his again, like a bird that's just spied a particularly juicy worm.

'Why do you say that?'

'Because the boy probably killed them as well.' She made the accusation of murder so casually that Teàrlach doubted he'd heard her correctly.

He studied her over the rim of his teacup, as she unconcernedly bit into her Victoria sponge with all this talk of death.

'Do you know how they died?' Teàrlach began to wonder how addled her mind was.

She gestured towards the window with a half-eaten slice of cake. 'Well, it wasn't old age that did for them, that's for sure. The police were there all day before the ambulance came to fetch them. That's not normal.'

The last of the cake was transferred efficiently into her mouth, and her jaw described circles as she ate. She reminded him of a ruminant thoughtfully chewing its cud. Teàrlach waited until she swallowed.

'Was he violent, the boy?'

Thin lips smacked together in appreciation of the last cake crumbs. 'I never saw him hit anyone.' She spoke with an air of consideration, making a pronouncement of the boy's character with the care of a high court judge. 'But there was always something off about him – do you ken what I'm saying?'

Something in his expression must have answered in the negative as she quickly continued. 'Well, the proof's in the pudding. What he did to his poor father.'

Teàrlach finished his tea, made an excuse about beating the rush-hour traffic, and headed back to the office. He'd enquired after one murder and had potentially come out with three. His witness was unreliable, quite possibly senile yet she was adamant that Logan was responsible for killing her cat. If he *had* killed her cat, then it wasn't that unlikely he'd have killed something larger. Something as large as his father? The woman was either batshit crazy or there was more going on in the forgotten municipal dumping ground of Seaview Drive with its anchors, lighthouses, taxidermy and pentagrams than at first appeared.

FOUR
POETRY

When the sun eventually set on Seaview Drive, five hours had passed since Teàrlach's brief visit. Lights came on in the terraced houses; televisions cast a selective eye into other people's more interesting lives until the street resembled a row of gleaming teeth. Teeth that needed fixing because numbers seventeen and eighteen remained as dark, gaping black voids ruining the illusion of a happy smile. Across the road, skyscraper incisors stretched up towards an orange sky stained by a distant sunset and the spill from a myriad high pressure sodium streetlamps. There may have been stars above, but the city's population had been blinded by light, so the crescent moon would only be spotted by the few – a silver boomerang curving inexorably away from the earth. The ice-cream van made another visit, chimes suitably muted for a more clandestine trade of tiny hand-wrapped parcels that promised release but delivered ensnarement.

Teàrlach's seat in the corner of the Rifleman's bar offered him the best view of the door. On the occasions when he felt the need for company, he'd be found here in his local, pint of bitter on the table and book in his hand. He sat as far away from the TV screen as possible. The other punters couldn't prevent themselves from checking every few seconds – each conversation punctuated with a furtive glance at the football, news or soaps. They were as desperate as junkies for their next fix, scarcely registering the quiet man with his pint and book.

Normally, he'd have brought along poetry, one of the leather-bound volumes his aunt had bequeathed. Her tastes had veered towards the Romantics – Blake, Wordsworth, Shelley. Teàrlach had scanned them at first with bewilderment, wondering what made her imagine he'd have any interest in the flowery outpourings of a bunch of dead poets; then he'd come to appreciate how they articulated existence with all its imperfections. The book he now held wasn't one of those. After returning to the office with his findings, he'd concluded investigating the pentagram was the only tangible lead in establishing what might have happened at number seventeen Seaview Drive. Chloe and Dee had drawn blanks with all the other lines of enquiry. Logan Martin refused to see or talk to any visitors. He kept to himself in prison, avoiding the other inmates. None of the family had been in trouble with the law, all leading a quiet and blameless existence until two months ago, as far as they could tell. If the boy was a Hedonistic killer, murdering creatures for thrills until he needed the biggest hit of all, wouldn't that have been picked up earlier? Then the neighbours – something must have been amiss with their deaths, or the police wouldn't have spent the best part of the day at the house before removing the bodies. He made a note to ask Dee to look into it.

The daughter, Jade, had left the local high school without telling anyone where she and her mother were going. Financially, they were doing all right. The father had worked as a baker. Early starts at a local factory churning out breakfast rolls for the workers. Steady work, Dee had said, but he didn't make much dough. The joke hadn't raised a laugh. The mother, Lauren, was a hairdresser – maybe still was but not at the Hair Today Studio in Partick where she worked until the day her husband was murdered. Teàrlach could sympathise with her. Every customer would be bursting to steer the conversation away from 'going anywhere nice on holiday?' to 'I'm so sorry to hear the dreadful news' – waiting in anticipation for the next gory details to emerge.

The Martins, it appeared, were indistinguishable from every other family trying to make enough to survive. Facing the next energy bill with the sinking realisation that even the cheap package holiday they all looked forward to would remain out of reach for another year. In their neighbourhood, they were most likely seen as the better off residents – own front door, front and rear gardens, place to park. There was an inversion to the usual snobbery; here the high-rise flats looked up to the terraced houses down on the ground.

Teàrlach knew poverty. His mother had appeared in court when he was still a child, found guilty of shoplifting. Basic groceries hastily shoved into a shopping bag so she could feed her two boys before the advent of foodbanks. His dad would have been off somewhere, leaving her to cope for weeks on end without any income and then returning as if nothing needed to be discussed. He'd controlled the finances, held all the bank cards as another means of controlling her. The only time his mother dared complain to his father, he'd punched her again and again until both boys leapt to her defence, screaming at him to stop. Teàrlach had been seven, his brother five – both thrown off like vermin. That was the last time he could remember they had lived together as a family, the social made sure of that. Teàrlach taken by his mother's elder sister to live on the Isle of Mull;

his mother taken to a refuge with his younger brother. They were meant to be safe there, but his father discovered where they were hiding, set fire to the house out of some twisted idea of revenge. Teàrlach learned they'd taken days to die, spending their last pain-filled hours on earth in hospital beds and drugged out of their minds on morphine drips. His dad was given thirty years, let out after twenty. Now he was rotting from his lungs outwards in a care home, and Teàrlach was cheering for team cancer.

He sipped his pint, washed away the memories. It did him no good to think about the past. All the people here in the bar could tell similar stories. The young women's laughs concealing the hurt; the old men's eyes shaded with guilt or pain; the woman serving behind the bar with only months left to live and out of all the regulars had shared her story only with him.

'I can tell you because you'll keep it to yourself,' she had confided all those weeks ago. 'I have to tell someone, or I'll go mad.'

'What about your man?' he had asked, head inclined towards the fifty-something guy with a beer belly and loud voice, busy exchanging good-natured insults with regulars over by the TV.

'Him?' she'd responded, a frown appearing as if she'd never considered telling her husband that her life was measured in months. 'He'd never be able to cope. It would kill him!'

Teàrlach watched her now whilst he drank his pint – polishing glasses, keeping busy as if that delayed the moment when she could no longer keep pretending. A cheer went up, heads automatically gravitated to the screen where a football pitch had been shrunk to a sixty-five-inch diagonal. Someone had scored and the barmaid's smile made her appear ten years younger.

He returned his attention to the book. The local librarian

had viewed his worn cardboard library card with pity, pushing a new application form his way before issuing him with a sleek plastic card. The book he eventually was able to take out was *A Layman's Guide to Ritual – A Pagan Primer*. He'd selected it due to the pentagram on the front cover, but the librarian's disapproving expression left him in no doubt as to her opinion of his selection. Teàrlach continued his research into the use of pentagrams, surrounded by enthused football fans and under the thoughtful gaze of a dying bartender.

The book was only serving to confuse him more. The author was at pains to provide a balanced commentary, batting for good and for evil. On the good side, it was used as a Christian symbol – the five points representative of Christ's five wounds on the cross. It also represented a place of safety, a refuge from evil. That made sense. If Jade realised her older brother was capable of stabbing their father to death, she would seek somewhere she felt protected. Teàrlach had invented a similar symbol as a child, imagining a circle drawn around himself, his brother and mother. He drew it in his mind at night, a circle in molten gold to encompass and protect them from evil. Even after that had been shown to fail spectacularly, he continued the ritual when he moved in with his aunt – although now the evil was formless but all the more real for that.

The pentagram was also used in the Wicca religion, the points representing spirit, water, fire, earth and air. Teàrlach viewed the photograph he'd taken with his phone, one foot in view preventing the girl's carpet from rolling back. There were the same triangular symbols at each apex. As if to lead the reader gently into what was coming, the author described how satanists favoured the pentagram drawn upside down and with a goat's head in the middle. Finally, the book described a supposed link between the female deity Venus and her celestial namesake's eight-year journey as seen from earth. The planet describing a figure termed the five Petals of Venus, or a rough pentagram in the night sky. This symbol used as a means of worshipping the goddess before Christianity turned it on its head to prevent the deification of women, making it the Devil's mark. He couldn't be bothered wading through the rest of the book, leaving it face down on the table and finishing his beer.

'Another pint?' the barmaid called out from the bar, pint glass already angled next to the pump in readiness.

Teàrlach nodded, making his way over to join her.

'Thanks, Mags.'

She operated the pump with practised ease, pulling the glass away at the last minute to leave a head of smooth froth and placed it in front of him. He swiped his phone, clocking up another debit without the physical trauma of parting with hard-earned cash.

'You into witchcraft now?' A half-smile played around the corners of her mouth.

'Research. It's a load of shite.' He indicated the book on the table with a tilt of his head.

'You going to cast a spell for me?' Her voice was for him only, her expression half-serious.

'I'll do that, Mags. It will have more effect than talking to the Big Man upstairs – think he's given up on us.'

Mags laughed. 'Aye, right enough.' Her expression hardened. 'He'd not be welcome here; I can tell you that!'

'Who's not welcome?' The shout came from her partner, ears tuned to detect key words from the other end of the bar.

'Nobody, Joe, just having a joke,' Mags called back. She shrugged apologetically, moved on to the next customer.

Teàrlach regained his seat, letting his attention wander around the bar, then back to his pint. Mags still appeared completely well, no sign of the disease ravaging through her blood. She should by rights be in hospital, letting them flush her body with chemo in a last-ditch attempt to give her another few months. She was having none of it – the hair loss, the sickness, being treated like the ultimate victim. This way she kept everything normal; delayed the inevitable. She and her man. Joking, drinking and loving until the end.

Teàrlach left the bar, made his way back home through air turned torpid in the heat. He spoke a few words under his breath to the night, a plea for Death to let Mags go this time and take someone more deserving of a painful end. His words were absorbed by the thick air, leaving no trace of ever having been spoken. They were as useless as the golden circles he drew for protection, as meaningless as the golden band on his mother's ring finger.

Home was a first-floor apartment in a three-storey redbrick in Hyndland, close enough to Glasgow University for students to frequent the area, too expensive for most of them to live there. Teàrlach lifted the lower sash in hope of a fresh breeze, letting in the sounds of the city. A shared park bisected his street and the one opposite, trees providing privacy from neighbours twenty metres away and offering a welcome relief to the relentless urban landscape. Glasgow used to be called the dear green place – a translation from the Gaelic Glaschu. He couldn't have lived there without being close to grass and trees – those ten years on Mull were part of who he now was. Teàrlach made a fresh pot of coffee, collapsed on the settee and streamed a random playlist that promised mellow sounds.

He felt anything but mellow. The job he'd taken was proving as difficult as he had first thought. A murder case with the guilty party safely locked away and refusing to talk; the only other witnesses had taken themselves off without leaving any forwarding address. He wasn't even sure what his client wanted – *find out what really happened, find out who killed my brother*. The answers to those questions were already in the public domain. The only thing he'd been able to find that jarred with the official narrative was the pentagram on the daughter's bedroom floor, but that could simply be an adolescent phase or even a previous occupant. He'd taken ten thousand pounds off the client, money that he was fairly certain he would have to return to her tomorrow.

FIVE
PERVERSION

Dee left the office, accelerating away from gridlocked traffic on her bike and enjoying the wind in her face. Home was a riverside apartment – not one of those swanky warehouse conversions that left little change from a million; this was a more modest development in Partick, only a few hundred thousand and a gift from her last employer. Tony Masterton had been responsible for setting her up with Teàrlach, a last request before the Glasgow gangster died, his body disappearing into the loch and never found. Sometimes, she imagined the Glasgow gangster had miraculously survived. The thought unsettled her more than she liked to admit. Dee shook it from her mind, turned into the underground car park serving the flats and made her way up to her apartment.

Teàrlach had told the client they'd paid for a week of their time and that was almost the first day done and dusted with no real progress. There also wasn't much call for her skill set now that she'd managed to find the original interview tapes. That was one advantage to the police entering the age of information technology – everything was turning digital and once evidence had been stored on a supposedly secure server, then it was game on.

She poured herself an ice-cold drink, opened the windows to a small balcony and stretched out on a settee to overlook the Clyde. The searches she'd been asked to do had all drawn a blank. None of the family had previous form, although the son stabbing his father to death had broken that unblemished record. Financially there was nothing untoward, the family struggling like most of the population in a declining economy. Nothing on forensics about Keith Martin's hands or arms showing defence wounds. The only question Teàrlach had asked of her that she hadn't been able to answer was who had profited from the father's death. With no life insurance, it appeared that everyone was out of pocket with the main wage earner gone.

Dee sipped at her drink, enjoying the sensation of cold coursing down her throat. Teàrlach had updated them when he'd returned to the office: the pentagram; the mother and daughter no longer living at the address and the cryptic comment made by the immediate neighbour regarding the recently deceased couple at number eighteen – '*the boy probably killed them as well*'. She'd been asked to investigate their deaths, and if she did manage to find any link involving Logan Martin, then that wasn't going to be well received by his aunt. What the hell, it's not as if she had to pass on whatever information she found.

Teàrlach had said the couple died a year ago, so she started with the local newspaper in August last year. Like most newspapers, they offered an online search tool, and she hunted until reaching the end of October before coming up with the story.

Couple found dead in house

Police were called by neighbours to 18 Seaview Drive after the resi-

dents grew increasingly concerned for William and Sheila Warmington who hadn't been seen for several weeks.

'We thought they'd gone off on holiday somewhere,' a close neighbour said. 'They were such a nice old couple, always had a friendly word for everyone they met. It's been quite a shock for us all when the police said they'd found them both dead.'

A police spokesman said they would have to wait for a full autopsy report, but at this stage, it looked like carbon monoxide poisoning and no foul play was suspected.

William Warmington was 68 and had only recently retired from his job as foreman at Denzil's Plumbing Services where staff said he was looking forward to being able to spend more time with his wife. Sheila Warmington, 67, had also recently retired from her job as teaching assistant at the local primary school.

'She was a much-loved member of staff, and it's such a tragedy that this happened just as she and her husband were looking forward to enjoying their retirement,' said Mrs McMurdo, headteacher of Clydeside Primary. 'She and Willie were always very close and enjoyed life.'

Glasgow City Council have asked us to repeat the advice that all dwellings are required by law to have interlinked alarm systems, including smoke, heat and carbon monoxide detectors.

That was underwhelming, Dee thought. Shame they both died so soon after retirement, but nothing there to implicate Logan Martin in their deaths. It looked like a tragic accident; no subsequent developments were reported by the papers. A roll of distant thunder sounded from the open windows, causing Dee to step out on the small balcony and check. It was termed a balcony in the estate agent's brochure, but at half a metre wide, there was scarcely room for a small chair and a pot plant. Room enough to stand out in the fresh air and check the weather. For the first time that week, Dee could feel a slight breeze in her hair; there was almost a hint of coolness in its touch – unless her imagination was working overtime. On the horizon, a bank of dark clouds was amassing, signalling a change in the weather. She hadn't seen the weather forecast today, but it would be a relief to have a thunderstorm to clear the air. As if on cue another rumble sounded, rolling around the distant Campsie Fells and threatening the end of another summer.

She returned to her laptop, was about to shut it down, then decided to check the police report on the Warmingtons so she could let Teàrlach know Logan Martin was innocent of those deaths at least. Getting into the reports was easy enough – she'd already broken through the firewall looking at Keith Martin's records, but what she found for the sweet couple who'd died in each other's arms was more shocking than she could have imagined. Dee could see why it hadn't made the press.

Written in the objective language of an initial police report, it took Dee a few readings and a detailed viewing of the associated photographs to believe what she was seeing. Sheila Warmington had been found naked and tied to her bed, a ball gag in her mouth and blindfold covering her eyes. Her husband, William, was found on top of her with a rope wound around his neck and attached to both bedposts. They had both been deceased for a couple of weeks which made the cause of death difficult to confirm, so the coroner had hedged her bets. Chief cause of death was carbon monoxide poisoning, traced to a defective gas central heating boiler flue. This was mistakenly attributed to the foul smell the police on the scene noticed when entering the property, and the first thing they blurted out when questioned by a reporter on the doorstep. Sufficient levels of carbon monoxide had been inhaled by both the deceased to show up in their post-mortem and went some way to explain how they died. What wasn't so obvious was whether that was the sole cause of death or whether William managed to inadvertently strangle himself whilst performing autoerotic asphyxiation during intercourse with his wife, leaving her trapped and unable to call for help.

Neither the plumbing centre nor primary school had quite hit the mark, it seemed, when describing how the Warmingtons were going to enjoy their retirement. The local news had missed out on a scoop as well – that was a salacious enough story to have sold to the red tops. Dee had a further dig in the coroner's report, but there was nothing there except a pared back statement of them being found dead in bed. That wasn't entirely unexpected. The wonder was that the station gossip hadn't surfaced in print – she could imagine the ribaldry in the police canteen when word spread. In fact, the bizarre circumstances of the Warmingtons' deaths *not* being made public troubled Dee. How had a lid been kept on it? She poured herself another drink, pulled shut the windows and door to the balcony as the breeze strengthened, and settled back in her seat.

Either the first police on the scene hadn't told forensics what they'd seen, or someone senior had put out a gagging order – if that was the right expression in these circumstances. The image she had recently seen from the scene of crime photographer threatened to ruin her enjoyment of the drink she'd just poured. There weren't many reasons the police would bother supressing the details of the Warmingtons' last fun-filled moments unless...

The laptop was within easy reach. The secretive organisation she started to research wasn't known for adopting the latest practices, but computers were the de facto tool for keeping membership subscriptions up to date. It took Dee an hour of digging before she found the route into the Warmingtons' nearest Freemason lodge. There was William online, nattily dressed in a bizarre uniform laden with enough insignia for her to realise he must have been high enough up the ladder to matter. There was the assistant chief constable. Dee put the pieces together, completed that part of the jigsaw.

Something had bothered her about the autopsy, apart from the obvious. She reread the report again, this time focussing on estimated time of death instead of the surrounding circumstances. There it was – both had died approximately two weeks prior to being discovered. She confirmed the date of the report, 30th October, making the actual date of death around mid-October. Teàrlach had mentioned the old woman at number sixteen saying they'd died a year ago. Close enough. Still no relatives, though, and the property had remained intestate for ten months. She wasn't an expert, but for the Warmingtons' estate to have not reverted to the Crown already made it likely whoever was tasked with finding their relatives had a lead they were following.

This was an altogether more challenging problem. Lightning flickered across the Glasgow night sky like the flick of a snake's forked tongue, followed a few seconds later by the crash of thunder. Dee pulled the curtains closed, shutting out a view of the city already distorted by rain lashing on the glass and made a strong coffee. She was going to need it if she wanted to dig around Glasgow Council's servers. It wasn't so much the security that concerned her, it was the sheer volume of data and the haphazard way it was organised.

By eleven thirty, she had all the information she needed. Tomorrow promised to be a fun start.

SIX
SPIRITUS

Jack Bentall's ears were still ringing when he left the gig at 11 p.m. The rest of the gang were staying on until the venue closed, crowding around the bar and shouting to be heard. He was by far the youngest member of the Open University course; the majority were at best middle-aged. They had approached the night out determined to prove they still had it. His early departure had been met with the satisfied confirmation that whatever 'it' was, they had more than twenty-year-old Jack.

He'd failed to get into university first time around – something that only reinforced his lack of self-worth and added to his insecurity. Friends couldn't understand why he didn't manage the grades, couldn't fathom why his mind blanked in panic at every exam paper. Now they only saw him during the holidays, told him all about the fun time they were having, their plans.

He had no plans and no future. It was his parents who persuaded him to see a doctor, and he came out of the clinic with a diagnosis of depression. His mum and dad had offered to fund him through the Open University as long as he passed all the exams. It was either study or fail – where failure meant falling into the emotional equivalent of a black hole.

Now he was walking along Glasgow's streets and doing his best to appear invisible to the gang of rowdy youths heading his way. At this time of night, any single man or woman on the street was a target for entertainment, however that might turn out.

He spied the taxi with a sense of relief, putting out a hand to stop it. It slowly drew to a halt beside him, female driver cautiously checking him out before letting him into the back of the cab.

'Where to, love?'

Jack gave the address, one eye on the youths who stared belligerently through the windows at him. He was worried one of them might try the door, drag him into the street and start roughing him up. When the taxi accelerated away from the kerb, they shouted something after him, indistinct but threatening.

He relaxed into his seat, pulled on the seatbelt and sighed deeply in relief. Jack stared as the city lights flew past the taxi windows, merging into a kaleidoscope as he lost consciousness. By the time he realised his eyes had closed, it was too late.

* * *

In the lock-up unit a familiar ritual repeated itself. The pentagram dutifully walked, words spoken repeatedly in supplication.

'Offero tibi spiritum vitae.'

The taxi driver stopped at another apex, this one designated by a circle. She raised arms made cumbersome in their NBC suit apparel, spoke towards the sky.

'I destroy from under heaven all flesh in which there is the breath of life.' She let loose a stream of air between pursed red lips towards the lock-up ceiling.

It had been done well. She lowered her head, blond hair

falling across her cold blue eyes, then reached for the mask. He'd have to be well secured in rope to pull up into the foliage. None of the sacrifices should be found before the full moon.

SEVEN
PECCADILLO

Dee produced the crime scene photograph of the two dead pensioners with a flourish, laying it on Teàrlach's desk as she completed updating them both on the goings-on at number eighteen.

Chloe was the first to comment. 'Hope my arse doesn't look like that when I'm a pensioner.'

'I should hope not,' Dee replied. 'They'd both been dead for two weeks when that was taken!'

Teàrlach remained silent, his focus on the unsettling photograph and hearing the old neighbour's voice in his head – '*because the boy probably killed them as well*'.

'So, what was he trying to do?' Chloe's brows drew down in concentration. 'I get the bondage thing, but if she's tied down and gagged whilst he's busy strangling himself... I mean, did they not think it through?'

Dee shrugged. 'Worse ways to go.'

Chloe seemed unconvinced. 'I'm not so sure.'

Teàrlach turned the photo over. 'I think we've seen enough of the neighbours in flagrante delicto.'

He noticed Chloe's frown return, but Dee quickly spoke before Chloe could phrase her question.

'Do you think this has anything to do with what happened to Keith Martin?'

'On the face of it, no. Looks like a separate event. Bizarre, but unconnected.' Teàrlach's face gave lie to his words. Coincidences happened, but not next door to each other.

'Well, that's a relief,' Chloe exclaimed. 'Otherwise, we're dealing with kamikaze sex-crazed OAPs and Freemasons as well!'

'Oh, and this.' Dee laid the last sheet of A4 down. 'Almost forgot about the search for relatives. They haven't put the house up for sale because the Warmingtons died without leaving a will and they can't find any relatives.'

Teàrlach held the A4 sheet away from his eyes. 'That's what? Ten months? Who's dealing with the search?'

'The council have instructed that firm of solicitors.' She indicated a name halfway down the sheet. 'They specialise in intestate investigations and work a percentage deal with whoever they find. Works well for them because they charge the council a flat fee too, whatever the outcome. Maybe we should look at doing something like that?'

Teàrlach snorted a dismissive response. 'How far back do they go? Cousins, second cousins?'

'Turn it over,' Dee suggested. 'On the back is a list from the Succession Scotland Act 1964.'

He read the list. 'I take it there are no parents, brothers, sisters, aunts, uncles, grandparents or brothers and sisters of the grandparents still living on either side?'

'Not unless they come from a family of vampires,' Dee quipped.

'OK. Then our firm of hearse chasers must be working on finding...' Teàrlach moved the sheet further away, forcing his eyes to focus on the blurred text. 'Ancestors of the deceased person more distant than grandparents on either parent's side.'

'That's the conclusion I came to.'

'And have they found someone?'

Dee shrugged. 'No idea. I didn't look any further down that rabbit hole.'

Teàrlach covered the downturned photograph with the sheet of A4, adding another layer of protection to his sensibilities. 'You're right. I don't see what the peccadillos at number eighteen have to do with our murder victim. Trouble is, where do we go from here? Logan murdered Keith Martin. He was found at the scene with the murder weapon and admitted his guilt.'

'We don't have a motive yet.' Chloe cut through the fog of extraneous detail.

'You're right!' A rare smile crossed Teàrlach's face. 'The least we can do is explain why Logan killed his father. He's still not accepting any calls or visitors?'

Chloe shook her head. 'Not unless he's changed his mind from yesterday. The prison staff were quite clear about his wishes.'

'We need to talk to the wife and daughter. They're the only other people who knew what was going on.' He scooped the paperwork Dee had supplied into the box file, shutting the lid with much the same feeling Pandora must have experienced. 'We've a week to find them, shouldn't be too difficult. We'll ask why it happened, put their statements in a file and give it to Nicole with our apologies for her loss. Then we can get on with another case – something straightforward.'

He stood up, letting them know the morning meeting was at an end. Rain lashed against his office window with every random gust of wind. Like the rest of the city inhabitants, he was relieved the late summer had broken. There was something unnatural about the intense heat, literally sapping the will to live with a surge of deaths as the very old succumbed to the highest temperatures Glasgow had seen for many years.

'I'll pay a visit to the firm of solicitors looking for the Warmingtons' relatives.' Teàrlach reached for his raincoat. 'Until we find Lauren Martin and her daughter, they offer the only hope of finding out what was going on in that house.'

'But the Warmingtons are dead.' Chloe's point was well judged.

'Aye, but sometimes the dead can talk.'

Teàrlach's cryptic comment left them both momentarily in silence. He made the street before Chloe's voice echoed faintly down the stairwell.

'What sort of animal is a peccadillo?'

The air had the unmistakable tang of pavement after rain. Petrichor, his memory advised him – from the Greek words for stone and blood of the gods. He shook his head, hurried towards his car parked on a side street and asked himself what possible use was that information? About the same use as talking to the firm of solicitors about their dead clients, came the response. Teàrlach knew he was chasing a nebulous lead, more out of the need to be doing something other than sitting at his desk. Maybe Dee had a point about taking on different types of work. Finding missing children was fine insofar that it helped towards salving his conscience. He knew enough about himself to know the blame for his mother's and brother's deaths lay heavy on his shoulders. Murdered by his drunk father – petrol poured through the sheltered flat letterbox, and he wasn't there to save them – even if he was only seven years old and living with his aunt when they died. Searching for missing people was his way of trying to make amends, to redress the balance. The problem was that no matter how good he was at finding what happened to missing kids, too often his findings ended in tragedy and loss. In the end, the salvation he sought merely proved to be an illusion, a fool's errand. The universe reminding him again and again that there is no mechanism adjusting right and wrong, no interstellar mechanic tweaking karma with a jeweller's screwdriver. On a more practical level there weren't enough clients able to pay, and now he had two staff relying on him for regular wages. Hence taking Nicole Martin's money when he should have politely declined the case.

Teàrlach entered the solicitor's address into the satnav, cautiously pulled out into the line of city traffic and drove on autopilot. The rhythmic thud of wipers accompanied his thoughts. He kept a watchful eye out for cyclists, especially the ones with a death wish who dressed in urban camouflage so they were almost invisible in the rain. The brief conversation with Mags the barmaid had brought him down. On one hand, he was glad she had confided in him, put her trust in him to keep her secret safe. On the other, here was another death he was powerless to do anything about. The missing kids were also adversely affecting his mental health. Of those he *did* find, at least half were returning to trauma or had suffered so much that they'd never be right again. Then there were the hundreds he couldn't look for – either the parents couldn't afford him, or he hadn't the capacity to take their cases. Either way, they were a constant reminder of how little he could accomplish. Maybe this case had come at the right time and wasn't such an aberration as he had first thought.

The solicitors' office he sought was sandwiched between shops selling vapes on the one side and an array of exotic vegetables on the other, spilling so far out onto the pavement that he had to wait for a gap in the pedestrian traffic before passing. The door had a bell attached to the top by a flexible metal spring, announcing his arrival with a discordant jangle. Teàrlach looked around whilst he waited. A couple of mismatched wooden chairs stood guard to a closed door on his left, a desk that he supposed belonged to a staff member on his right, filing cabinets and shelving taking up most of the space. Dust-covered Venetian blinds reduced the limited light making it through the rain spattered glass. The place smelled like a second-hand bookshop but dustier.

The door opened, revealing a short, balding man with a harassed expression and a suit that he probably slept in.

'Can I help you?' His eyes took Teàrlach's measure, decided he was safe, then puzzled whether he was going to be a time-waster or potential income.

'Teàrlach Paterson, private investigator.' He handed over a business card, seeing the needle shift firmly into timewaster. 'I'm involved in a job next door to one of your clients – number eighteen Seaview Drive?'

The needle swung back into potential income.

'Ah, yes. The Warmingtons. Terrible case.' He shook his head in sorrow like an actor rehearsing a line. 'Did you have some information about their relatives?' A hungry look had appeared on his face, making him seem more porcine than human.

'That's where I thought we might be able to help each other.'

A look of animal cunning entered his small eyes.

'What do you propose?'

Teàrlach gave him a few seconds to build up an appetite before replying.

'My team have a few specialist skills that you'll not easily find elsewhere, namely in the fields of genealogical research and accessing government files that are normally difficult to reach.' He could see he had the man's attention. 'What I suggest is that we work this case for you, pro bono, so you can assess how useful we might be to your business.'

'And you want what in return?' The animal cunning remained.

'Nothing. Consider it a free run. Whatever, whoever we

find in the Warmingtons' family tree who may have a claim to their estate, we will pass to you without any expectation of fee or favour.'

Teàrlach could imagine the gears engaging under the solicitor's sweaty cranium. 'You said help each other – how exactly can I help you?'

'We've been asked to look into the facts and background surrounding the murder next door at number seventeen. The Warmingtons were next-door neighbours. It's a long shot, I know, but if you had access to any diaries or paperwork they may have jotted something down in, that might help us understand the family dynamics.'

The solicitor visibly relaxed now that terms had been outlined. 'And, even if there was nothing of any use to you in said paperwork, you'd still be willing to trace any relatives entitled to a share of the estate?'

Teàrlach nodded enthusiastically.

'Without payment?'

'That's what I said, and if you like what we can offer, then we can agree terms for any future work.'

'Follow me into my office. I'll draw up an agreement on that basis, including a non-disclosure, and if you can do what you say you can, then we may have the beginnings of a mutually beneficial business relationship.'

Teàrlach grasped the hand that was offered, the texture and strength of a wet marshmallow, and followed him into a room even darker than the reception area.

Thirty minutes later, he exited onto the street with two journals under his arm and a file with the solicitor's investigations to date, plus a legal document that effectively had him working the case for free. On the face of it, he'd had the worst of the deal and the pleased solicitor viewing him from the grubby reception window tended to confirm that point of view – especially as he'd only been given until the end of the week to come up with the goods.

But then the solicitor had no idea what the carefully drawn diagram on one journal front cover had meant to Teàrlach. An exact copy of the pentagram etched onto Jade Martin's bedroom floor.

EIGHT
PRO BONO

Teàrlach ran a hand through his hair before entering the office, shaking off the worst of the rain in the shared close. At least the Glasgow weather had returned to normal even if nothing else was going that way.

'How did you get on?' Dee looked up from her laptop. Chloe stood leaning over her, her attention switching from the screen to Teàrlach as he removed his wet coat.

'Well... it was interesting.' He waved the two journals and file at them, cleared a place on his desk with the sweep of an arm and dumped the slightly sodden documents down.

'What have you got?' Chloe picked up the journal with a pentagram emblazed on the front, a quizzical expression forming as she opened it.

Dee made a grab for the other journal, opening pages at random and frowning at the contents. 'What's this meant to be?' She aimed the question at Teàrlach, settling back in his chair with an air of quiet satisfaction.

'Those both belong to the recently departed Warmingtons, or Willie Warmington at any rate.'

'Can you not call him that?' Dee retorted.

Chloe buried a snigger behind her hand.

'You'll notice the pentagram is exactly the same as the one I found underneath Jade Martin's carpet.'

'Yes, I can see that,' Dee's eyes narrowed. 'What I want to know is why does next door's pensioner have the same design that's on the bedroom floor of his sixteen-year-old neighbour?'

'And that's what we need to find out.' Teàrlach stretched back in his seat, wiping the rain still dripping from his hair away from his face.

'Man, what is all this stuff?' Chloe raised her open journal for them to see symbols superimposed over what was clearly a map of Glasgow.

'I'd like to know too, but first,' Teàrlach continued, 'we need to go through these documents and see if they can shed any light on the Martins. Have either of you tracked down the wife and daughter?'

'I'm on it,' Dee explained. 'Found the removal company they used, more man with a van than anything. It looks like they're still in Glasgow, just about to give them a call to find out where their new place is.'

'OK. Make that a priority, then I want to know if the Warmingtons have any far-flung family to inherit their estate. Part of the pro bono deal I arranged with the solicitor and may provide some easy pickings going forward.'

'What did I tell you?' Dee exchanged a conspiratorial side-eye with Chloe.

'Aye, alright.' He held the solicitor's file out to Dee. 'Swap you for the journal. When we've found Lauren and Jade, you can work your magic on finding some Warmingtons.'

Teàrlach poured himself a coffee and began reading the journal. It was written in a flowing longhand, each entry dated and starting from April 2020. The first few lines described the

Covid outbreak and then lockdown, detailing how the garden had proven to be a refuge from a dangerous world. Willie Warmington obsessed about keeping them both safe, mentioning wearing masks for trips outside, washing the shopping in anti-bacterial spray. He skipped pages, reading more of the same interspersed with a running commentary on politics and what he'd planted in the small vegetable bed. After about six months of mind-numbing minutiae, Teàrlach detected a change in tone, subtle at first then more fervent as Willie noted who walked past his house without a mask or which delivery drivers came within a two-metre limit. There was an air of paranoia in his writing, people acting strangely, theories about Covid inoculations being used for mind control.

The journal entries became more sporadic, month-long gaps intruded where nothing had been written at all. Teàrlach was on the point of giving up when the first mention of Keith Martin appeared, dated over a year ago.

Heard Jade shouting NO! Then furniture being moved. Has Keith found it? She cried when he left the house. Must speak with her.

Then something inconsequential about onions and how he needed a greenhouse before another mention two weeks later.

Spoke to Jade when she was alone. She won't say anything about Keith, but I know what's going on. She's changed, much quieter. I told her she must tell Lauren. Poor lass. The protection I've given her is not enough.

A two-month gap and he wrote several paragraphs about them being watched.

Disconnected the phone tonight so they can't listen. Same with the TV. Someone is watching us. Sheila doesn't believe me, but I saw a man in the back garden just standing there and looking at the house. I don't think he was human. I'm keeping the doors locked and windows shut from now on.

Keith is doing it again. These walls are so thin I can hear everything. Lauren and Logan were out. He always waits until he's alone with her. Someone has to do something!!!

Teàrlach stopped reading at that point, watching the city from his window. The rain had eased, more of a gentle drizzle than tropical downpour. Cars drove by two stories down, leaving a characteristic static hiss with each passing as tyres forcibly sprayed water through rubber treads. He had an idea where this was going and felt a strong reluctance to read any further, but the trail had to be followed to the end.

Everyone is lying. I don't believe them. Lauren said not to speak to her about my twisted fantasies. She said she was disgusted and will call the police if I ever mention it again. Jade is not to speak to me or Sheila. I've done all I can. She watches him now. I've noticed that Lauren and Logan rarely leave Jade alone with him. She says she doesn't believe me, but she does. Oh yes. She does.

Something happened next door. There was a fight. Shouting. I heard glass break. Jade isn't safe in that house, and I can't help her. Not any longer. I'm not sure if I can help myself anymore. My mind doesn't work properly. We're both experiencing headaches – bad headaches. Is it Covid?

Teàrlach had almost reached the last entry in the journal. William's writing had deteriorated almost to the point of illegibility. It was dated a week before their death.

Sheila not well today. Stayed in bed mostly. Can't call the doctor because the phone doesn't work. I don't want to ask neighbours because it's not safe. Covid everywhere and people are dying. What else can I do?

Having trouble concentrating. Dates are getting muddled. I don't want to end up with dementia and be a burden on everyone. Especially Sheila.

Teàrlach reached the last page and shut the journal thoughtfully. If the gas boiler had been leaking for months, was it possible that William's mental health as well as his physical health were beginning to suffer? He was displaying paranoia, confusion, and they both had experienced bad headaches. His mention of dementia suggested he might well have taken his own life at the end. But would he have elected to go out the way he had, especially knowing how they'd both be discovered? That was unbelievable, even if he wasn't thinking straight. Teàrlach took his journal through to the outer office. Chloe's head was still buried in the weird drawings.

'What have you found? Is there anything about the Warmingtons or mention of any relatives?' Teàrlach didn't hold out much hope – all he'd seen of Chloe's journal were strange diagrams and arcane symbols. She reluctantly stopped reading, an uncharacteristic frown still etched on her face.

'There's nothing here about his family or neighbours. This is some kind of weird religious research he's been doing.'

Teàrlach recognised a map of Glasgow, the Clyde winding like a serpent through the centre of the city.

'What's with all the lines?' The map was overlayed with different coloured lines criss-crossing the city from every direction. He searched in vain for any meaningful pattern.

'The ones in orange are based on Alfred Watkins' *The Old Straight Track*.' She stopped as Teàrlach's expression made clear his ignorance of esoteric research. 'He wrote a book linking ancient monuments and sites with straight lines – ley lines?'

He nodded. 'I've heard of them. Something to do with dowsers?'

'Sort of,' Chloe said dismissively. 'Then these green lines are based on another book by an amateur archaeologist, Ludovic Mann, who believed Glasgow was a centre for worshipping the moon goddess. The name Glasgow can either mean Green Hollow or Dear Green Place, or Mellow Glow of the moon goddess.'

Teàrlach started shaking his head. 'All very fascinating but I don't see how any of this helps us.' He turned to leave when Chloe put a hand on his arm to stop him.

'That's what I thought until I saw this.' She turned over the next page to show the same map of Glasgow but with most of the lines from the previous diagram removed. Those that remained formed the same pentagram that had been drawn on the front cover – and on Jade Martin's bedroom floor.

'So, what are we saying here? That Willie Warmington and his wife were devil worshippers and Jade Martin was an acolyte?'

Chloe shrugged. 'I don't know. There must have been some contact between them, otherwise it's a hell of a coincidence she's drawn the same diagram on her bedroom floor. It's not just satanism, the Wicca religion make use of the pentagram too.'

'As do Freemasons,' Dee added, joining them to view Chloe's journal.

Teàrlach brought their speculations to a halt. 'They'd been in contact all right.' He pointed out the paragraph where William wrote that he'd been in touch with Jade, offered her protection.

'You think he told her to draw a pentagram to keep her dad from... pestering her or whatever he was doing?' Chloe asked.

'Damn sight more than simply pestering her by the sounds of it,' Dee spoke with subdued anger. 'Looks like we've found the motive and the bastard got what he deserved.'

'Best not to jump to conclusions.' Teàrlach shut Willie's journal and dropped it on Chloe's desk. 'See if you find anything I might have missed, but it's still Logan Martin in the frame for murdering his father. There might now be a motive, if Keith *was* guilty of abusing his daughter and Logan heard about it from his next-door neighbour, but unless one of the family confirms that, then it's just hearsay.'

'What about all this pentagram stuff?' Chloe waved her journal in the air.

'I don't see it's anything to do with any of the deaths. Most likely Willie was getting swept up in something and being confined in the house during lockdown only worsened his mental state. That and the carbon monoxide poisoning.'

Dee turned around, picked a Post-it up from her desk and handed it over to Teàrlach.

'This is the address Lauren and Jade Martin moved to.'

'Crow Road?' Teàrlach checked the time – just after 1 p.m., as good a time as any to talk to the pair of them.

'Do you want me to tag along?' Dee asked. 'If Jade's there as well, I may be able to get her on her own.'

'Good idea. She'd be more open with you if I'm with her mother. You OK staying here Chloe, looking after the phone?'

Teàrlach caught the quick look of disappointment before Chloe turned away to look at the map.

'No, you guys are better at this interviewing lark than I am. Anyway, I want to try and get to the bottom of all this.' She laid a hand on the journal with its pentagram cover.

Teàrlach pulled on his coat. 'Have you found anything?'

'I'm not sure. There's something niggling me about where the pentagram points coincide with Glasgow's landmarks.'

'Doesn't do any harm, but I suspect it's just gibberish. More to do with his state of mind than anything else. We'll be back in an hour or so.' Teàrlach left her reaching for a map of Glasgow and settling back in her chair with a look of intense concentration.

NINE
PRESS

'Chloe's well into this moon goddess,' Dee ventured once they were on their own.

'Aye, she's like a wee terrier with a bone.' Teàrlach concentrated on driving. 'Don't underestimate her,' he warned. 'Won't be the first time she's come up with something from the most unlikely source. Although what connection there can be to Keith Martin's murder...'

They parked close to the address written on Dee's Post-it, pulling into a space outside a kebab shop. Dee was about to suggest grabbing a bite to eat, but Teàrlach was already marching away up the road, leaving her hurrying to catch up.

The address led them to a top-floor flat on Crow Road, one in a row of mostly identical traditional red sandstone tenements with miscellaneous shopfronts occupying the ground floors. In between the cafés and newsagents lay the empty husks of one-time hairdressers or financial consultants, boarded up and with no prospect being taken over soon. A stone stairway led from the pavement up to a weathered door and four doorbells. Teàrlach chose the flat number Dee had given him, the only bell without a name against it. A door release responded to his summons, and after exchanging a questioning look, they started up the shared stone stairway inside. The air smelled faintly of decay, overlaying a less subtle odour that hinted of a plumbing problem emanating from somewhere deep within the building's fabric. Stone steps showed evidence of use, edges worn smooth by the tramp of feet. A bicycle laid claim to the first landing, chained to an ornate iron railing. Two doors faced each other on the top floor. The one to his right had a welcome mat. The door Teàrlach sought was unadorned with any such fripperies. It opened a crack as they reached the top stair.

'What do you want?'

Teàrlach attempted to view the female owner of the voice, saw the security chain in place.

'Lauren. Lauren Martin?'

A hand appeared in the gap in preparation to slam the door shut.

'Who's asking?'

'My name's Teàrlach Paterson, this is my colleague, Dee Fairlie.' He offered her a business card through the gap which she snatched and read with mistrust.

'Hi.' Dee waved encouragingly at the door. The worried expression in the one eye visible through the narrow gap lessened slightly, an uncertain frown taking its place.

'So, what do you want? I thought you were the post.' She said this with a degree of irritation as if accusing them of deceiving her into giving them access.

'We're looking into your husband's murder.' Teàrlach caught the fright in her expression, hurried on before she closed the door on them. 'Your sister-in-law, Nicole Martin, asked us to get in touch.'

'What's that interfering cow want from us now?'

Teàrlach was tired of conducting an interview through a four-centimetre gap.

'She just wants to offer whatever help she can. Look, can we come in and talk?'

There was a moment's hesitation, a calculation visible in the single eye.

'It won't take a minute,' Teàrlach encouraged. 'Or we could talk out here on the landing?'

The eye switched to view the other door, then the sound of a security bolt being removed preceded the door opening to reveal the rest of her. Lauren Martin's distracted expression suggested she regretted letting them in. She looked older than her forty years with hair swept up in a careless bun, pulling greying roots into display above suspicious eyes, framed in heavy mascara.

'What sort of help?' Lauren added once they'd stepped inside. From the way she unconsciously rubbed her fingers together, Teàrlach suspected she was hoping for financial aid.

'She wanted to know why her brother died, make sense of it all. I was hoping you'd be able to fill in some of the blanks. The police report didn't say anything about the circumstances leading up to his death.' He'd substituted death for murder just in time. No sense in making a difficult conversation any worse.

Lauren turned her back on them, rummaged in a coat hanging on a hook beside the door and retrieved a pack of cigarettes. She lit one with a cheap lighter, drawing in a deep breath so the tip glowed an angry red before releasing a stream of grey smoke through pursed lips.

'How did you find me?' Her defiant gaze met his, cigarette returning for another nicotine hit.

'That will be down to me, Mrs Martin,' Dee volunteered. 'Takes more than a change of address to drop off the radar these days. Thought we should pay you a visit before the press.'

Teàrlach held back from commenting, making a mental note to tell Dee to let him lead the conversations in future.

Lauren switched her attention to Dee, seeing her properly for the first time.

'What's the press got to do with anything? They've had their fun. Keith's just another statistic, nobody cares that I've lost a husband and a son on the same day.'

A note of pity had entered her voice – it hadn't carried through to her eyes.

Teàrlach regained the initiative. 'We don't mean to upset you, Lauren. If you can just tell us what you know about that day, what could have caused your son, Logan, to have acted like that. Keith's sister deserves to know that at least. She's grieving too.'

Lauren had returned to her cigarette like a diver desperate for air, cheeks sucked in as she drew another lungful.

'Is there somewhere we can sit down?' Teàrlach asked. They'd remained corralled in the tiny entrance hall, front door still wide open to allow the three of them room to stand in a line.

'In here,' Lauren motioned with a tilt of her head. They dutifully followed through a cloud of acrid tobacco smoke into a living room, sinking into the worn settee she indicated with her cigarette. She remained standing, silhouetted against yellowing net curtains and searching the road outside as if expecting to see a TV crew.

They scanned the room, noting photographs telling the lie of a happy family. A china lighthouse held several letters pressed tightly against the wall, sharing shelf space with an antique clock stopped at three thirty.

'Do you have children, detective?' Lauren's question was directed towards Teàrlach.

'No.'

'No,' she repeated quietly, nodding her head slowly in confirmation of something she already knew. 'Then you wouldn't understand. Same as his bloody sister,' she quickly added. 'Dogs make a poor substitute for the children you can't have.'

Teàrlach interrupted her diatribe. 'Is Jade here? Can we have a quiet word with her...'

'You stay away from my girl! Hasn't she been through enough? If I catch either of you anywhere near her...' She ground the cigarette stub into an ashtray for emphasis.

'Can I use your loo?' Dee had heard enough to know this conversation was unlikely to produce any dividends.

'Can't you wait? I don't like strangers using my toilet,' Lauren retorted.

'Sorry, no.' Dee adopted a strained expression, thighs urgently pressed together. 'It's a medical condition.'

'End of the corridor.' Lauren frowned in response, craning her neck to check Dee took the correct door.

'Anyhow, Jade won't be able to add anything. She was in her room the whole time, listening to music on her headphones – didn't know anything had happened until I came home with the shopping and found them.' Lauren's voice caught in her throat.

'I thought someone must have been caught burgling the place, stabbed them both when they tried to catch him – then I saw the knife in Logan's hand.' She shook her head in disbelief, reliving the moment she'd discovered her son was a killer.

'It made no sense then. Makes even less sense now. Tell her that.' Lauren jutted her chin out in defiance, eyes screwed down in anger.

'Did they fight often, Logan and his dad? How were things when you left – had there been an argument?'

'Logan loved his dad!'

Teàrlach failed not to display incredulity, pulling his eyebrows back down too late.

'Oh, you can think I'm lying. Think you know better than a mother knows her son.' Her shaking fingers reached for another cigarette, drawing so deep that the lighter flame bent to her will.

'I'm just trying to get to the truth.' He struggled to find words that might soothe her. 'It's just your husband was knifed multiple times, by all accounts this was a frenzied attack.'

'I don't know what happened, don't you get it? I wasn't there!' she shouted, waving her cigarette at his face before taking herself back to the window. Lauren dabbed ineffectually under each eyelid, leaving telltale smudges of mascara in their wake as black tears fell to honour the dead. 'When I left, they were all at peace, Keith was sitting in the living room with his newspaper. The kids up in their rooms. Then I came back to that...'

The tears fell in earnest now, whatever dam she had put into place to stem the flood of emotions proving inadequate. A dry, rasping gasp followed each silent sob. Teàrlach made to put an arm around her shoulders only to be forcibly pushed away.

'Don't you dare touch me!' She glared at him then, a mask of pure hatred had replaced the face of the downtrodden woman who'd first opened the door. She caught sight of Dee coming back into the room, stopping in the doorway at the sound of her outburst.

'You can both fuck off back to wherever you came from and tell Nicole not to try and make contact with us ever again.' Lauren pointed her cigarette at the door.

'Thanks for seeing us,' Teàrlach replied. 'I'm sure Nicole is only trying to help, but I'll pass on your message.'

'You do that!' The door slammed forcibly behind them as they left.

'That went well.' Dee's attempt at levity was met with a frown, and they descended back to street level in silence.

'Did you see any sign of the girl?' Teàrlach asked once they were in the car, negotiating through the traffic back to the office.

'She wasn't there. I checked the other rooms whilst you were getting along so well with Lauren.' Dee shot a quick glance towards Teàrlach, then hurriedly continued when he didn't smile.

'Lauren's bedroom had a double bed, looked like she shared it with someone. The other bedroom belongs to Jade.' She brought up her phone, showed a photograph to Teàrlach as he drove.

'What am I looking at?' He snatched a quick glance before returning his attention to the busy Glasgow streets.

'This was drawn on her wall. It's a pentagram, same design as the picture you showed us of her bedroom floor, only now there's no attempt at hiding it.'

Teàrlach drove on in silence until they drew to a halt in front of a red light.

'We need to speak to the girl.'

'Jade?'

Teàrlach nodded in response. 'I don't buy her listening to music unaware her father's being stabbed in the hallway. Lauren's covering up for her.'

TEN
AER

Bryony Knight had spent too much in Sauchiehall Street. Why did she do this? Every time she had an argument with her boyfriend, she relied on retail therapy to make herself feel better again. She had too many bags to take on the bus back home, especially now she'd hit rush hour. The seats would be full – no chance of taking up two places with her shopping.

When a taxi came along with its light on, Bryony dropped her bags on the pavement and waved frantically for it to stop. She had competition; at least one other shopper was running towards the taxi as it indicated to pull into the kerb. Sweeping the bags back into her hands and setting her face with a look of determination, she ran like she used to at school.

Reaching the car first, Bryony pulled open the door and threw her bags across the seat. Now that she'd claimed the prize, her features turned from triumphant to sorrowful as her competitor glared at her.

'Sorry. I'm sure there'll be another one coming in a minute.' She smiled sweetly before climbing in and shutting the door on the other woman's face.

'Where to, love?'

Bryony's smile was still in place as she caught the taxi driver's eyes in the mirror and gave her address.

'Can you strap in?' Her driver's voice issued from a small speaker in the back of the cab.

'Sorry. Just sorting out these bags. OK, good to go.'

Bryony caught the woman still glaring at her from the pavement as the taxi drove off and settled back in her seat with an air of smug satisfaction. Her brows drew down as she stared at the taxi driver's cascading blond hair through the dividing glass, tried to work out if it was all natural or whether she was wearing extensions. In a few minutes, she lost interest in the driver. She lost interest in everything.

* * *

In the lock-up a familiar ritual was enacted, the pentagram walked, incantation repeated in sonorous tones.

'Tibi offero spiritum meum.'

She stopped on the pentagram point depicting an upright triangle bisected by a horizontal line. As before, arms raised upwards, pale blue eyes stared with fervour at the lock-up corrugated roof.

"I give you my breath, as life is created and you renew the face of the earth.'

She puffed out her cheeks and blew forcibly into the air until her lungs had no more to give.

ELEVEN
WATER

A small crowd had gathered on the Prince of Wales Bridge, alerted by the excited calls of young children being taken to day nursery attempting to force curious soft faces through carved stone balusters. When the adults caught sight of her body, they hastily pulled impressionable young minds away, forming a human barricade to block the view until their own panicked shouts drew larger crowds.

She was naked, arms open in supplication to the sky above. Glasgow's homage to Ophelia. There the poetic comparison faltered. A rope bound both wrists, looped under her back and attached to her ankles to keep her arms in place and snared on something submerged in the River Kelvin. Her unnaturally white skin spoke of death; wrinkled flesh spoke of a few days' immersion. Her journey downstream to join the River Clyde abruptly terminated by an unceremoniously dumped shopping trolley.

Onlookers found their eyes drawn back to her despite the urge to look away. Seeing in her something primal, something that should remain hidden. She called to the subliminal, to perverse desire and to a fascination with death. Her arms moved in sympathy with the flow of water, acknowledging the onlookers with languorous royal waves from outstretched arms. A cyclist stopped on the bridge, leaned over the stone railing curious to see what had caused the crowd to behave so strangely, then promptly threw up.

* * *

Chloe stared at her mobile in morbid fascination, morning coffee forgotten. Photographs had spilled across social media long before the police arrived to cordon off the area. Some posters had attempted black humour, titling their snaps with comments like *Dolly in the Trolley* – but humour sat uneasily alongside such a death. Chloe's attention wasn't so much on the dead woman but on the ropes that bound her. Ropes that reminded her of the Warmingtons locked in a final embrace.

'You seen this, Teàrlach?' she called to him as soon as he stepped into the office.

'What is it?' He took the proffered phone, squinting until the image was brought into focus almost at arm's length. 'Poor lass. Where's this?'

'Under the Prince of Wales Bridge, by the university.' Chloe watched as he brought the phone closer, squinting to bring it into focus.

'Someone's trussed her like a turkey.' He sounded more resigned than shocked, inured to the callous disregard for human life displayed on the screen.

'Or a sacrifice,' Chloe added quietly.

Teàrlach caught her comment, looked again at the photo. The parallel to a watery crucifixion stared back at him.

'Can you print this full size for me, Chloe? And dig out that photo of the Warmingtons whilst you're at it.'

She reached for her coffee before it was too cold to drink.

'You think there's a connection?'

'God knows. The Warmingtons was just a sex game gone wrong – or that's what it looked like. This one has similar vibes, but there's no doubt she was murdered.'

'Think the police will make that connection?' Chloe was doubtful.

'I don't think so. The Warmingtons' picture was never released, hushed up for reasons best known to the boys in blue. Unless the same detectives are given this one to investigate, they'll never make that connection.'

Chloe nodded. 'And we can't tell them because Dee pulled the forensics photos illegally off the police server.'

'Did I hear my name being mentioned?' Dee swept into the office, stuffing leather gloves into her helmet.

Teàrlach passed her the phone.

'Jesus!' Her eyes flashed with anger. 'Hope they catch the bastard that did this to her. Is this something we're involved with?'

'Not as such. The rope looks similar to the Warmingtons' death.' He stood by the printer in readiness to grab the print.

Chloe held out her hand. 'You'll have to give me back my phone if you want me to print it.'

Dee dutifully handed her back the phone. 'I thought the Warmingtons died in some sex game mishap?'

'That's what everyone thought – those that know about it. The chances of two instances of dead people being tied up in intricate ropework within a few miles of each other...' Teàrlach left the rest unsaid. 'Who ran the enquiry into the Warmingtons' deaths? Was there a commanding officer's name on the file you pulled from the police server?'

'Hang on, I'll have a look.' Dee powered on her laptop, opened a file.

'Here we are – Detective John Jenkins. You're wondering why the ropes never made it into the report?'

Teàrlach nodded. 'He must have had a reason. Someone

didn't want the coroner to see the original crime scene photographs, and my guess is it wasn't to spare the Warmingtons blushes.'

'You want me to dig into this Jenkins, see if he's bent?'

'There's no point in looking into dodgy coppers. Once anyone gets wind they're being looked at, the police close ranks. Easier to give them enough rope...'

Dee responded with a wry smile.

'How are we doing with finding the Warmingtons' relatives?' He lifted a newly printed page out of the printer, peering closely at the enlarged picture.

'Should have something for you this morning,' Dee replied. She stripped out of her jacket, made a start on her leather trousers. 'Do you want me to send it straight to your pet solicitor or do you want to see it?' Dee found she was speaking to Teàrlach's back and winked at Chloe.

'Just send what you find to him. And find Jade. One of these kids knows why the dad was killed.' He rummaged around his desk, came back with a notepad after giving Dee enough time to finish changing out of her biking gear.

'I'm off to see the son, Logan. See if he can be persuaded to talk to me.'

'Thought he didn't want to speak to anyone?' Chloe asked.

'I'll take that risk. Let Barlinnie know I'll be there at ten and tell Logan his mum sent me.' He paused, catching sight of the woman's body in the photograph. 'Tell him it's about a sacrifice and try and make it sound religious.'

'You planning on wearing a dog collar?' Dee quipped.

A fleeting smile crossed his face. 'Fancy dress isn't really my thing. I'll have to rely on my winning personality.'

'Good luck with that!' Chloe sparred as the office door closed behind him.

'God, I need a coffee.' Dee made herself an espresso from

the fancy machine Teàrlach had invested in last year. 'What's with the sacrifice angle?'

Chloe found the number for Barlinnie Prison, paused with her finger hovering over the phone.

'The coincidence between the Warmingtons and this poor lassie both being bound with rope. I thought it looked like they'd been sacrificed – put on display.'

Dee took a sip from her cup, observed Chloe through narrowed eyes. 'I get the coincidence angle, but why do you think they're sacrificed? And why is Teàrlach making that point to the son – Logan?'

Chloe shifted uncomfortably, took her hand away from the phone and reached for one of the journals instead, flicking through the pages until she'd found what she wanted. The page lay open on a hand-drawn map, crudely annotated with arcane symbols. It took Dee a while before she recognised what she was looking at.

'That's the Clyde!' She put her cup down, started tracing the line of a tributary until it reached a symbol. 'You're going to tell me that's the Kelvin, where that girl was found?' Dee stared at Chloe in shock.

Chloe nodded. 'Her body was downstream of there, near the Prince of Wales Bridge.'

Dee frowned. 'What sort of map is this? Where's the motorway, or any roads for that matter? Just these weird symbols. If it wasn't for the shape of the river and that bit of coastline, I wouldn't have recognised it.'

'That symbol there, the one in the River Kelvin with the wavy lines. I think that represents water.' Chloe pointed to another symbol, a Celtic knot with three points. 'This one is called the triquetra or Trinity knot. It represents earth, air and water – or life, death and rebirth.'

Dee looked suitably impressed. 'You've really gone to town

on these journals. What makes you think there's any connection to the girl in the river or the Warmingtons?'

'Because the triquetra has been drawn on top of where the Martins lived.' Chloe couldn't miss Dee's cynical response. 'I pointed that out to Teàrlach yesterday, and he had the same reaction. Then this lassie turned up on another symbol this morning.'

'What's going on then? You think someone's out there wrapping victims up in rope and leaving them at the points marked up on this map?' Dee flicked her hair away from her face. 'Doesn't make any kind of sense. Anyway, Keith Martin was stabbed by Logan – no ropes there.'

'No,' Chloe was forced to agree. 'But there was that pentagram on Jade's floor, same as the one on the front of this journal.' She closed the book, leaving the cover artwork displayed, and reached for a sheet of tracing paper which had a copy of the pentagram drawn in pencil. 'I thought I saw a pattern to the symbols on the map.'

She opened the journal to the roughly drawn map, carefully positioned the tracing paper so that each point coincided with the symbols underneath.

'This one's the Warmingtons – or Keith Martin – and this one is the woman they discovered this morning in the Kelvin.'

'That's mad! Must be a coincidence.' Dee sounded unconvinced.

They exchanged a look that spoke volumes.

'You gone over this with Teàrlach?' Dee asked.

Chloe gave a single shake of her head. 'I only suggested the way the Warmingtons had been bound made it pretty unlikely they'd done it to themselves.'

'When did you become an expert on ropes? Something you're not telling me?'

Chloe's cheeks flushed.

'I know this guy. He's into ropes and knots.' She responded to Dee's comically enlarged eyes with a sharp retort. 'Not like that! He was a fisherman, knows how to make all sorts of knots. I thought he might be able to give an expert opinion on the Warmington ropework.'

'That's not something to let out into the public domain. I lifted that photograph from what's meant to be a secure server. There'd be hell to pay if they found we'd been snooping behind the forensics firewall.' Dee seemed genuinely angry.

'It's OK. I didn't let on anything about it. He doesn't even know they're dead in the photo because I cropped it and photoshopped the colours before I showed him.' She bit at her bottom lip. 'If anything, he's got the impression I'm kinky. Which I'm not!' she added sharply.

Chloe's warning glance was enough to stifle Dee's laugh before it began.

'So, what did your man have to say?' Dee's curiosity demanded an answer.

'He said there's no way anyone could do that to themselves. Said it was staged but admired the specialised knots that had been used. He offered to demonstrate on me, so I had to change the subject fast.'

'Aye. I'm with you on that,' Dee agreed. 'So, why didn't the police realise that and call it in as a murder?'

Chloe shrugged. 'Maybe the same reason they kept it all quiet.'

Dee focussed back on the map. 'There's five of these symbols. Does this mean they'll be another three victims?

Chloe held her palms out. 'No idea. Maybe I'm reading too much into it. Anyhow, we can't go to the police without giving away our inside information on the Warmingtons.'

'No, I suppose not.' Dee returned to her laptop, took her seat. 'Right. Let's find the Warmingtons' long-lost relations. I'll try this genealogy site first, make a change to use the web legally for once!' Chloe shook her head as Dee bent over her laptop and resumed her call to the prison. At the back of her mind, three symbols lay in wait on the Glasgow map like portents of death.

TWELVE
PRISON

Teàrlach sat in front of a sign advising those visitors waiting to see inmates that *Barlinnie Prison seeks to provide a secure, safe, caring and productive environment.* A prison dog had just made the rounds of the secure waiting area, paying so much attention to one visibly nervous visitor that he was led off by prison officers for a 'further search.' The desperation in his eyes only served to bring a satisfied smile to the dog handler's lips, the dog now reined in tight to prevent it lunging at the man in its excitement. A collective sigh of relief audibly escaped the remaining visitors when the dog and its quarry exited the room as if they were all guilty of something but had evaded detection this time.

'Tear Lock Paterson?' A guard stood in the doorway, derision evident in his voice. He searched the room, eyes landing on Teàrlach as he unwound his body from the confines of a plastic chair.

'Follow me.' The words were issued as an order, the guard automatically sizing up the risk of any threat before turning his back on him.

Teàrlach fell into step in the man's sour wake, entering an open hall where prisoners faced visitors across blank tables under the watchful gaze of wardens. Conversations were either urgent, whispered with furtive looks towards nearby tables and guards, or silent as if there were no words left for what had to be said, only mute appeal to convey meaning.

He recognised Logan Martin long before they reached his table. His slight frame made him look like a child, hunched in on himself and staring at the table surface oblivious to the dramas being played out around him. Even from the other side of the room Teàrlach could see that prison life wasn't sitting comfortably on Logan's narrow shoulders. His folded body made him look even smaller than he was, a futile attempt not to be noticed. In this predator-rich environment, you don't want to advertise that you're prey.

Logan lifted his gaze from a study of the table as the guard gave Teàrlach final instructions – no bodily contact, not to hand anything over. He left them alone, taking position with his back to the wall and watched them with incurious eyes.

'Hello, Logan. Thanks for seeing me. Are you being treated OK?' Teàrlach asked with genuine concern. He'd seen this soulless look before in those who had already decided the only way out was death.

Prison was a microcosm of society, a high-pressure experiment for social scientists to play with their caged animals. The strong ruled their packs, the packs used whatever they could to avoid demotion, and at the bottom were weak creatures like Logan. He would have come in with a certain cachet as a murderer. More so for patricide – it takes courage to kill your own father.

'What have you got to do with Mum?' Logan's voice was so quiet the words were difficult to catch over the low-level hubbub in the room, but still contained an underlying threat.

The direction of his question took Teàrlach by surprise. He attempted to read Logan's expression and failed.

'I'm here because of your aunt, Nicole. She asked me to

check how you're doing.' Logan remained impassive, so Teàrlach pressed on. 'She wants to know what happened that morning. Why your dad was stabbed to death. She doesn't believe you killed him.'

Logan flicked a glance towards the guard, saw he had lost interest in them.

'You can tell my aunt that I stabbed him. That's why I'm here, isn't it?'

Teàrlach nodded. 'She just wants to know why, Logan. Why her brother was killed. Can you tell me that?'

Logan sat back in his seat, appraising Teàrlach.

'You've seen Mum, haven't you?'

'Yes, I saw her yesterday. She's worried about you; said you loved your dad.'

Logan's head sank down to his chest in response. 'I did. I did love him.' His voice emerged indistinct and muffled. When he looked up, Teàrlach saw the moisture glistening in his eyes.

'You said Mum wanted to talk about a sacrifice. That's what the girl said on the phone.'

'You spoke with Chloe. She works for me. We're only trying to understand why this happened, to make sense of it all and put your aunt's mind at rest. She lost a brother that day as well.'

Logan considered the question. 'I'm not saying anything until you tell me how Jade is.'

'I didn't see her. She wasn't at your mother's flat.'

'Where was she? Is she alright?' Logan's fists bunched as he suddenly became animated, leaning in close so they were scant centimetres apart.

'I'm sure she was fine. Your mother didn't appear bothered.' Teàrlach thought back to Lauren nervously smoking, returning to look out of the curtains time after time. 'She basically warned me to stay away from her.'

Logan didn't seem convinced but leaned back again in his seat. There were white marks in his palms where the blood had been forced deep under the skin by the pressure of his nails.

'Promise me you'll find her.'

'OK. We'll look for her. Where is she likely to be?'

Logan looked nervously around before whispering an answer. 'Keep a watch on the Crow Road Freemason's Church. She sometimes works there as a cleaner. Tell her...' He looked up at the ceiling, searching for the right words. 'Tell her I know what he did to her and I'm sorry. Tell her to stay safe. Leave Glasgow if she has to. Tell her that, and I'll give you your answer.'

'Who did what to her, Logan? Who does she have to stay away from? Is she in any danger?'

'Just promise me you'll speak to her and pass on my message.' He waited like a man who had nothing but time to kill.

'I promise.'

Logan searched Teàrlach's face for truth, then sighed as if a weight had been lifted from his shoulders.

He made to stand, then stopped as Teàrlach's hand shot out to stop him.

'No contact!' the guard snapped, taking a step towards their table.

Teàrlach pulled back his hand, held it palm upwards to apologise and show the guard it was empty. Logan unwound from the table, motioned to the guard that he wanted back in his cell.

'Can't you tell me anything?' Teàrlach pleaded. 'Something to put your aunt's mind at rest?'

The guard started leading Logan away, giving Teàrlach a disapproving scowl for breaking prison rules.

'He was a sacrifice,' Logan called back over his shoulder. 'Tell her I'm sorry.'

Teàrlach was escorted to reception, collected his phone,

wallet and keys, and took the road towards Glasgow with only his thoughts for company. The visit hadn't really provided any further insights into Keith Martin's murder, nor had he been convinced of Logan's guilt. But the absence of any other potential murderer and the clear forensics evidence linking Logan to the knife and his father's blood made that doubt immaterial. It was more the words left unsaid that were troubling Teàrlach. He had a good idea who had done something to Jade. But why did Logan say Jade had to leave Glasgow?

At least he now had a lead to find Jade, an address close to her mother's flat in Crow Road. There was something else he had to understand. Why did Logan say his father was sacrificed, and was there a connection to the rope-bound deaths next door?

There were only a few more days he could give to this case before admitting defeat. Keith Martin's murder was likely to remain a mystery if neither his wife nor daughter had an inkling why Logan stabbed him, and all Logan was willing to offer was that his father had been sacrificed. Did it boil down to this? Religious extremism? Or was there something darker behind it all? Was Keith the one who Logan knew had 'done something' to Jade and was that why he had to kill him?

Willie Warmington's journals had mentioned Keith doing something to his daughter. The inference of sexual abuse was clear, but by then a level of paranoia was evident in everything he wrote – even to the point of stating they were being watched by non-human entities in his garden. Carbon monoxide may have had a part to play in his mental health, the leak from the gas boiler steadily poisoning their minds until it finally killed them. That or whoever left them the way they were discovered.

Could Logan have murdered his father to protect his sister? That at least provided a motive and could explain the frenzied nature of the attack. Was a seventeen-year-old Logan capable of inflicting such a level of violence? And what, if anything, was the connection to their tied-up neighbours? The questions kept coming and, so far, Teàrlach had no answers. The discovery of the young woman that morning was also preying on his conscience. By rights, he should tell the police of his suspicions that something linked this death to the Warmingtons – but he couldn't do that without alerting them to the fact Dee had been in Police Scotland's supposedly secure servers.

He checked the time and turned on the local lunchtime news. The dead girl was the headline story, police appealing for witnesses to come forward. So they had nothing on her yet. The rope would have been sent direct to forensics in case any DNA attached to the fibres. Teàrlach caught his reflection in the rear-view mirror, eyebrows drawn down in concentration. This wasn't his case, he had to let it go and concentrate on the Martin family for now.

THIRTEEN
PERSONAL

Dee found the Warmingtons' relatives before Teàrlach had left Barlinnie Prison. Willie had a cousin in Canada, working at a bookstore in Ontario and happily oblivious to the Warmingtons' inglorious departure from this life. She forwarded his details to the solicitor, copied to Teàrlach's email and then turned her attention to the photograph of the girl in the River Kelvin, feeling a visceral need to avenge the young woman's murder.

Chloe was still intently studying the journals, her finger tracing each diagram and line of text and oblivious to Dee standing beside her. She jumped when Dee quizzed her.

'What do *you* think's going on here? With these ropes. Is there anything in these journals?'

'Mostly mumbo-jumbo as far as I can make out,' Chloe said once she regained her composure. 'At the start it all makes some kind of sense, linking prehistoric sites to Glasgow landmarks and mentioning the Druid religion.' She warmed to her subject, flicking the pages to point out standing stones and the relationship to far off landmarks, astronomical notes regarding sunrise and sunsets on each solstice.

'Was he a Druid?' Dee asked hesitantly.

'Maybe. Thing is the Druids passed down their knowledge verbally. There's nothing written down as far as I know.' She turned back to the front of the journal and held the page open. Dee craned her neck to read the spidery scrawl.

'What am I looking at?'

Chloe pointed out a drawing which meant nothing to her.

'Sorry, I'm none the wiser.'

'This is the broken pillar. Used to represent the fall of a high-level Freemason, and this one is the Eye of Providence.'

This at least was familiar. A triangle containing an eye with rays of light coming out.

'I've seen this on a dollar bill.'

Chloe nodded encouragingly. 'Yes, and these other symbols – the anchor, scythe, square and compass – they're all used in Freemasonry.'

Dee's mouth turned up in an involuntary smile. 'Don't tell me your rope-loving boyfriend is a Mason as well?'

'No,' Chloe said with irritation. 'All this stuff is on the web. Thing is, this isn't just Freemasonry in here. He's added a load of weird shit about Glasgow before it became a city. I can't make it out. This bit refers to the Clyde being named after Clota, the Celtic goddess – he references a Roman General Gnaeus Julius Agricola.'

Dee gave up attempting to decipher the writing. 'The guy's brain was addled with monoxide poisoning anyway. More to the point, what did your boyfriend say about these ropes?'

Chloe's eyes narrowed. 'He's *not* my boyfriend.'

'Whatever he is. Did he say anything about the type of rope? Where can you buy it?'

'Why are you asking?'

'If there is a link between the Warmingtons and this woman they found this morning, then rope is the common denominator. I've found his relatives, so I've nothing else better to do this afternoon.'

'He said it was six-millimetre hemp as far as he could tell. Used mostly in theatre or school gyms and available all over the place. They don't use it in fishing anymore because manmade fibres are much better.'

'Damn! I was hoping to narrow it down to a couple of outlets at least.' Dee's face creased in concentration. 'I'll take a copy of that map and the pentagram. See if there's anything I can do with that.' She lifted the journal from under Chloe's hands, headed for the photocopier.

'Make a copy for me too, will you?' Chloe called. 'The solicitor will be wanting the journals back and I've not finished with them yet.'

The mechanical sound of paper feeding through the copier filled the office. Dee handed Chloe her copy.

'Tell him I'm working from home this afternoon.' Dee replaced the journal back on Chloe's desk. 'Teàrlach can call me if there's anything else he wants done.'

Dee took a detour, leaving her bike parked on Kelvin Way and walking through Kelvingrove Park to stare over the Prince of Wales Bridge, watching the police activity underneath. There was tape stretched further along the park embankment where the body may have entered the water. Uniforms were systematically walking a ground search, divers paddling waist deep in the water.

The park was busy during the day. She stood feeling the August sun on her skin, hearing children shouting as they chased each other over the grass. The park held a more menacing aspect at night – somewhere to be avoided. Dee shivered despite the heat. Had the girl been taking a short-cut and been killed there, on the riverbank? She felt an impotent rage building up inside her, demanding retribution for the unknown woman.

She headed back to her flat. It was too early for anything of interest to appear in the police reports, but she wanted to do something. Somebody had done this, murdered her in cold blood, and Dee wanted them caught before anyone else became a victim.

She stood on her balcony, looking out over the Clyde, and thought about her ex-employer. It had only been six months since Tony Masterton had been killed. Dee felt a cold shiver run down her spine, despite the warmth of the day. Both she and Teàrlach had sensed something in that loch yet had never spoken of it. Looking out over the city, hearing the continuous sound of traffic – the short time she'd spent by Tony's lochside house felt more like a dream, or a fading nightmare.

Dee laid the photocopies down on the table, shut the French windows to prevent a breeze fresh from the Clyde from blowing them away and watched as white clouds scudded across the sky. The memories of last winter were still fresh. Tony's last instruction to her to work for Teàrlach and his offering her a job almost as if the two of them had rehearsed it beforehand. She'd taken his offer of course, there wasn't anything else bringing in any income unless she went freelance again – and it was inevitable that she'd be caught hacking eventually. At least this way Teàrlach offered something in the way of financial security, and she enjoyed working with him and Chloe, although Teàrlach's reserve was an irritation.

She considered having another search online for Jade. A trawl of social media hadn't found her by name, so she was either Glasgow's only teen without an online presence or she was anonymous. Dee had some sympathy with that approach. There were enough creepy men out there trying to climb into your DMs without giving them any clues to your identity. It was the same with profile pictures. If Jade was online, then she was masquerading as a cat or hiding behind an icon – image search drew a blank against her photograph. She briefly considered staking out Lauren Martin's flat. Jade was almost certainly still living with her mum, so it would only be a matter of time before she appeared on the doorstep. Dee dismissed the idea as soon as it occurred. The girl was only sixteen, her mother had warned them off approaching her and the thought of stalking Jade didn't sit comfortably.

The pile of photocopied scribblings waited for attention. It was lunchtime – they could wait until she'd had something to eat. One of the disadvantages of living in a modern apartment block on the River Clyde was the absence of any decent food shops. Apart from a couple of questionable fast-food outlets, the nearest places were on the Dumbarton Road which was a good fifteen minutes' walk away. Dee started walking.

There was still a lot of building work going on in the area. Builders' vans littered the roads, the sound of power tools and hammering coming from inside unfinished apartments. She lived only a few hundred metres away from where the River Kelvin seeped into the Clyde. Dee shivered at the prospect of the young woman's bound body drifting past her apartment balcony windows if it hadn't caught under the bridge. The thought of pre-historic inhabitants associating a goddess with the murky river was a concept so alien she dismissed it out of hand. Her mobile vibrated inside her jacket. It was Teàrlach.

'Hiya. How did it go with the psychokiller? Qu'est-ce que c'est?' She smiled as she imagined his expression.

'I had to run. Run away.' Teàrlach spoke dryly.

Dee knew he had a sense of humour buried under there somewhere.

'He gave me a steer to where I can find Jade. I'm heading there now – the Freemason's building in Crow Road. Said she works as a cleaner. Hang on...'

She heard him accelerate, change gear.

'Sorry. Some eejit deciding to park without signalling. Almost rammed into the back of him. Aye, so, can you do a bit of research for me on this chapter or whatever they call themselves?'

'I think they call them lodges. Like beavers. You should ask Chloe; she's been researching Freemasonry online.'

Teàrlach responded with a non-committal grunt. 'At least beavers are useful. I'm going to park up and watch for Jade. If I can talk to her, she may be able to give me something about her dad's death. We've spent three days looking into this and have bugger all to give Nicole for her money.'

'Her mum said she was up in her room the whole time listening to music. Lauren wasn't too keen on us going anywhere near her daughter as I remember.'

'She's sixteen. Not exactly a child anymore.'

'Not exactly an adult either,' Dee countered.

'I'm only going to ask for her take on it. See if she can add anything.'

'Aye, fair enough. I've sent you a copy of an email to that solicitor about Willie Warmington's cousin, did you see it?'

'Yep, thanks. That didn't take long.' There was a pause, then the sound of an indicator ticking a metronome beat. 'OK, I'm parked up near the church – lodge. Send through anything you find, just in case.'

'In case of what? You want me to look for anything in particular?'

'I don't know. See if any of the members have criminal convictions or whatever. Anything that smells odd.'

'Like a penchant for bondage and rope?' Dee asked. A builder walking towards her stopped eating his burger, eyes open wide as he feasted upon more tasty fare. She smiled at him sweetly, felt his eyes on her back as they passed.

'I don't know. Anything that flags up a concern.'

'The fact that you have a bunch of guys dressing weirdly and rolling up their trouser legs isn't enough of a flag for you?'

Teàrlach laughed. 'Aye, right enough. Message me if you do come across anything.'

'Will do.' The call ended just as Dee spied her favourite food stop. She didn't hold out much hope. These secretive organisations were still writing on vellum, not leaving data strewn across the Cloud for people like her to find.

She made a start as soon as she returned to the flat. There was no ready information showing a list of lodge members, so she followed the money, starting with the sale of church title deeds to identify a holding company. The main shareholder was a Peter McKinnon, someone who'd made a small fortune setting up a paper-shredding business and selling it for millions. His background checks came back without anything, not even a parking ticket, although there were a couple of small claims outstanding. They were both relatively small amounts of a few thousand each, but Dee made a note of them anyway. Peter McKinnon was either playing hardball with the tradesmen listed as claimants or he was short of money.

She kept digging, entering his name into historical newspaper searches until she received a hit from forty years ago. The article was about a spate of domestic animal attacks that had occurred in the same neighbourhood as Seaview Drive. Her interest roused, she magnified the accompanying black and white photograph until it filled the screen. Dee was staring at a dead cat tied up in string, with an eight-year-old Peter McKinnon peering at the camera from behind his mother.

FOURTEEN
PYRAMID

It used to be a church, the stone blackened with age. Now that Jesus had left the building, it had been repurposed. A pair of interlocking triangles had been carved into the stone above the doorway, a set square facing upwards pinned down by a set of dividers with a capital letter G residing in the middle. An air of dissolution hung around the place, giving the impression that nobody really cared for it. Someone had carelessly hacked at the long grass, leaving clumps of decaying vegetation haphazardly scattered over the uneven path.

Teàrlach made himself comfortable, stretched out in his seat and keeping watch on the pavement outside. He didn't have to wait long until Jade Martin appeared in his rear-view mirror. She looked like her photograph, apart from her newly cropped hair. Her skinny body made her look more like a boy. She was taller than he expected, almost as tall as her brother – certainly taller than most sixteen-year-old girls. Unless her height came from the boots she wore – classic Doc Martens over cropped jeans. Were skinheads even a thing anymore?

He wound down the passenger window as she drew alongside, leaning over the seat to call to her.

'Jade Martin?'

She took a step away from the car in alarm, the keys in her hand gripped in defence.

'Who are you?' Her features had twisted into a scowl, but he could see her relax as he made no effort to leave the driver's seat. There were enough pedestrians around to give her confidence. 'How do you know my name?'

'My name's Teàrlach Paterson, I'm a private investigator.'

She readied herself for a response that Teàrlach guessed wouldn't be polite. He cut in before she had a chance to begin.

'I've been to see your brother, Logan. He wanted me to pass on a message.'

She regarded him with suspicion, keeping a safe distance from any potential kidnap, yet curiosity was burning a hole in her blue eyes.

'What did he want?' Jade bit her lower lip, eyes flicking up and down the road in case Teàrlach had an accomplice. 'How is he, is he alright?'

Teàrlach shrugged. 'About as good as anyone banged up for twenty years. You been to see him, you or your mum?'

Jade switched from biting her bottom lip to biting the top one. 'What's it to you?'

'Nothing,' Teàrlach responded with an air of unconcern. 'I guessed he hadn't seen much of you, otherwise he wouldn't have asked me to pass on a message.'

Her eyes narrowed, followed a man walking into the church grounds. Teàrlach turned to see what had caught her attention, caught a glimpse of the guy before the door closed behind him.

'What did he have to say? I haven't got all day; I'm meant to be working.'

'At the Masons Hall?'

Jade's suspicious air changed to one of surprise. 'How do you know where I work?'

'I'm a private investigator, like I said. It's my job to know things.'

She considered this, accepted that at least was true. 'So, what's the message?'

'I'll tell you, but I need something from you in return.'

'You a perv or something?' She shot back.

'No. I'm working for your aunt, Nicole.'

Jade's eyes performed an elaborate mime of rolling around her head. 'That weirdo! Don't tell me. She wants to know why her precious brother who was too good for us ended up dead.'

'Basically, yes.'

'And then you'll tell me what Logan said?' She stuck her chin out in what Teàrlach imagined was meant to be a belligerent pose. He nodded encouragingly.

Jade let out an audible sigh. 'OK. It's like this. I didn't see or hear anything. I was in my room minding my own business until my mum came to drag me out of the house.'

'Did you hear them arguing before it happened? Is there anything you can tell me that I can pass onto Nicole?' Teàrlach saw the shutters closing down and hurried on. 'She's grieving for her brother, the least you can do is give her some reason why it happened.'

She stared at him, eyes expressing irritation more than any other emotion. 'Like I said,' she continued, 'I don't know anything!'

Teàrlach saw the first crack appear in her façade, detected raw emotion under the surface.

'Did he do anything to you, Jade? Is that why Logan stabbed him?'

Jade responded with a panicked expression. She looked as if she was getting ready to run, then struggled to retain her composure, feet regaining balance on the pavement.

'You going to tell me what he said or not?' The chin jutted out once more.

'Sure. He said that he knew what he did to you and to stay safe. You may have to leave Glasgow.'

She gave no visible reaction to his words.

'Are you in trouble, Jade? Is there anything I can do to help? We're not the police, you can tell us if anyone is threatening you and we'll deal with it for you. Who is it that did something to you – was it your dad? Why did your brother say you had to leave Glasgow? If you need help, you can just call us.' He handed her a business card through the open window.

Jade snatched it out of his hand, shoved it into her jacket pocket. She started walking away, heading towards the church entrance. 'Just stay away from me,' she called out over her shoulder. 'Stay the fuck away!'

FIFTEEN
TERRA

The water tribute had been found that morning. She had been weighted down with stones, anchored to the bed of the Kelvin as a tribute to Clota, the goddess of the Clyde. In time, she would have broken free, floated on the current, adding her blessing to the river.

Instead, she had been snared on a shopping trolley. Adding sacrilege to all the other sins against the original gods – the real gods. Not this Christian imposter. She'd seen the original bible, knew it was a lie. The only path to salvation lay in the pentagram. In worshipping the old gods. In leaving sacrifice.

There wasn't much time left. This next one required a lot of preparation. She may have to start earlier than planned to be able to complete the ritual in time. A quick glance at the dashboard clock – 11:50 p.m. She started the engine, switched on the taxi light.

The girl staggered along the pavement in front of her as if pleading to be taken, her hand waving for the taxi to stop.

'You all right, love?' She spoke through the passenger window. 'Can I give you a ride home?'

Distrusting eyes struggled to focus, hands held onto the

doorframe for support. The young woman smiled when she caught sight of the blond hair.

'Great. Yeah, thanks.' She fell into the back of the car, gave an address just a few minutes' drive away. She was close to passing out already. Just needed a little push.

* * *

She'd been busy in the lock-up. A flatpack coffin lay waiting assembly – one of these that doubled as a bookshelf. That had been funny enough for her to laugh out loud. There was a spade, an oak sapling, an augur bit and plastic tree guard. It was past midnight, but the pentagram demanded observance.

'De terra venimus ad terram.' She traced the course of the symbol with her feet until reaching an inverted triangle bisected with a horizontal line.

'The earth and all it contains is yours. The world, and those who dwell in it.'

She reached inside a pocket, withdrew a handful of earth and sprinkled it by her feet. There was no time to waste.

SIXTEEN
SPIRIT

The boys' shouts had become louder, more incoherent with each bottle they consumed. Newly emboldened, they'd started pairing off with the girls and the campfire flames could no longer compete for heat. The group sat on fallen branches, arranged around the leaping flames. Faces were caught in the twisting light, throwing features into unflattering focus as mouths sought mouths, hands explored territory both familiar and new.

Jeannie pushed her boy away, making some excuse about needing a wee and letting him know that no, she didn't require any help. She staggered slightly, Glasgow's lights a carousel in her vision until she forced herself to recover equilibrium, setting a course towards the nearby trees and weaving between standing stones. They'd walked to the top of the hill, carrier bags laden with alcohol and as far away from the city streets as they could, but even so the police were more than likely to pay them a visit. The fire alone could be seen from a distance, a beacon bright enough to attract unwanted attention. She'd tried to stop them piling on more wood, running around like eejits and throwing on more until they'd created a pulsating light that shone its message far across the city.

She squatted under a tree, far enough away from the group that she couldn't be spotted, close enough to call for help if someone crept up on her. Queen's Park was an oasis of green scarcely large enough to provide for the press of humanity on each side. In common with other urban parks, its character changed as darkness approached – becoming altogether more unwelcoming for children, dog-walkers and runners so it was left empty except for those shunned by society, or those who preyed on the weak. She shivered, suddenly spooked by her own fears and stood up so quickly that she staggered, thrown off-balance and tripped by her own pants still wrapped around her ankles. Jeannie landed on her back, winded but otherwise unharmed and stared at the night sky and the branches spread over her head. The drink and adrenaline found release in howls of laughter directed at herself, grateful that no one had been close enough to take a video. Then she saw something that stopped her laughter dead, and she began screaming loud enough to bring the rest of them running.

* * *

Dee caught the news report the following morning, the woman reporter gesturing beyond ubiquitous police tape towards a tree-clad hill in the city. A major incident van was parked behind her, dog units criss-crossing behind her back. She turned up the sound, breakfast forgotten.

'... unable to provide any further information at this stage.'

'Do we know how he died, Valerie, is this a murder investigation?'

The reporter consulted her phone, scrolling a finger rapidly up the screen.

'Chief Inspector William McVicar has said that this is a

murder investigation, but they cannot release any further details until the next of kin have been informed.'

'What about social media posts that this is another body found tied up in rope, has anyone been able to confirm?'

'As far as I know that is only a rumour. The police have not divulged anything about the circumstances around the man's death and have asked me to remind people not to speculate as this could harm the investigation. More police patrols have been allocated for the city's streets tonight and people have been advised to remain vigilant.'

'Thank you, Valerie. We'll bring you more on this breaking story as soon as we can. That's Valerie Townsend reporting from Queen's Park on the south side of Glasgow, and that brings us to the end of the morning news.'

Dee turned off the TV, shuffled through the papers on her table until she found the hand-drawn map and overlaid pentagram. Queen's Park was nowhere near any of the points Chloe had identified so that looked like even more of a far-fetched theory than ever. She went to close down her laptop, then just as quickly opened it again and searched social media for any mention of Queen's Park.

It didn't take long for her to find one of the teenagers' posts. True to form she'd documented everything from the lass sprawled on the ground to the body suspended above her. The shaky video was accompanied by screams and curses as the youngsters realised what they were looking at was real, then showed a panicked flight down the hill and towards a well-lit street before abruptly stopping. As a film it wasn't going to win any awards, but Dee was able to freeze the frame where the body hung lifeless from a branch. This wasn't a suicide. The young man was cocooned in rope, suspended like a chrysalis patiently awaiting a metamorphosis that would never happen. She grabbed a screenshot, pulled on her leathers and made for the underground car park and her bike.

. . .

Teàrlach was at his desk when she arrived, Chloe parcelling up the journals.

'Morning, Chloe. Heard about the guy they found in Queen's Park?' She placed her helmet on top of a filing cabinet, started changing out of her gear.

'No, I'm just in. Didn't see the news last night – what's it about?'

'Was on this morning. On the telly – *Scotland This Morning*.'

'Never watch the telly in the morning,' Chloe replied, tearing Sellotape with her teeth. 'What have I missed?'

'This.' Dee thoughtlessly opened her laptop on the frozen frame, the body hanging out of a tree above a hysterical teenage girl collapsed on the ground underneath.

'Shit! Another one.' Chloe closely examined the image, seemingly unperturbed by her own suicide attempt a few years ago.

Teàrlach came through to join them, alerted by the commotion. 'What now?' He caught sight of the picture, frowned and moved in for a closer look. The two women exchanged a look that said he needs glasses. Teàrlach remained blissfully unaware of the two women's detective capabilities.

'Where was this, and when?'

'Heard it on the morning TV news. You didn't see it?' Dee asked.

'I was busy, didn't have time to watch daytime TV,' he answered.

The women exchanged another glance. 'Well, the body was found at Queen's Park last night. Group of teenagers had their midnight revels rudely interrupted when one of them saw the body.'

'Can you print that off for me?' Teàrlach asked.

Dee hit a couple of keys and the printer obediently whirred into life.

'It's another roped up victim.' Teàrlach took the print, holding it an optimum distance to obtain the clearest focus. 'This looks like the same rope as the lassie in the Kelvin.' He looked at them both in puzzlement. 'What the fuck is going on?'

They shrugged in response.

'It's got to be connected to the Warmingtons and Martins somehow,' Dee prompted. 'Will your boyfriend be able to help?' She directed this at Chloe.

'He's not my bloody boyfriend!'

Teàrlach held his hands up in a plea for peace. 'It doesn't really matter if there is a connection, we're off the case.'

Chloe shrugged and went back to packaging the journals. Dee followed him back to his office.

'What do you mean, we're off the case? I spent hours researching that bloody Freemason lodge for you last night. You could have told me before I wasted my time.'

He sat behind his desk, made a gesture that could have been apologetic. 'I'm sorry, you're right. I only decided this morning and asked Chloe to pack away the journals. We've not made any progress on the case, and I'm not taking any more money off Nicole Martin without any hope of producing results. It looks like the boy killed his dad, and all I can add to that is that he killed him for molesting his own daughter. I don't think that would give her any satisfaction, so no, we'll stop here.'

Dee held her ground. 'We know there's a link between these murders. The least we can do is investigate them or tell the police.'

'The police will have made the link between the guy in the tree and the lassie in the river, and you know we can't mention the Warmingtons.' He held her gaze until she backed down.

'I just wanted to find the bastard that killed that girl. And this one looks no older than a teenager himself.'

'We can't take on work without pay. This is for the police to sort, not us.' He saw her determination and relented. 'OK, we've until the end of today. See if you can make any progress at all so I've something to give Nicole, but we don't step on anyone's toes. Understood?'

Dee nodded, made to leave, then stopped as Teàrlach questioned her.

'What did you find out about that Freemason chapter?'

'Lodge. Hell's Angels are in chapters.' She looked at him askance, linking her two hands together and making a point with her two little fingers. 'Here's the Temple, and here's the steeple.' Her thumbs drew apart, then she inverted her hands to waggle her interlinked fingers apart. 'Open the doors and here's the dodgy lodgy people.'

Teàrlach smiled. 'Lodge, chapter, whatever. Did you find anything that moves this investigation forward?'

'I'll fetch my laptop.'

Dee returned with the laptop and a fresh coffee, taking a noisy slurp and then sitting down opposite him with her fingers flying across the keyboard. She spun the screen around so they could both view it.

Teàrlach's eyes narrowed with the effort of focussing. She bit back the comment forming on her lips about buying him a magnifying glass. He had a limited tolerance for Sherlock-themed jokes.

'First up, this isn't an official Freemason lodge. This is a list of Glasgow lodges, they're not that secretive, and the Crow Road address isn't here.'

'Maybe it's a new one and they haven't updated the website?'

'Good try. I checked the metadata, and this site was recently updated two weeks ago. Not only that, I found this online.' She flicked to a new page. 'This is an internal memo complaining about the Crow Road lodge masquerading as Freemasons and suggesting legal action to close it down. They decided not to proceed to avoid bringing the organisation into disrepute.'

'I take it that memo isn't generally available online?'

Dee smiled. 'Define generally available.' She quickly swiped to another page. 'And this is the guy who set up the lodge, Peter McKinnon.'

'What's his story?'

Dee's smile grew larger. 'On the surface he's a successful businessman. Sold a paper-shredding company for a couple of million two years ago and rubs shoulders with the great and the good of Glasgow.'

'Not too many of them,' Teàrlach commented. 'The good, that is.'

'He's also a Freemason, or ex-Freemason if that's a thing. Left around the time he made his money and under some sort of cloud.'

Teàrlach's raised eyebrows prompted for more information.

'I can't find out what he did to upset them, but he's persona non grata with the Freemasons generally. Been struck off, had his trouser legs pulled back down, regalia removed, whatever. Thing is, he set up his own parallel organisation and recruited sufficient disaffected Freemasons to his cause that it has become an official schism. The church belongs to a holding company he owns. Safe to say, the regular Freemasons are not happy.'

'I don't see how this helps us,' Teàrlach said dismissively. 'Bunch of people deciding to change which trouser leg to roll up or change a wacky handshake to a high five. It's of no interest to us or relevant to the case.'

'Well, that's what I thought. So I dug some more, specifically into Peter McKinnon's past, and found this!'

She flicked the last screen into place, a newspaper article dating back forty years. The black and white photograph showed a dead cat, blood matting its white fur. The animal was curled up in death, legs awkwardly splayed in an unnatural pose. Teàrlach realised the cat had been tied up with string as Dee spoke.

'This was eight-year-old Peter's pet cat. Someone had tortured it to death, caused a bit of a stir at the time because they published the photo.'

'Did they find who did it?' he asked quietly.

'No.'

They exchanged a look. In the main office, Chloe answered the phone.

Sensing the urgency in her voice, Teàrlach waited until she hung up before asking 'What is it, Chloe?'

'That was Lauren Martin. Jade's gone missing!'

SEVENTEEN
POI

Dee and Teàrlach drove straight to Lauren's flat on the Crow Road, slowing down to a crawl as they passed the Masonic Temple. There was no sign of activity, the church melancholy in its patch of roughly tended grass and forgotten tombstones. Gravity had brought most of the markers to their knees, those remaining upright did so more in the way of a tribute to a Glaswegian drunk.

Lauren Martin watched them climb the stairwell, wiping her eyes with the back of her hand. They sat in her small living room, waited for her to light a cigarette held in trembling fingers.

'You've got to find her!'

'What's happened, Lauren? What makes you think she needs finding?' Teàrlach attempted to soothe her, his voice low and measured. She paced back and forth, sending distraught stares towards them through smeared mascara.

'She never came home last night.' She started to wail. 'I don't know what to do.' The last words were choked off in a sob.

Teàrlach couldn't help running a comparison of how she'd

behaved two days previously, only too pleased to see the back of them. Whatever had been bothering her then, it had come back to haunt her with a vengeance.

'Lauren, she's not a child anymore. Could she be having a sleepover at a friend's house?'

Teàrlach used the terms sleepover and friend loosely, book-ending the statement about Jade not being a child. Lauren's cigarette glowed bright red in response as she inhaled a lungful of nicotine.

'She's been taken by this murderer. I know she's been taken.' Lauren started sobbing in earnest now, body crumpled in on itself. She held onto a chair back for support.

Dee took charge, holding Lauren close and leading her back to the seat she'd just vacated. 'Sit down here.' A flick of the eyes told Teàrlach to try and comfort her. 'I'll make us a cup of tea.'

Teàrlach placed an arm around Lauren's shaking shoulders, hearing Dee busying herself in the small galley kitchen.

'Try not to worry,' he said soothingly. 'We'll do everything we can to find her.' He cast an anxious glance towards the door, feeling a sense of relief as Dee returned with mugs of tea.

'I'm sure she's alright. Probably lost track of time and is still asleep on someone's floor,' Dee ventured, holding out a steaming mug.

Lauren took the mug in her spare hand, the cigarette still clasped between two fingers. 'I know she's in trouble,' she wavered. 'And these killings. I'm frightened. I just need her home.'

Teàrlach had heard these same words so many times before, a plea from the heart that he felt powerless to ignore.

'If you think she's in danger, then you have to tell the police.' He saw the denial written across her face before she responded.

'No polis. I can't tell the polis!'

He tried rationalising with her. 'They're better placed than we are to help you, especially if you think she's gone missing. They can put word out to other regions, spread her picture around social media, knock down doors if it comes to that.'

'I said no polis!' Lauren spat the words out, sounding more like she had yesterday. She sucked the life out of the cigarette, stubbed it on a convenient ashtray.

Dee attempted another tack. 'What trouble is she in, Lauren?'

Lauren locked eyes with her, a realisation that Dee might be the dangerous one.

'I didn't say she was in any trouble; I just want you to find her.' She reached for the box of cigarettes, fumbling for the last one. 'It's not safe out there with this guy tying people up and killing them. It's not safe.'

Teàrlach glossed over Lauren's contradiction. 'Why can't you tell the police, Lauren? If you want us to help, we have to know what we're dealing with.' He watched her carefully as she played for time, striking another match and filling the air with the pungent tang of sulphur dioxide.

'We don't want any more trouble with the polis.' She gratefully inhaled another fix. 'My son is in prison for murder – do you think they'd give us any help?'

It was a reasonable enough excuse for not wanting police involvement, but she was clearly lying.

'OK. We can try, but you'll have to tell us what you know. Why do you think she's in trouble?'

Lauren stood, crossed over to look out over the Crow Road, searching for any sign of her daughter. Even with her back to him, Teàrlach could see the tension evident in her shoulders as she struggled to answer the question. 'I can't. I just can't.'

'Then we can't help you.' Teàrlach stood, Dee followed his lead as he started towards the door.

'Wait!'

They stopped. 'Please, you have to help me,' she croaked. Lauren sat like a condemned woman, the spark dead inside her. Her eyes in their mascara panda circles pleaded with them to stay.

'You have to tell us what's going on, Lauren. The more information we have, the sooner we can find Jade.'

Lauren nodded in response.

Teàrlach and Dee returned to their seats. He pulled a notebook and pen out of his jacket, turning towards her. 'I can't work for free, Lauren, much as I'd like to.'

Lauren's mouth twisted down. 'I understand. I've money coming from the sale of the house. I don't care how much it costs. I want my girl back.'

'What can you tell me?' Teàrlach's pen poised in place above his opened notebook, and Lauren started to speak.

'Jade went to work as usual, early yesterday afternoon.'

'Where does she work?' Teàrlach interrupted. He wanted to compare Lauren's answer to the truth.

'The old church down the road. She works as a cleaner. Money's crap, but it's cash in hand so worth doing.' She checked her cigarette packet unsuccessfully, then crumpled it in disgust. 'She's been working there ever since we moved here, couple of months for two afternoons a week.'

'Is she not staying on at school?' Dee asked.

'She was old enough to leave, so she did. Think she wanted to stay with all the rumour and gossip about her dad?'

Teàrlach pulled the conversation. 'Who are her friends?'

'She doesn't have any friends, not around here. And not any from the school either. She's usually back here by five, sometimes looks around the shops, but she's never stayed away without telling me first. She knows I worry.' Lauren bit her lip again, a finger wiping under one eye.

She pointed to a phone on the table. 'She didn't take her mobile to work.'

Dee exchanged a disappointed look with him; their easiest way of tracking Jade was written off.

'Did you go there – to the church – ask when she left or if anyone knew where she went afterwards?'

'Of course I went!' Lauren snapped. 'I've been out looking for her all last night. The church was closed, door was locked. Someone's taken her and with these murders...' She broke down, wracking sobs making her body heave.

Dee made for the bathroom, returning with a roll of toilet paper.

'Thanks,' Lauren muttered reluctantly. 'I'm sorry, I don't know who else to ask.' She quietened sufficiently to tear of a quantity and wipe her face dry, before blowing her nose wetly on the already sodden paper.

'You said she was in trouble?' Dee asked her gently.

Lauren raised her face, searching Dee's eyes to see if she could be trusted and came to a decision. 'Keith was a good man, but he had a gambling problem. Cut a long story short, he owed someone a lot of money, and I mean a lot of money. When he died, I thought that was the end of it, but they came round looking for payment. We were being threatened, me and Jade. Just two women alone in that house and we'd never earn enough to pay them. I decided we had to leave, move somewhere and start afresh where nobody knows us.'

Teàrlach couldn't help the cynicism in his voice. 'You didn't exactly move very far. We're, what, two miles away!'

She glared at him. 'We didn't have enough money to go any further. Least, not until the house is sold. Then we're leaving Glasgow for good.' The anger dissipated as fast as it had arrived. 'But I need my girl. She's all I have left, and now they've taken her.' Her voice failed as fresh sobs took over.

Teàrlach looked over helplessly towards Dee. She picked up the toilet roll again, held it encouragingly in front of Lauren.

'Listen, Lauren. We can try and help you find Jade, but you have to tell us who your husband owed money to. If someone's been threatening you and your daughter, then we can at least go and talk to them, see if they know anything about her disappearance. When does the church open up? Have you a name or something so we can talk to the people where she worked?'

'I don't know anyone at the church.' She sniffed, clutching a fresh handful of toilet paper. 'It's not a church, it's a Freemason Temple. Keith used to be a member at another lodge, so Jade got the job. Knows what to say, what not to say.'

'Who is it you think has Jade? I need a name and an address.' Teàrlach reworded his question.

She looked up at him, cheeks streaked with mascara and face twisted with anguish.

'He's dangerous. There's no knowing what he's capable of.'

'Just give me a name, Lauren.'

'Peter McKinnon. He's a multi-millionaire. Keith used to play cards with a group of them before falling out. I only found out he owed money after he'd died.' She grabbed Teàrlach's hands in hers, wet toilet paper sandwiched between their fingers. 'He can have all the money from the house, I don't care. I just want my girl back.'

Teàrlach extricated his hands with difficulty, wiping shredded toilet paper on his trousers as he stood.

'We'll look into it for you. If this McKinnon has your daughter, we'll bring her back.'

'He's dangerous. Don't do anything to upset him – I don't know what he'd do to Jade!' Lauren's fists curled across her heart in fear.

'You have my number, call me as soon as you hear anything or if she turns up. We'll be in touch very soon.' Teàrlach paused in the doorway. 'You have to tell the police if you've been threatened, you or Jade. And you should tell them Jade's missing, just so they can check hospitals, local CCTV. You need to trust them.'

'I can't trust them. It has to be you.'

Teàrlach engaged with her tear-stained eyes, her hands now unclenched and held out towards him in pleading.

Lauren had the look of a woman preparing to grieve for her daughter's death. It felt like shutting the door on despair.

EIGHTEEN
EARTH

Emily Katz literally couldn't move. She'd woken in pitch blackness, so dark that she feared she'd lost her sight. Her arms and legs were tightly bound against her body, making unused muscles cramp with pain. She would have screamed if it wasn't for the foul-tasting rag in her mouth, pulled tight against the back of her neck.

She lay there, forcing herself not to give in to the panic building inside her chest and calming her breathing until it became less frantic. She was flat out on a padded floor, the silken material thin enough that she could feel the hard surface underneath. Something about the smell of the place gave her the impression that she was being held underground, or in a damp basement. The silence was oppressive, the only sound the wet rush of air in and out of her nostrils.

How did she end up here? Emily fought through an all-enveloping brain fog to remember, the repetitive throb of pain across her forehead making every attempt at thought difficult.

She'd gone to the pub with friends, the usual group. They'd been together ever since leaving school four years ago. It was someone's birthday. Her memories played on a shaky newsreel inside her head. Then they'd moved en masse to the local nightclub, she'd had enough by midnight. Too many mixers had gone straight to her head. Someone called an Uber for her when she started losing her balance and then...

Try as she could, there was only a blank between her leaving the club and waking up here. Wherever here was. Panic briefly overwhelmed her again as she struggled uselessly against ropes tying her limbs tight to her body. Whoever had done this to her would be back, and she had to be ready.

There was just sufficient slack in the bindings around her legs to flex her feet. Snakelike, she began exploring the confines of her prison, feeling for anything she could use to cut herself free. Her fingers confirmed every small propulsion forward, fingernails scratching over a cushioned silken surface with each push of her heels. After moving all of ten centimetres her head impacted an unyielding surface with a muffled thump.

She lay still, exhausted by flexing her body against the constraints of her bindings. Lying in the dark, pressed up against two unyielding walls, Emily had a nightmarish thought which threatened to overwhelm her sanity. There was something she had to try, despite the horror such a manoeuvre would bring if her worst fears were true. Bracing herself, she used every effort to sit up. Her stomach muscles protested as she strained her torso upwards, fighting against the ropes that held her tight. When her head felt the wooden ceiling immediately above her head, she whimpered in fear.

She was trapped inside a wooden box, closely fitting her body on every side and padded with soft material. Her scream was muffled by the rag in her mouth, but she could confirm by the sound reflections that she was in a small space – and it felt to her like a coffin. The awful possibility she'd been buried alive came moments before the realisation that she only had so much air left to breathe.

Emily thought of her flatmate waiting for her to come home.

She'd know something was wrong when she didn't turn up for work. How was anyone going to find her buried underground? Somebody had drugged her. Why couldn't she remember what had happened?

Emily lay perfectly still in pitch darkness, hearing nothing but the sound of her own breathing using up however much air was left. This was how she was going to die, trapped inside a coffin without any hope of being discovered. Tears formed in each eye, overspilled the natural reservoir of her lower eyelids and crept down her cheeks. There was so much she wanted to do with her life, so many experiences that would forever be denied. Her parents didn't even know she'd been taken. She surrendered to despair.

When the sobbing stopped, Emily quietened into an acceptance of her fate. The air by now should be getting stale. A coffin could only hold so much air, and what little there was had been in and out of her lungs enough times to have filtered every last scrap of oxygen. It was the coldness of the air that alerted her, more so than the vague scents catching the back of her nose each time she took in another lungful. Each breath was cool and fresh instead of warm and stale. What if she wasn't underground at all?

She considered her options, kept a lid on the panic threatening to drive her insane. The threat of suffocation receded, for the moment at least. Air was being refreshed inside the box, she could tell it was fresh and cold. The silence told her the air wasn't being pumped, so there had to be a connection to the outside world. The complete lack of any sound also reinforced the impression that she was buried underground, otherwise she'd be able to hear traffic, people, birds. The realisation confirmed there was little chance of escape.

Her mental checklist continued. Water – already her mouth felt dry, the rag having absorbed all available spittle and was now rubbing painfully against raw skin each side of her lips.

People could only last so long without water – was it a day, or two? Did that mean whoever had imprisoned her would return with water and food?

Emily refused to consider any other alternative. In any case, she rationalised, why keep her alive with an air supply if she'd just been left here to die? She tried to conserve her energy, tried to stay calm and focussed. Whilst she remained imprisoned, Emily worked on her bonds, flexing muscles and encouraging movement to stretch the ropes. Her teeth caught at the gag, chewing the foul-tasting fabric. She'd do all she could to break free and ignore the hysteria building inside her mind.

NINETEEN
PRIVATE

The church door might have been built to withstand a siege, Teàrlach's knuckles making as much impact upon the worn oak as a child's soft hand.

'I'll have a look around the back,' Dee offered. She followed a path that led around the rear of the church until defeated by brambles. There might be another way in, but she'd need a machete before making any further progress. The windows were too high off the ground to get a view of the inside, tall gothic arches filled with original leaded glass. She stepped back, searching for non-existent cameras or alarm systems, then considered what a prime abduction environment this was. The traffic noise from the Crow Road was loud enough to drown out any cries for help, but she cupped her ears towards the glass windows just in case.

Teàrlach was having an equal lack of success, his ear pressed against the wooden door in a futile effort to hear anything from the inside. Dee rejoined him at the entrance.

'Nothing doing,' she summarised.

'I'll come back when the place is open, see what I can find. Let's go back to the car.'

'What did you make of Lauren's story?' Dee asked as he triggered the remote.

'I don't know what to make of it. Sounded like she was telling it straight, but would a multi-millionaire threaten a baker for a gambling debt? They wouldn't have been playing for high enough stakes. Not enough to kidnap his daughter.'

'Guess not, unless he put his house up as collateral. Either way he's a direct link to Keith Martin and knows Lauren and Jade by all accounts. Why would Lauren let her daughter work part-time at the Temple if she knew this Peter McKinnon was involved?'

Teàrlach started the car, threaded into a gap in the traffic.

'I don't think she knows it's his lodge. You saw how frightened she was of him – there's no way in hell she'd have let her daughter anywhere near him.'

'Do you think Jade knew he was there?'

Teàrlach shrugged a response. 'Maybe not. She's a part-time cleaner. No need for her to meet the top man, and his name only came up because you found him on an internal Freemason memo.'

He keyed the phone, asked to call the office. Chloe answered immediately.

'Hi, Chloe, can you find out where this Peter McKinnon lives – Dee's texting you his details now. Oh, and hang fire on cancelling our inquiries into Keith Martin's murder. It's beginning to look as if there's a connection between this Peter character and Keith Martin – Lauren said that her husband owed him a lot of money. Can you also invoice Nicole for another week? Tell her we're making some progress and send a pro forma off to Lauren Martin.'

'Will do. Is this connected to the rope deaths?'

'I've no idea,' he responded. 'Not as far as I can tell. Talking of which, can you ask your man to come in some time? I want to ask him some questions about the ropework.'

There was an uncharacteristic silence from the car speakers, so much so that Dee's thumbs stopped their typing over her iPhone screen.

'He's my brother,' Chloe said haltingly. 'Are you there as well, Dee?'

'Aye, I'm listening in. All ears.'

'OK. Look, I didn't want him to have any contact with you both because he doesn't know about my suicide or any of it. He was at sea a lot of the time, or living up north, so we didn't have much contact. I don't want him to ever know, about the drugs, the pregnancy, any of it.'

Teàrlach responded immediately. 'That's not a problem, Chloe. That stuff's private to you, we'd never say anything about it to anyone.'

Dee chirped in. 'Don't be daft, girl. We've got your back, same way as you'd do for us. All for one and every man for themselves!' She caught Teàrlach's quizzical expression on her from the driving seat before he responded.

'If he'd like to drop in and say hello, then I'd be interested in his views on the ropes, that's all. We'd certainly not get into any discussion about your past. It's up to you, Chloe. Do what's comfortable for you.'

'OK.' The relief in her voice was evident. 'I'll text you this Peter McKinnon's address and have a word with my brother. Bye.'

Dee exhaled dramatically as the phone line dropped. 'She kept that quiet. Her brother!'

'Aye. I can see why she was being reticent. Have you sent her what you have on Peter?'

'Yep.'

They drove a while in silence, the city busy with people going about their daily routines and unheeding of a predator stalking the streets.

'You think Jade is in danger?' Dee asked.

'She's been missing less than a day, the police wouldn't normally be treating it as a disappearance until two or three days have gone by without any contact. But I'm certain Logan only agreed to see me so he could pass on a message for Jade to stay away from someone, and to get out of Glasgow.' Teàrlach paused as a bus pulled out in front of him. 'Lauren's beside herself with worry. Wherever Jade is, she's not come back home and that's out of character.'

'And Lauren thinks this McKinnon character might have her – all for a gambling debt? Is he the guy Logan was warning her to stay away from?'

A text chimed with Peter McKinnon's address, and Teàrlach turned the car towards Bearsden.

'Guess we're going to find out,' Teàrlach replied tersely.

Dee watched the Glasgow streets slide by from the passenger seat with Lauren's tear-streaked face still fresh in her memory. Teenage girls don't tend to drop off grid without letting their mums know where they are, despite the misconception that they're young adults and old enough to do what they want. Especially teenagers who've just lost a dad and have a brother locked up for murder. Jade would be needing her mum as much as her mum needed her. They were all each other had.

The house stood a way off from the road, in a leafy suburb preferred by football players and upwardly mobile young professionals. Teàrlach's car navigation displayed a golf course running along the back of the property, beyond an expanse of mature woodland which might have been part of the grounds. A pair of electric gates hung open at the entrance; judging by the weeds wrapped around the wrought ironwork, they hadn't been closed for weeks. He pulled onto the blockwork drive, swung in a circle so the car was pointing back out. Dealing with the criminal class for so long had made planning for a speedy exit standard behaviour.

'I don't expect any trouble,' he told Dee. 'Once I tell him

who I am, he'll probably just close the door on me, but it might be better if you stayed here in the car?'

Dee opened the door and purposefully strode towards the house, leaving Teàrlach to hurry after her. 'Or not,' he added.

The house didn't, at first sight, give the impression that it belonged to a multi-millionaire. The broken gates and slightly dilapidated pre-war building vibe it gave were at odds with the owner's alleged fortune. That said, the place wouldn't have left much change from a cool million – not here and with so much land attached. He rang the bell, hearing a chime from somewhere deep inside.

The man who answered the door was instantly recognisable from his photograph. Rounded head topped with a short frizz of blond hair, stocky frame turning to fat. He was dressed for the golf course, even to the point of the cashmere Argyle sleeveless jumper with a brash red diamond pattern across his chest.

'Can I help you?' He appeared more puzzled than threatening.

'Mr McKinnon?' Teàrlach waited for the nod of acceptance before offering him his card. 'My name's Teàrlach Paterson, I'm a private investigator looking into the circumstances of Keith Martin's death.'

He looked up from reading the card with a start. 'Sorry, whose death?' The hastily adopted puzzled expression arrived too slowly to take anyone in. 'And what has this to do with me?' His hand returned to the door in preparation for closing it.

'I believe he owed you a sum of money.'

'Who did you say you worked for?' Peter queried.

'I didn't,' Teàrlach shot back. 'I have a couple of clients with an interest in this case, and they've asked me to find out everything I can about the circumstances surrounding Keith Martin's murder.'

Peter McKinnon made a poor attempt of searching for an elusive memory.

'The stabbing! The boy who stabbed his father to death? Terrible business. Still, he's locked up now, isn't he? More than enough knives on the streets as it is – they should lock them all up.'

Dee was uninterested in the conversation once she realised their suspect wasn't likely to pull a gun on them. Why Lauren thought this man was dangerous God alone knows. She'd met dangerous and this wasn't it. Her attention wandered over the CCTV cameras fixed to the walls and one in plain view in the entrance hall. She bent down to her phone, to all intents oblivious of the conversation and intent on checking her social media.

'So, did he owe you money?' Teàrlach persevered.

'Keith Martin?' He wilted under Teàrlach's steady look. 'Yes, now you mention it. We used to play cards a bit, ended up owing me a few pounds. Never bothered me, it was more the playing I liked than the money. I certainly wouldn't have concerned myself with a few bob here and there. He didn't have the look of money about him.'

'That's not the story I've been told. I heard that he owed you a lot. Enough for you to threaten his family.'

Peter found this amusing, so much so that he broke out into laughter. 'That's a good one – who put you up to this? You had me going for a while.'

Teàrlach remained impassive as he quietened down and realised this was in fact serious.

'You're really an investigator?'

Teàrlach gave one imperceptible nod.

'Do you think I'd threaten a woman and her daughter over a few quid? Are you suggesting I had anything to do with the man's death?' He sounded more belligerent now, more sure of himself. 'You'd better leave my property before I call the police. Who the fuck do you think you are? I've not had any contact with the man or his family for years. Yes, he defaulted on a debt, but I let him off with it, I could see the guy was worthless. Are you seriously suggesting I had him killed? You've heard of libel laws I take it? Well, mention any of this again and I'll take you for every meagre penny you have. Now fuck off!'

The door slammed in their faces.

'Nice chap,' Dee declared.

'Come on, nothing we can do here. We'll head back to the office and think it through.'

Dee sat beside him, attention once again on her phone. She launched an app as he started the engine, let out a whoop of joy as they exited the broken gates.

'What's that?' Teàrlach quizzed, brows drawn down in puzzlement.

'That's me into his home router. Still set to the default setting of admin with the same for the password – some people deserve to be hacked. Park up here!'

Teàrlach pulled into the side of the road, within a few metres of the gates but shielded from view of the house by the surrounding wall. Dee dug around on the back seat, pulling out her laptop and settling it on her lap.

'Let's see what you've got, Peter boy.'

TWENTY
PEEPING

Teàrlach was still astonished by the ease with which Dee bypassed security protocols and passwords as if they didn't exist. Her laptop screen displayed a map of Peter McKinnon's home network, giving access to devices and files. She clicked on one node, brought up a sub-menu and then selected the top file. The screen instantly divided into eight small rectangles displaying camera views inside and outside the house. He saw the two of them standing in the doorway, Peter's feet shuffling in and out of view. The adjacent rectangular display showed Peter's back, and occasional glimpses of Dee's red hair as he shifted position.

'I need a haircut.' Dee leaned in for a closer look before double-clicking the image to fill the screen. 'Yep, definitely need a haircut.'

'Have you access to his video files going back a day or two?'

'Depends how much hard disk space is allocated, hang on.' She closed the view of the two of them on the doorstep like a pair of stubborn Jehovah Witnesses, bringing up a list of files that meant nothing to him.

'There. The video files go back four weeks. Do you want to see if Jade appears at the front door?'

'You read my mind,' Teàrlach replied. 'I saw her on Thursday going into the Crow Road church, so any time after 1:00 p.m.'

The front door camera again filled the screen, Dee dragging a marker across the bottom of the image to select Thursday lunchtime.

'I'll start searching from here, so let's see what activity there was up to today.'

An Amazon delivery appeared, the courier taking a shot with his phone before banging on the door and walking out of view, all in fast motion. Peter reached outside to grab the box and shut the door. At three fifteen, he left with a heavy bag of golf clubs on his back. He returned after six, closely followed by a food delivery. A woman appeared in view, most likely Mrs McKinnon, opening the front door for the delivery driver. At ten, motion triggered a security light and a fox scuttled away from the door. Three fifteen in the morning a black cat sat on the step and licked itself, unconcerned with the spotlight. There was no more activity until Peter left the house at nine that morning, returning half an hour before they arrived on camera.

'She's not there. Not unless she fits inside that small parcel,' Dee added helpfully.

'It was worth a look. At least we know where she isn't. What else has he on his home system?'

Dee expertly navigated through folders. 'His financials are here,' she pointed at one folder, 'and this one looks like correspondence. I can't say what's here without digging through the whole lot – hang on.'

She opened another screen, started dragging files from one side to the next.

'Isn't he going to notice if you clear him out?' Teàrlach asked.

'Copied, not moved. He'll not notice anything – except maybe he'll realise his network's running slow. Give me five minutes, and I'll have all the tasty files.'

* * *

When Dee said they were good to go, Teàrlach made for the office feeling like he'd just taken part in a robbery.

They arrived back before one o'clock, Dee heading straight out again to grab herself something to eat. Chloe was bent over her desk marking red dots on a Glasgow map. She beckoned him over.

'What's up?' Teàrlach squinted at the map, saw she'd drawn lines as well as red dots over it.

'These points here,' she indicated two extra-large red dots, 'this is upstream from where the young woman was found in the Kelvin. And this is Camphill Ringwork in Queen's Park. You remember the pentagram from under Jade's bedroom carpet? Well, these symbols on each point of the pentagram are Neo-Pagan marks. I've been looking into them, and they're always arranged in the same order whether it's for the Wicca religion or dark magic.'

She stopped as she caught him looking at her like she needed help.

'No, seriously, listen. The symbols always go like this: Spirit, a circle at the top, then going clockwise Water, an inverted triangle; Fire, an upright triangle; Earth, an inverted triangle bisected by a horizontal line, then finally Air, an upright triangle bisected by a line.'

'I'm not sure how this helps, Chloe?' Teàrlach was beginning to feel concerned on her behalf.

'I thought that the first murder was connected, that's why I positioned the pentagram here originally.' She pointed to a constellation of red dots around the Martin's house. 'But when the body was found on Camphill Ringwork, I thought I was reading too much into the journals.'

'And now?' Teàrlach asked.

Chloe repositioned a pentangle drawn on tracing paper with two points overlapping the sites of the two recent bodies.

'Now they line up. I didn't expect the pentagram to face any way other than north, but of course, it doesn't. This line...' She indicated a thick yellow line heading off the map south-west from Queen's Park. 'This line points directly to Lady Isle off the west coast.'

Teàrlach struggled to make sense of what she was saying and admitted defeat.

'Sorry, Chloe. I don't see what you're getting at here.'

'Look. This point here, the Kelvin. That's water.'

Teàrlach had to agree.

'And this point where the bloke was found bundled up in a tree, that's spirit.'

'Not with you, why not air? He was found hanging up in a tree.'

Chloe made a sound of exasperation. 'Yes, it would look like that except for the ropework. I asked my brother to look at the ropes, remember?'

'Yes, I remember asking if you could see what he could add about the ropework,' Teàrlach said cautiously.

'Right! Well, the knots on the guy in the tree, this knot here...' She reached for an enlarged picture of the body in the tree. 'This is called Solomon's knot. It serves no practical use, so it's purely symbolic.'

'OK.' Teàrlach was impressed despite his initial misgivings. 'What does it symbolise?'

'The union of God and Man, eternity and immortality, a

symbol of love. In other words, Spirit.' She looked at him triumphantly.

'And this point lines up with the two bodies and the pentagram?'

Chloe nodded vigorously.

'So, anything your brother noticed about the ropework on the woman in the Kelvin?'

'Thought you'd never ask.' Chloe replaced the poor-quality screen grab of the body in the tree with a forensics photo of the drowned woman. She pointed to the knot linking all four limbs together that had been concealed behind the woman's back. It looked fairly basic to him, a clumsy loop wrapped around a few times without any finesse.

'Is that even a proper knot?'

'That,' Chloe said proudly, 'is a water knot.'

Teàrlach couldn't see what relevance Chloe's research had to the investigations.

'You've done an amazing job putting all this together, Chloe. And you may be onto something if this all lines up like you say, but it's not directly connected with Keith Martin's murder or Jade Martin's disappearance – unless I'm missing something?'

'I knew you'd say that.' Chloe produced another photograph from her pile, the original forensics shot of the Warmingtons' final moments. 'You asked me to find out about the ropes used on the Warmingtons, and my brother said no way could they have done that to themselves?'

'Yes, go on.'

'He also said that the knots used on the bedposts stood out to him because they weren't proper knots, all the others were recognisable, and he could name them for me. The ones on the bedposts were amateur in comparison. Then I looked more closely at the pattern the rope made going around the bedpost.'

She produced a final print out, a line drawing of the Celtic triquetra symbol.

'See how the rope follows this drawing exactly? This is the same symbol used in Willie Warmington's map, drawn over the street where they lived. There's a connection between all of this, the Martins, these murders and the Warmingtons.'

Teàrlach found himself stroking an imaginary beard. 'Does it mean anything, this triquetra thing?'

'I looked it up. It's to do with body, mind and spirit bound up to make the soul.'

He shook his head. 'None of this makes any sense. Show me the other points on the Glasgow map, where this pentagram intersects.'

Chloe cleared her desk until only the map and tracing paper remained. She carefully marked the pentagram points on the map with a red pen.

'So these,' Teàrlach pointed to the Kelvin River and Queen's Park locations. 'These are where the two bodies have just been found. But this one, way over here, is the Warmingtons' house. It doesn't fit on your pentagram.'

'I know. But what if it was the same killer, and the Warmingtons' murder was never meant to be linked to these other two murders? The evidence was never shown, it's only thanks to Dee we have these forensics photos in the first place.'

Teàrlach frowned in concentration. 'Keith Martin wasn't tied up. Are you saying his death isn't connected?'

'You're the detective,' Chloe countered.

'These other three points on the pentagram, there haven't been any bodies left anywhere near?'

'Not yet, I searched online.'

'OK. I don't know if this is in any way related to our investigations. If another body shows up at any of these remaining three locations, then we have to go to the police and tell them what we've found – without giving away anything about the forensics data we lifted. In the meantime, our priority has to be finding Jade.'

Dee came into the office, finishing a wrap before wiping her mouth. 'What's the latest?'

Teàrlach updated her on Chloe's findings.

'So, it's looking like our murderer is using this same map to place his victims?' Dee questioned.

Chloe shrugged. 'Maybe, it's all guesswork until another body ends up on the map on another pentagram point.'

'And these symbols are Wiccan – witches?' Dee pushed for more information.

Chloe spread her hands. 'I don't know. I looked into it and the pentagram has been around since before the Egyptians. Christians use it to symbolise Christ's wounds, even the Freemasons use it.'

'Oh, do they now?' Dee asked thoughtfully.

'We don't have time for that,' Teàrlach interrupted. 'This stuff may be relevant, I don't know, but we need to track down Jade.' He grabbed his car keys from his desk, paused before leaving the office.

'I'm going to wait outside the church until I see someone go inside. That was the last place we think she went, so it's the obvious place to start looking. Dee, if our Peter McKinnon is up to anything, you might find it in the files you copied across. Chloe, Lauren Martin refuses to contact the police, so can you run checks on the hospitals, the usual places – see if a girl matching her description has been admitted? Call me if either of you find anything.'

Dee turned her attention back to the map and pentagram as soon as Teàrlach headed down the stairs.

TWENTY-ONE
PEWS

Teàrlach found the Masonic Temple door unlocked when he returned, pushing the heavy oak door open on well-oiled hinges and entering into a whitewashed vestibule. Notices concerning forthcoming meetings were pinned to a noticeboard, sharing the space with more prosaic business cards and brochures advertising a range of services. Cobwebs draped from the roof; artisan nets cast in wait for the next airborne victim. A second, more modestly built set of doors led into the church itself, looking much as it had when still a place of Christian worship. High windows filtered light through grimy lead glass, motes of ancient dust danced irreligiously in celebration of worshippers long since departed. Pews lined up in serried ranks, a low stage taking the place of an altar in lacklustre light. Flags drooped listlessly against the undecorated stone walls. He recognised the Union Jack and Saltire, the others were more esoteric and displayed symbols that he recognised from the journals Chloe had been pouring over.

'Can I help you?'

Teàrlach turned to see where the voice came from. A fair-haired man stepped out from an open doorway where he'd been concealed in shadow, the diffuse light from high church windows catching the unnatural pallor of his delicate features so he appeared like an apparition. As he came closer, the ghost resolved into the flesh and blood of an ordinary man, dressed in a severe black suit with an incongruous, embroidered apron belted around his waist.

'My name's Teàrlach Paterson, I'm a private investigator.' He held out a business card for the man to inspect.

'This is private property,' his eyes scanned the card with disinterest, 'Mr Paterson.' He held out an arm in invitation, pointing Teàrlach back towards the entrance. 'We don't allow the uninitiated inside the Temple.' His pale blue eyes fixed Teàrlach with an unsettling intensity whilst a slow smile crept across his face until locking into an unnatural fixed position.

Teàrlach held his ground. 'I'm here on business, looking for a missing girl. Her name's Jade Martin, and this was the last place she was seen. She works here as a cleaner?'

The man's attention remained firmly fixed on Teàrlach. 'Are you the police, Mr Paterson? Or do you have a search warrant?' The smile crept back into place.

'No, neither of those things, but I could bring them both with a single phone call if that's what you want?'

Two pairs of eyes remained locked together. The suited man was the first to crack.

'She cleans twice a week, a couple of hours on a Tuesday and Thursday afternoon. She was here yesterday. I opened the cleaning cupboard for her and left her to it. She completed her work and left, around half two as usual.'

'Then you won't mind if I have a look around?'

The man's fixed smile metamorphosed into a scowl. 'We don't encourage tours.'

'No, I understand you have secrets you wish to keep to yourselves. My interest is solely in finding out where Jade is, what has happened to her. It would be a great help if I can see where she was working yesterday, so I can rule out any connection to this place.'

'As I said, Mr Paterson. We don't encourage tours, so if you'd like to leave...'

'The police might find it suspicious that you refused to let me see where Jade worked.' Teàrlach shrugged off the hand attempting to propel him back to the church doors. 'They can be here within minutes. Is that how you want this to go?'

The man contemplated tackling Teàrlach for a brief moment before sizing him up and realising he might not come out of any physical altercation well.

'I'll show you where she worked. There's nothing here for you to see, but if it puts your mind at ease... This way.' He glided back to the doorway from where he'd first appeared, leading Teàrlach into an area that must have originally been the vestry. A large book lay open, the contents of the pages concealed by a cloth embroidered with more Freemason symbology. An old PA system occupied a shelf, a locked cupboard underneath. There were two doors off the small vestry, one led to a toilet, the other opened to reveal a cupboard with cleaning equipment and shelves of boxes reaching up to the ceiling.

'This is where the cleaning stuff is kept, that's the toilet and you've seen the church. There's nothing else here. As you can see, no cleaner, nowhere else for anyone to hide away. Satisfied?'

'You don't seem particularly bothered that a young woman has gone missing, one who works here for you?'

He shut the cleaning cupboard door, made a point of securing it with a padlock. 'I don't know where she went after finishing up here. It was still early, around two or two thirty and broad daylight on a busy street. I expect she's staying over at a friend's house. It's a bit early to start throwing accusations around, don't you think?'

'I'm not suggesting anything,' Teàrlach replied evenly. 'Her mother is worried, that's all, and asked me to look into it.'

'Well, now you've looked, you can cross us off your list and leave.' He impatiently gestured for Teàrlach to back out into the open church nave.

Teàrlach resisted the urge to wrap the guy's arm around his back, and made towards the main entrance. His attention was caught by colourful canvases displayed on the main entrance wall – they'd been behind him when he entered the nave. One figure might have been a homeless man, a pale halo outlined around his head like a full moon. He benevolently observed a robin perched on his hand. Teàrlach recognised the similarity to the Glasgow High Street mural depicting a modern-day St Mungo. Beside his portrait a woman stretched out an arm from under the surface of a river. A third painting was unmistakably that of a unicorn, unchained hoof raised towards a full moon.

Teàrlach stopped to look at the paintings more closely. 'Who's the artist – this one looks like that painting of Ophelia?' He pointed at the woman lying languid under the water.

His guide stopped to face him, sparing a glance at the paintings before interrogating Teàrlach for signs of guile. Teàrlach's expression remained one of honest wonder; the artwork could have belonged in a museum or art gallery.

'I painted them.' He spoke softly in the open space, sounding more like a child than the aggressive man who'd been chasing Teàrlach out only seconds before. 'They are the old gods, the true gods.'

Teàrlach reluctantly dragged his eyes away from the artwork to focus on the pale man in front of him. The smile had returned.

'You have a real talent.'

He received an inclination of the head as way of an acknowledgement. Teàrlach returned to look at the paintings.

'I thought Freemasons were Christians?' Teàrlach asked

more from his own sense of confusion than from any expectation of receiving a response.

'Freemasons allow any monotheistic faith, but discussion of religion is not encouraged within any lodge. We here believe there are a multiplicity of gods – that's why we have separated from the other brothers. Our path is a different path.' A hand extended towards the door, long delicate fingers pointing to the only entrance.

'Thank you for showing me around, Mr...'

The main church doors were pulled open, and he waited for Teàrlach to leave, the question left hanging.

'Goodbye, Mr Paterson. Been a pleasure meeting you.'

The sound of the big oak door being secured behind his back made any riposte pointless. He checked his watch, almost half past two, the same time Jade was meant to have left yesterday. The Crow Road buzzed with traffic; someone would have seen her leaving – if she left at all. He knew there must be places inside the church where Jade could be hidden, but the suited guy didn't appear too concerned at the threat of a police search. Teàrlach made his way back to the car, deep in thought. The Freemason had confirmed Jade was there yesterday and had left around two thirty. Her flat was only a five-minute walk back up the Crow Road, and Jade was distinctive enough with her skinhead attire to register on people's memories. He cursed himself for not waiting yesterday until she'd left the church, but how could he have known she was about to go missing? Teàrlach crossed the road, running to reach the opposite kerb as a bus headed towards him.

There was something connecting these Freemasons to the murders, that was becoming apparent to him. Keith Martin owed the Master of this breakaway lodge, Peter McKinnon, money. Enough to have him killed and then his daughter kidnapped? The neighbours, Willie Warmington and his wife, whose death the police had termed accidental – someone senior in the force had deliberately concealed evidence of murder. It didn't take a leap of imagination to connect the police force with Freemasonry. Then the recent ritualised murders that were exercising the Glasgow press, and their connection to Willie Warmington's increasingly deranged journals.

Teàrlach shook his head. A missing girl enquiry was one thing, but these disparate murders were more than he and his small team could cope with. In normal circumstances, he'd have passed everything they'd found onto the police and let them deal with it. Everything except the evidence that the Warmingtons had been killed as that would put Dee behind bars and without that, they only had Chloe's interpretation of Willie's bizarre maps and symbols.

He smacked his hands on the steering wheel with frustration. If a sixteen-year-old girl wanted to disappear off the face of the earth, a busy Glasgow street offered more chance of anonymity than a deserted bus stop in the middle of the Highlands. His eyes sought the bus that had come close to running him down, squinted to read the route number. A lot of, if not all, buses were fitted with cameras – internal and external. There might be a way of seeing if Jade left the church and where she went. He reached for his mobile to call Dee just as the Freemason left the church and walked purposely away from him, turning into a side road. Teàrlach checked the satnav map, saw it was a one-way street going in the wrong direction for him to follow in the car. Making a snap decision, he opened the car door to follow on foot, then saw the man at the wheel of a blue Skoda, waiting to join the main road. The left indicator signalled his intention to head in Teàrlach's direction.

Teàrlach turned his face away as the Skoda passed on the other side of the road, then shut the door and forced his way out into the traffic, earning a blast from a car horn. More followed when he spun into a U-turn, leaving him positioned three or four cars behind his target.

Stuck behind the only car on Glasgow's streets religiously obeying the twenty mile an hour limit, the blue Skoda was free to make a getaway at speeds approaching thirty. It felt like a car chase in slow motion, with the prospect of ever catching up fading to zero when the learner stopped at traffic lights only just turned amber.

This wasn't working out at all well, he'd not even managed to catch the Skoda's number plate. Teàrlach gave up, followed the learner driver haltingly navigating the city traffic until they parted ways, and headed back to the office. The day wasn't entirely wasted. He had a possible way of spotting who was on the Crow Road yesterday afternoon at the time Jade was last seen, and they had a new person to investigate. The worry was that Jade had now been missing for twenty-four hours. If she was in trouble, they had to try and find her fast. A job made all the more difficult by not being able to contact the police.

TWENTY-TWO
PHANTOM

Donald Ritchie saw Teàrlach's car pulling a U-turn on the Crow Road. There were enough car horns sounding at his rash manoeuvre to make any attempt at concealment impossible. He kept an eye on the rear-view mirror as the traffic lights drew nearer, keeping well under the 20mph limit before accelerating towards a set of traffic lights. Immediately behind him a learner driver braked and locked Teàrlach into position. Satisfied that he'd so easily lost his tail, Donald made his way leisurely back home to number fifteen Seaview Drive. The private investigator was an unwelcome distraction, one that might require dealing with if he ever came back.

He let himself in, walked through to the back of the house and into the kitchen, where he put on the electric kettle.

'Making a pot of tea. Do you want a cup?' Don cocked an ear for a response, heard a woman's affirmative from up the stairs and added another spoon of tealeaves to the pot. He raked around in a kitchen cupboard for biscuits, added them to a plate and carried them and two cups of tea upstairs.

The house was configured differently to all the other houses on the street. Here the first floor was given over to living space, apart from the ubiquitous bathroom. At the back of the house, the bedroom had been converted to a workshop. Tools lay in ordered rows on wall-mounted hooks; a workbench lay against the rear window to gain the maximum light. The storeroom – Jade's bedroom two houses along – was a library. Each wall covered with bookcases and filled with old leather-bound volumes interspersed with modern works on astrology, magic, history.

The front room had been made into a living space: a settee took the place of a bed, TV screen mounted on the facing wall, armchair backed onto the window. Donald carefully placed the plate of biscuits beside the armchair, added a cup of freshly poured tea onto to a small, circular table where it joined the plate.

'How has your day been?' Donald asked, looking expectantly towards the armchair.

'Oh, nothing special. Just sitting here and reading.' Her voice was as soft as he remembered.

He smiled – a return of the slow stretch of the mouth that had so unsettled Teàrlach. The woman wasn't concerned. She'd seen that smile so many times before.

'Are you working tonight?' she asked.

Donald reached for the biscuits, hesitated with a hand hovering over the plate. 'Do you mind?'

'No, don't be silly. I'm not going to eat them all.' She laughed as if the very idea of eating was somehow ridiculous.

Donald's smile began to slip, then returned as he shared the joke.

'No, of course not.' His hand completed the objective, taking a biscuit. 'No, I'm having a night in tonight.' He apologetically wiped crumbs from around his mouth. 'Been a busy week.'

She nodded understandingly. 'We should have a takeaway tonight. Save you having to cook.'

The smile grew larger. 'You're right. If we're going to have a night in, then we should do it properly. I'll open a bottle of wine.'

'This early? The sun's not over the yard arm.'

'It is somewhere,' Donald retorted. 'And that's good enough for me.'

He returned with a bottle of wine and two glasses, filling hers first before offering a toast. 'To the departed, and their safe return.'

'Will they return?' she questioned him, hand stretching out to take a glass.

'There's no doubt. I promise you that!'

He sipped delicately at the wine but drank in the sight of her with a thirst so ravenous it physically hurt.

'You seem so certain,' she said quietly. There was a note of wonder in her voice, mirrored in her face as she tilted her head up to stare blankly into his pale eyes.

'I've told you.' Donald heard the exasperation in his response, took a deep breath to compose himself and felt the smile return as he reached an inner state of grace.

'Mungo brought the robin back to life after the children killed it.'

'I told you that story, do you remember?' A voice so quiet he could have imagined it.

He remembered. Sitting in her lap and feeling safe and loved – or was that merely a dream as well?

'You told me about the Glasgow saint who brought a dead robin back to life after the children had killed it.' That memory was true. She had told him the story of St Mungo so many times that he had it committed to memory. He'd tried again and again to work the same miracle so he could win her admiration and love. All those dead creatures sacrificed for nothing. The chemical cocktails useless, the magical incantations proving worthless.

'I can do so much more now that I have his bible.'

'His Christian bible?'

He laughed at her confusion. 'Yes, but that's no use to me. I have the original – the missing pages from the Book of Kells. They don't know how valuable the heirloom really is.'

'Do you still need my help?'

Donald reached for her hand. 'Sunday – the sabbath. And then we'll be together forever.'

Her hand felt as insubstantial as a dream in his. They only had a few more days.

TWENTY-THREE
PURL THE OTHER ONE

Dee shut out the distraction of Chloe working the phone in search of Jade. The image of the young woman discarded along with random urban junk in the River Kelvin kept intruding on her imagination as she opened up Peter McKinnon's files on her laptop. They had no leads into her disappearance – unless Teàrlach had found something on his visit to the lodge. It was only twenty-four hours since Jade had last been seen by Teàrlach on Crow Road yesterday afternoon. She'd not been missing long enough for the police to take any interest, but Lauren Martin was beside herself with worry for her daughter's safety.

So far, Peter McKinnon was the only name they had with any connection to Jade and her murdered father. Lauren had told them that Keith owed Peter a gambling debt – large enough to have him killed and his daughter abducted? That seemed too farfetched, about as farfetched as Lauren warning them that Peter McKinnon was dangerous. Dee had seen him full of bluster on his doorstep, straining the seams of his cashmere golfing jumper when he tried threatening Teàrlach. He looked about as dangerous as a tea cosy.

Peter McKinnon's financials weren't in great shape, that

was the first information Dee gleaned from his spreadsheets. He'd re-mortgaged his house to release equity, and with no signs of any regular income, the guy was running on empty. The millions he'd made from the sale of his paper-shredding business had been spent on his house and the church on Crow Road, plus a few investments that had turned sour. She moved onto his correspondence. The Freemasons weren't enamoured with him, that was clear – threatening all sorts of legal action about his setting up an independent lodge and using their symbols on the building. There were several demands for money from tradesmen, advertisers, a legal firm and Glasgow City Council were chasing him for overdue rates. Dee was losing the will to live perusing the depressing minutia of Peter's life when she came across a folder with encrypted word files. Now her interest was piqued. Using a standard sledgehammer approach to forcibly decrypt Peter's documents would take Dee and a quantum computer around ten times as long as the universe has existed. Which was why she chose a different route. The email she sent to Peter appeared to be from his bank, advising him that his balance was overdrawn and requesting he add credit to avoid additional charges. Displayed in the email footer was the bank's corporate logo and hidden in that was a keystroke logger. Next time Peter wanted to look at his encrypted files, she'd have a record of his passwords. Satisfied that she'd done as much as she could, Dee closed her laptop and stared out at the Clyde, sluggish and grey under the clouds covering the city.

'Hi, sis.'

Dee turned her attention to the door as a man walked in and held Chloe in a bear hug. Even from a distance she could see they were closely related. When Chloe had extricated herself from his embrace, she turned awkwardly towards Dee.

'Leo, this is Dee. Dee, Leo. He's my brother,' she added superfluously.

'Hi, Leo.' Dee crossed the room to take his hand, feeling self-consciously formal and with Chloe's eyes on her.

'Chloe's told me all about you.' He spoke in a rich baritone, warm brown eyes focussing on hers so directly she was reluctant to let go of his hand.

Dee wondered what Chloe might have said. 'Well, she's not told me anything about *you*.'

'Ha! Nothing much to say about me.' An easy grin spread across his face.

'You're the expert on knots, then?' Dee told herself not to start flirting with Chloe's brother. The two women had existed under an uneasy truce ever since she'd joined the firm and attempting to bed her brother wouldn't be a good move.

'It's something I've studied. Used to be a fisherman for a bit, working the trawlers out of Fraserburgh, but there's more hands than jobs now, so I've come back to Glasgow.'

She liked the open honesty of his face, saw he kept himself fit, stopped that train of thought before it threatened to derail everything.

'Not much fishing here,' Dee countered, attempting to focus. She looked pointedly out of the window at the Clyde.

He laughed, an infectious sound from somewhere deep in his chest. 'You'd be mad to eat anything that came out of there. Upstream of Carstairs is good for trout and grayling, wouldn't touch a fish out of that – if there even are any.'

Chloe interrupted their easy chat. 'Do you want a coffee? I'm just making myself one.'

'Sure. That'll be good.'

Dee grabbed her mug, gave it to Chloe as she passed by. 'Thanks, Chloe.' Chloe's eyes narrowed dangerously.

'So, what's with all this stuff about knots? Did you learn it in the boy scouts?' Dee asked brightly.

Leo cast around for a seat, settling himself in Chloe's chair. 'No, never did the scouts. Not really a pack animal.' His grin belied that remark, looking more wolflike than anything else. 'I had to learn a bit for the fishing – simple stuff like the bowline, clove, anchor bend, fisherman's knot. Then I started studying them for fun – lot of free time on a trawler and always some spare rope.'

'These knots on the bodies, would anyone know how to tie them – or just fishermen?'

Chloe returned with three mugs of coffee, furrowed her brows at her brother for taking her seat, and perched on the edge of her desk holding out a mug for Dee.

Leo's easy grin faded, picturing the reason for his being asked these questions. 'Yeah, what is it with these bodies? Are these the poor kids that are on the news – except I haven't seen anything about the old couple yet?'

Dee caught Chloe's eye before answering. 'We can't say anything about an ongoing investigation.' She quickly changed the subject. 'You said the knots were the water knot and Solomon's knot, are these commonly used?'

They waited for Leo to take a sip of coffee.

'Yeah, well. The water knot is called a load of different names – overhand follow-through, tape knot, ring bend, grass knot – more the sort of thing used in mountain rescue to make a sling.'

Chloe made a grab for a notepad, started writing furiously.

'And Solomon's knot?' Dee asked.

Leo looked around in discomfort, Dee could swear he was embarrassed to answer.

'It's more of a crochet thing.' Leo spoke so quietly that both women had to strain to hear him. Chloe was the first to comment.

'Crochet? You do crochet?' Her expression matched the disbelief evident in her voice.

'Look, we all did weird things on the trawlers. Reading in even a gentle sea gives you a headache, so we all used to do ropework or knitting – which is only ropework in miniature,' he added defensively. 'Crochet's just easier than knitting if you've fat fingers like me. Anyhow, gambling's too dangerous. We were on a share of the catch, so it's not that unknown to earn less than your gambling debt.' He challenged them to make any further comments.

'I think that's sweet,' Dee eventually said. Her eyes belied the serious look on her face. 'But getting back to business, who'd know how to tie these knots – are we looking for a mountaineer who crochets in his spare time?'

'Beats me,' Leo countered. 'It's just something I'm interested in. Guess you think it's a bit weird?' He aimed this at Dee.

'No, I don't think it's weird. Sounds fascinating – think I might be interested in learning a bit more about it myself.' Dee sensed Chloe's disapproval rather than saw it. Her attention was drawn to her laptop, a chime sounding from her desk. 'Gotta look at this. Been doing some fishing myself and someone's just taken the bait.'

Dee's cryptic comment left them both lost for words, following her with their eyes as she opened up her laptop and lost herself in the screen.

* * *

Chloe hunted through the papers on her desk, retrieving a close-up of the rope tying Sheila Warmington's wrists to the bed.

'You said that the old couple couldn't have tied these knots themselves?'

Leo slurped his coffee, making himself a little too comfortable in Chloe's chair as he studied the picture.

'That's right. The guy may have tied her down, assuming she was either into it or she was out of it. No way could you do that fancy work with someone struggling. Then the Double Fisherman...'

Chloe was struggling herself and stopped him mid-flow. 'Sorry. Into it. Out of it?'

Leo laughed at her obvious confusion. 'Whether she was into bondage or if she was unconscious or something. All I'm saying is that you wouldn't tie these knots with someone struggling. You'd use a quick and simple knot, like an Arbor knot.'

'OK,' she spoke doubtfully. 'What were you going to say about the fisherman?'

'Double Fisherman,' Leo corrected. 'That's what joined the two ropes holding the old guy down.' He stopped; a look of concentration etched on his face. 'Strange choice of knot, there's better ways of doing it. But the main point is he couldn't have done that himself if he was already tied up. Much less this weird mess tying up his hands – it's not even a proper knot.'

It was Chloe's chance to turn specialist. 'This is a Celtic triquetra.'

'A what?'

'Celtic triquetra,' she repeated. 'It's the oldest pagan symbol and so old that nobody really knows what it stood for. According to what I've found, it's either meant to be for protection, or a representation of Odin and the sun and moon goddesses.'

'Man. You're getting into some weird shit, Chloe.' He stood, sent a quick glance towards Dee still focussed on her screen. 'I've got to go, meant to be working.'

Chloe walked as far as the door with him, exchanged another hug. He lowered his voice so Dee couldn't hear. 'When are you going to see Mum and Dad? They were asking about you, wanted to know if you were alright.' He looked deep into her eyes, held her shoulders. 'You're OK, aren't you, Chloe?'

'Course. I've been busy, you know. I'll call them tonight, promise.'

'OK.' He sounded doubtful. 'You'd tell me if you were in any trouble, needed some help?'

'I'm fine. Tell them everything's good.'

Leo breathed out. 'OK. But call them, Chloe. They worry.'

'I will.' She stood by the door long after the sound of his feet on the stairs had faded into the all-pervasive traffic noise, feeling the tears gathering on her lower eyelids like the precursor to a summer downpour.

TWENTY-FOUR
PALLIATIVE CARE

The call came in before Teàrlach had made it back to the office. Unknown number displayed on the car dash. He pressed accept.

'Teàrlach Paterson?' A woman's hesitant voice came over the car speakers.

'How can I help?' He spoke brusquely, navigating the latest diversion as yet another Glasgow street was closed off, sending traffic down a narrow residential road. Teàrlach glared impotently at the section of main road cordoned off with barriers and traffic lights for no apparent reason.

'This is Greenplace Care Home, Milngavie. It's about your father.'

There was a silence that stretched further than any courtesy call had a right to extend. A silence that spoke volumes.

'What about him?'

If she wondered at the flatness of his response, then she didn't let it show.

'I'm afraid he's not doing too well. We had to call in a doctor. He may not have long to go, I'm sorry.'

That makes one person, Teàrlach thought. 'How long? How much longer does he have?'

She hesitated before replying. 'These things are difficult to quantify, Mr Paterson. Your father's not been eating well and has been on morphine for a while now, as you know. The thing is... he's been asking for you. According to our files, you're his only family.' She hurried on now that the awkward bit had been accomplished. 'We can be flexible with visiting, even outside of normal hours if that helps?'

Teàrlach stared at the dashboard in disbelief. 'Do your files show that he's been in prison for years after setting fire to the refuge my mother and young brother were staying in? Did he tell you I'm all that's left of his family because he murdered everyone else?'

'We are Catholics, Mr Paterson,' she answered primly. 'Forgiveness is what we preach and practise. However bad the sins your father committed, he's asked for forgiveness from God and has done his penance.'

The words sounded good, Teàrlach had to admit. She even managed to sound like she really cared. The truth of the matter was that his father would do or say anything, even to the point of taking his sins to the confessional if it brought him somewhere comfortable to spend his last days. The Catholicism was a new low even for him, he'd shown no sign of believing in anything other than his own selfish needs all the time Teàrlach had known him.

'I'll try and get over this weekend,' Teàrlach voiced out loud.

'I'll let your father know, Mr Paterson. I hope you can find it in your heart to forgive him before it's too late. I'm sorry.'

The phone cut off before he could respond, her final words dripping with insincerity.

'Fuck's sake!' Teàrlach hit the steering wheel in anger. Glasgow had been shrouded underneath a blanket of grey cloud all afternoon, perfectly matching his mood. The investigation into why Logan Martin killed his father in a sustained and brutal attack was going nowhere – certainly not in any direction that was likely to bring succour to the dead man's sister. Jade Martin's whereabouts were unknown, and he had a foreboding that the girl was in danger. The only people who knew what was going on refused to open up and the overweight golfer, Peter McKinnon, came up short as the arch-villain responsible for the string of murders Teàrlach suspected were somehow connected to his investigation. Now he was saddled with caring for the father who had never cared for him. He checked the time. Just enough to make it through gridlocked rush-hour Glasgow and reach the office before Chloe and Dee left. His father could wait.

He arrived to find Chloe wrapped in Dee's arms, dabbing ineffectually at tears falling like plump raindrops. Dee looked towards him as he came to a stop in the doorway, her cryptic expression providing no clues.

'What's wrong?'

Chloe started, pulling herself away from Dee in confusion and averting her face as the handkerchief worked overtime.

'It's nothing,' Dee said unconvincingly. 'Just having a moment.'

Teàrlach felt uniquely ill-equipped to handle the situation. 'Is there anything I can do?'

Dee shook her head.

'I'm all right.' Chloe's muffled voice issued from underneath a handkerchief, followed by a loud sniff as she almost ran to the toilet, shutting the door on them both.

Teàrlach's inquisitive stare was met with a shrug. 'It's nothing,' Dee reiterated. 'How did you get on with the lodge?'

He took the diversion with relief. 'Nothing doing. No sign of Jade or any leads as to where she might have gone after her cleaning job. There was a guy there, pale skin, tall. Wearing one of those aprons.'

Teàrlach placed his notebook down on his desk. 'I tried following him when he left, but he gave me the slip in traffic.'

'You think he has something to do with it?' Dee's eyes switched to the toilet as the flush sounded. A tap squeaked noisily, running water hitting porcelain.

'I don't know. There was something off with him. He wasn't keen on having me look around, that's for sure.'

Chloe made a reappearance. She'd made an effort to reapply makeup, but her eyes still glistened with moisture. She provided an update as if nothing was untoward.

'I asked around the hospitals to see if anyone matching Jade's description has been taken in since yesterday. Nothing doing.'

'Thanks, Chloe. Look – why don't you leave early? Take yourself back home and spoil yourself. You sure there's nothing I can do, whatever it is that's upset you?'

She shook her head, offered him a fleeting smile. 'I'm just being stupid. It's fine. I'll be off then. See you Monday.'

Teàrlach waited until Chloe was out of earshot before interrogating Dee. 'What was that all about?'

'Her brother was in earlier, Leo.'

'Did he do anything to upset her?' Teàrlach felt the need to punch something, Chloe's brother would do fine.

'No, nothing like that. He just reminded her it had been a while since she'd seen her parents, suggested she saw them, that's all. His visit brought back her suicide and losing the baby. The memories caught her at a bad time, you know?'

Teàrlach wasn't sure he *did* know. For all the time he'd known Chloe, he realised he knew next to nothing about her, same for the woman in front of him.

'Is there a problem, with her and her parents?'

Dee shrugged. 'I've no idea. She's never said anything to me about it – didn't even know she had a brother until today.'

'What's he like, the brother?' Teàrlach recognised the glint in her eyes from the first time they'd met. She reminded him of a predatory animal.

'Oh, quite fit,' Dee said lightly.

Teàrlach laughed, setting Dee off as well until the tension cleared.

'Whatever Chloe's problems, at least she has a family.' Dee returned to seriousness.

'Aye, right enough,' Teàrlach agreed. 'Although that's not always a good thing.'

He checked the time. It had gone five, time for them to shut up shop for the weekend. 'If you fancy a drink, you can give me an update on where we're at – or we can catch up on Monday?'

Dee thought about it for a second. 'Come on, then. I'll leave my leathers here and grab a taxi back if it turns into a heavy session.'

They grabbed a table in one of those anonymous city pubs that tried too hard to emulate a country inn. This one was called the Hare and Lettuce, a name that had encouraged a street artist to spray cartoon outlines of a recently departed Chancellor and PM on the wall outside. The graffiti had been there at least a month, so it must have had tacit approval from the landlords, otherwise they'd have had it erased. The place was already filling up with punters looking to quench a thirst.

'OK, where are we?' Teàrlach asked before taking a long drink from his pint. He relaxed back in his seat, letting the tension ease. He'd learned nothing of any use at the lodge, managed to lose the fair-haired mason in traffic and then had the care home wind him up so tight he needed this time out.

Dee concentrated on sipping her cocktail through a straw,

cheeks dimpling with the effort until she'd half emptied the glass.

'Our man McKinnon. I managed to open a couple of his encrypted files and he's been importing chemicals from China.' Dee sucked on the straw until her glass emptied. 'I'm not sure, but I think he may be involved in making fentanyl.'

Teàrlach paused before the pint glass reached his lips.

'He's a dealer?' His incredulous expression matched his voice.

'No, I don't think he's dealing, more likely acting as a supplier to a lab. I need to dig around some more, see what some of these chemicals are used for. Whatever he's involved with, he's keeping it hidden.'

'McKinnon's not our focus. He strikes me as more white-collar crime than a murderer.'

Teàrlach needed that second pint.

'Another?' He stood.

'No. I'll have a half of Guinness. It'll do for my tea.' He felt her eyes on him all the way to the bar until he was swallowed by the crowd.

'What's your story, then?' Teàrlach placed a half-pint in front of her. 'Now I've given you my life history.'

'I don't know who my parents are. Spent all my life in care homes, passed from one to the next.'

'I'm sorry. I didn't know.'

'Nothing for you to be sorry for. It's all right, really. Food and shelter – you're given the basics.'

'Have you looked for them – your parents? Tried to track them down?'

Dee frowned. 'They made it clear they didn't want me in their life. It can stay that way as far as I'm concerned.'

Teàrlach caught the warning tone, made a mental note to steer clear of that topic. She downed her drink, asked if he wanted another and headed off to the bar to replenish their glasses. He criticised himself for not having already made a connection between Dee's propensity for drink and the life she must have experienced in care. They were both orphans, by accident or design, yet he was so wrapped up in his own messed-up world that he hadn't noticed the vulnerability concealed behind Dee's bluff exterior.

The place was filling up now the weekend was beginning in earnest. Laughter sounded from the bar and Teàrlach craned his neck to check on Dee just as she sidled back through the crowds with a glass in each hand.

'Sláinte!' She raised a glass to health.

'Sláinte,' he echoed, their glasses meeting across the table. Her grey-green eyes observed him with amusement from close range, unaware or uncaring of his recent analysis. Teàrlach looked away, uncomfortable under her disconcerting gaze.

They piloted a careful course during the remainder of the evening, avoiding the wrecking rocks and heading for deeper, more unfathomable waters. When Teàrlach walked Dee to a taxi at the end of the night, they weaved across the pavement like sailors newly back on land. After Dee was driven away into the Glasgow night, Teàrlach stood at the edge of the pavement with the unsettling knowledge that he was alone in a city of almost two million people and wondered whether she felt the same.

TWENTY-FIVE
AIR

This was Sam's favourite time of day, at the end of another working week and before the sun made an appearance. Glasgow streets were painted in pastels, lit by the promise of a new dawn. The first bus of the day was almost empty, only a few passengers making an early start on a Saturday and still wrapped in sleep's coils or returning from a night shift. The chilled air carried the first premonition of autumn. He gazed out of the bus windows, mesmerised as the houses and flats drifted past, imagining the multiplicity of lives and relationships held inside the bricks and concrete. It looked like another overcast day was in store – he hoped so, even with blackout curtains, the sun and heat had made sleep almost impossible for most of the summer. Not that he needed much sleep. Working as a night guard in the office block required three walkarounds every night, swiping his badge at each floor's checkpoint and spending the rest of his time asleep behind the reception desk. Now people worked from home, most nights the entire building was left empty.

When his stop came into view, he stood, pressed the bell and waited for the hydraulic doors to reluctantly open. Sam headed for his habitual short-cut home through a small park, a square oasis of green overlooked by houses on each side. The ground rose to a slight hill in the middle, crowned by trees. It was meant to be an ancient monument, but he never paid it much attention, concentrating instead on making sure his feet avoided anything unpleasant left on the paved pathway. This morning a blackbird's song sang so sweetly that he stopped, scanning the trees surrounding the mound for the bird, puzzled at what he saw.

At first, he mistook it for a kid's swing left suspended in the tree branches, but then he saw it more clearly. Sam stepped closer, his feet slow and unwilling as the truth began to reveal itself through the foliage. What faced him was a woman's body, her features tortured into a silent scream.

When he took out his mobile, his fingers shook so badly he was scarcely able to hit the emergency numbers. He croaked a response, asking for police with a mouth turned so dry the words had to be forced out. There was no point in asking for an ambulance.

* * *

Dee watched the news with morbid fascination, her morning coffee for once ignored. The film crew had been kept a good distance away from the trees, the iron age burial monument appearing as a backdrop. A journalist gestured towards police setting up a white forensics tent. The camera swung to zoom in on a woman's body, filling the TV screen before the studio producer had a chance to cut the feed. Even through shaky camerawork the rope holding the corpse suspended in mid-air bore similarities to the other recent deaths.

Dee picked up Chloe's map and pentagram overlay, saw the tumulus in Rutherglen lay precisely on the point marked with the symbol for Air. There was no doubt now. Whoever was responsible for this spate of bizarre murders in Glasgow was placing the bodies with precise reference to the same drawing Dee held in her hand. She called Teàrlach, his phone ringing for longer than usual.

'Have you seen the news?'

'What time is it?' Teàrlach sounded half-asleep.

'Eight thirty.'

A groan escaped Teàrlach's lips. 'What is it?'

Dee could picture him rubbing his forehead in a futile attempt to massage his hangover. Their 'drink after work' had turned into a few, then a few more. She remembered him insisting on calling her a cab, holding open the door as she climbed into the back seat and then waving at her from the kerb. They'd talked about themselves for the first time, freed from the immediacy of work and finally relaxed enough with each other to open up – enabled by copious a amount of alcohol. She had thought the mutual exploration of each other's background and personality might continue along more physical lines as the evening drew to a close – she wasn't sure how she felt about waking up alone and in her own bed.

'There's another body, hanging from a rope at the pentagram point marked Air on Chloe's diagram.' Her own words closed down any vestige of romance or passion that remained.

'Suicide?' The hopeful optimism in his response faded even as he spoke.

'Not likely. She's hanging upside down.'

'Like a bat?'

Dee looked at her mobile askance. 'Yeah, like a bat.'

The line went quiet for a few seconds. 'We'll have to tell the police about the connection to the other bodies.'

'Gathered as much. I'd prefer not to be involved with them personally due to having some history. I'd best keep a low profile.'

'Yep. Understood. I need a copy of the drawing, can you message me?'

'I'll do it now. What are we planning on doing about it?'

Dee heard the sigh escaping Teàrlach's mouth. 'First make sure it's not Jade. After that, I really don't know. This is something for the police, not us.'

'You'll have to tell them the drawing came from the Warmingtons' journal, and Jade drew the same pentagram. Her mum didn't want the police involved – remember?'

'Aye, I remember.' He sounded tense. 'Send me the drawing and I'll talk to a detective, although what he'll make of it...'

'Someone ought to look at the last two points on the pentagram, make certain no bodies are there.' Dee looked more closely at Chloe's photocopy. 'There's still Earth and Fire.'

'Weegie wonderland.'

It sounded like Teàrlach was attempting to sing on the other end of the line.

'You what?'

'Nothing. See if that's Jade hanging on the rope. I hope to hell it's not – Lauren's been through more than enough without losing her daughter as well.'

Dee's heart sank at the prospect of having to confirm the identity of the body in the tree.

'Oh, and thanks,' Teàrlach added in a quieter voice.

'What for?'

'Last night. It was good to have that time with you. Away from work – you know?' Teàrlach's words sounded uncharacteristically halting.

Dee knew. 'Same. Must do it again.' She stared at her phone quizzically once the short call had ended, then reached for her coffee only to spit the lukewarm contents straight back into the mug in disgust.

Outside the panoramic windows, Glasgow emerged from a grey dawn with the lazy enthusiasm of having a weekend in prospect. She made another coffee, sipped it reflectively whilst watching the Clyde making sluggish progress towards the sea. Something had subtly changed between her and Teàrlach since last night, she felt it in her blood. Dee's right foot tapped rhythmically on the floor, alerting her to the slow workings of her subconscious as a disco beat intruded and the words of 'Boogie Wonderland' started playing.

A smile played on her lips, then swiftly faded as a police spokesperson appeared on her screen, soundlessly speaking to a camera with cordoned-off parkland as a backdrop. Another body, another grieving family. Dee imagined Lauren watching the same broadcast and seeing Jade hanging from that tree. She urgently set to work, opening a route into the police server and sharing Teàrlach's plea that this wouldn't be Jade's name she'd discover. When she found the name Bryony Knight, Dee felt an immediate sense of relief that this wasn't Jade's body they'd found – immediately followed by guilt for feeling relief when Bryony's death demanded her sorrow and required to be avenged.

She let Teàrlach know it wasn't Jade. Whoever the serial killer was, Dee decided she'd do anything in her power to stop him.

TWENTY-SIX
POLIS

'You expect me to take this seriously?' Detective John Jenkins still retained a hint of his native Welsh accent, now overlayed with sufficient Glaswegian after forty years to make him an unusual Celtic hybrid. He still looked Welsh, as far as Teàrlach was concerned. Thick dark hair even into his forties, heavy eyebrows and built like a pit pony with a temperament to match.

'Someone has to,' Teàrlach replied. 'Three bodies turning up with the same MO and on the same points as this drawing.'

He left the rest unsaid.

'And how did you come to have this pentagram and map?' The detective's eyebrows formed hairy question marks above each suspicious brown eye.

'We're working for a firm of solicitors, looking for the relatives of a couple who died intestate. This came from the paperwork they gave us.' Teàrlach tried for innocence. 'You wouldn't know anything about them, would you – William and Sheila Warmington, eighteen Seaview Drive? They were both found dead together. In bed.'

Detective John Jenkins fixed Teàrlach with a look that

precluded travelling any further down that line of enquiry. 'I'll need the papers.'

Teàrlach shrugged unconcernedly. 'They're with the solicitor. We've tracked their relatives, so the paperwork was sent back to them yesterday.'

'Mail?' the detective queried.

Teàrlach nodded.

'Then it will be Monday at earliest before we can make a start.' John Jenkins glowered as if the glacial speed of Royal Mail was Teàrlach's fault. 'What made you connect these deaths to this diagram?' He held a printout of Chloe's map superimposed with a hand-drawn pentagram up for inspection as if searching for authenticity.

'Something my PA noticed. She has an interest in symbols, realised the sign for water coincided close to the young lass in the Kelvin, then when the next two lined up with the pentagram, she realised there was more than coincidence at play.'

'Why a pentagram? Are we dealing with satanists or something?'

'The pentagram is drawn at several places in one of William Warmington's journals – and on the cover. Chloe saw a map of Glasgow with the pentagram sketched over it, and realised with a bit of tweaking the murder locations fitted a little too well for it to be a coincidence. When this third body turned up this morning and fitted the drawing, we realised it must be connected.'

The detective managed to express utter disbelief with the slightest movement of one impressive eyebrow. 'I'll need to speak to her. Today.'

'I'll ask Chloe to get in touch with you as soon as she can. We'll do anything we can to help the investigation.'

'Why come to me?'

Teàrlach didn't hesitate. 'Your name came up as someone

connected to the Warmington case. Thought you ought to know about the journals in case it's important.'

Detective John Jenkins seemingly decided to give him the benefit of the doubt. 'So these two locations here...' He indicated the two remaining points on the pentagram that hadn't already been the location for brutal murders. 'You think whoever is doing this is deliberately placing dead bodies on the five points of a bloody pentagram, tied up with string?'

'Looks like it.' Teàrlach found the tune to 'My Favourite Things' running through his head.

'Why the hell would anyone do that?'

'Can't help you there, officer. But it's worth a look at these other two locations or staking them out.'

'Thank you for your advice,' Detective Jenkins answered brusquely. 'So, this Chloe will be in touch?'

'I'll text her right away.'

'OK. Well, thanks for bringing this to our attention.' He managed the thanks with the clear implication that he didn't want the additional work Teàrlach had just added to the case-load. 'I'll be in touch if we need anything else.'

Teàrlach turned to leave the interview room.

'Keep your nose out of this one, Sherlock. I don't want a bunch of amateur sleuths getting under my feet.'

Teàrlach gave no indication of having heard the detective's parting shot as he left, taking the car back through Saturday morning traffic to the office. He'd asked to meet with Detective Jenkins, said he had information pertinent to the serial murderer stalking Glasgow's streets. The detective had reacted at the mention of the Warmingtons – not surprising as he was in charge during that investigation but then he'd warned them off the case. That threat had just made Teàrlach more determined than ever to find out what had really happened at Seaview Drive.

Dee's motorbike was still outside, waiting for her to collect it. The thought of Dee brought an unexpected spring to his step as he climbed the stairs, followed by disappointment when he found she wasn't there. He texted Chloe, apologised for disturbing her weekend and asked her to call the detective about her pentagram research. He didn't need to remind her not to mention the Warmingtons or Dee's illegal data gathering.

Outside, the weather was torn between sun and rain and had settled into an indeterminate state of greyness, turning the city monochrome. Teàrlach linked his hands behind his head and stared at the ceiling. His investigation into the reasons for Keith Martin's murder had only come up with the man being indirectly accused of sexually molesting his daughter. Not particularly edifying, nor something his sister Nicole would want to hear. It did provide motive for Logan to stab him in retribution for his sister, although the frenzied nature of the attack didn't sit right with what he'd seen of Logan in prison. The young guy gave every impression of victim rather than aggressor. But he'd confessed, was seen standing with the bloodied knife when the police arrived – it had to be him that killed his dad. Still the nagging doubt remained, something about it still felt off.

His train of thought was derailed by Dee coming into the office. She stopped dead when she saw him, covered her confusion with an easy grin.

'Morning. Wasn't expecting anyone would be here.' Dee pointed at her leathers and helmet still draped over her seat. 'Come to collect my bike,' she added.

'Hi, Dee.' Teàrlach matched her unease, removing his hands from behind his head only to find he didn't know what to do with them and mimed an unconvincing stretch instead. He remembered seeing her go last night, being ambushed by the realisation that he was alone and wished that memory could have waited longer to surface.

Dee looked at her leathers as if she wasn't sure what to do with them.

'I've been to the police.' Teàrlach broke the stalemate. 'Saw Detective Jenkins – he's the detective who was in charge of the Warmingtons' investigation. Told him we were hired to look for any relatives and mentioned the pentagram.'

Dee took refuge in discussing the murders. 'How did he react?'

Teàrlach's smile provided the answer. 'Warned us off the case – but he didn't have any response to the bodies being placed on the pentagram points.'

'You think he's somehow involved?'

'I think he deliberately concealed evidence at the Warmingtons, for reasons best known to himself, but the pentagram came as a surprise.'

'So, what are they going to do about it?' Dee left her dilemma with the leathers on her seat, stood in the doorway to Teàrlach's office and took her usual pose leaning on the doorframe.

He shrugged. 'They'll take a look around the other two sites still waiting on bodies, but I can't see them having the manpower to stake them out. May ensure patrols include those places for the next few days.' Teàrlach opened his notebook, leafed back through the pages as he spoke. 'They want to talk to Chloe, see how she came up with the map and worked out the placements.'

Dee's eyes opened wide in alarm. 'She's not going to tell them about the ropes, about the Warmingtons? Only that information is meant to be on a secure police server.'

Teàrlach shook his head. 'You can trust Chloe not to drop us in it. Although she might mention the significance of the rope knots, she knows not to include the Warmingtons or Martins.'

The thought that had been birling around in his head popped into focus. Teàrlach's finger stopped on the page he'd been searching for – his notes on first entering the Martins' home. 'Talking of the Martins, did you find anything on the coroner's report about defensive cuts to Keith Martin's arms? If Logan was stabbing him, then Keith would have tried to protect himself.'

Dee fetched her laptop from her desk where she'd left it the previous night, tapping at keys as she placed it on his desk.

'Here's the coroner's report. There wasn't much to it.'

A file opened on the screen and Dee scrolled through text and photographs until Keith's upper torso filled the screen. His naked chest had been washed clean, the body laid out on a stainless steel table in a forensics lab under harsh light. The skin was shredded and punctured from multiple cuts turned purple against the unnaturally white flesh newly drained of blood. Teàrlach moved closer until the image resolved into sharper focus, breathed in her scent and shook his head in irritation at being so easily distracted.

Dee misinterpreted his body language. 'I know. Only the one slight cut to his right arm. Doesn't look like he put up much of a fight.'

He leaned back in his chair until her scent cleared and forced himself to concentrate.

'That doesn't make any sense. It's instinctive to fight back, to defend against that sort of attack. By rights his hands should be covered in cuts, his forearms, too, from raising them as a shield.' Teàrlach realised he was miming the action, making a cross with his arms to protect his chest. He folded them instead, relieved to have finally found something to do with his hands and feeling slightly less vulnerable.

'Why do you think that is?' Dee asked.

TWENTY-SEVEN
PERP

Jade Martin hesitated, her mum's mobile number tapped into a cheap mobile phone and finger poised over the call button. She reluctantly cancelled before completing the call. It had been two days since she had left the flat, and Lauren would be going frantic with worry. A wave of guilt flooded through her – everything was turning to shit, and she was the one to blame. She and the Warmingtons.

When Willie had first started talking to her about the secret patterns overlaying Glasgow, she'd humoured him, chatting away over the garden fence and quietly making fun of the old man. Then he'd brought out his book, showed her the lines connecting old monuments and archaeological sites and she started to believe him. So much so that she'd asked for a copy of the pentagram to draw on her bedroom floor, hidden under the carpet like something deliciously forbidden. She'd felt protected in her room, yet at the same time open to something dangerous.

She didn't remember when the lies turned from elaboration to damnation. She'd started by complaining that her dad wouldn't let her stay out late, was too protective. Willie had listened when her mum hadn't, treated her like an adult instead of a child. Then she began to make things up, encouraged by the scandalised look on his face. Mentioned being touched, grabbed, interfered with. When Willie Warmington came round to face her mum with the allegations, it was too late to admit she'd made it all up.

Now her dad was dead and Logan was locked up for his murder, the lies poisoning the family long after the Warmingtons had passed away. She couldn't bear to face her mother anymore, not when she carried so much guilt. There was only one chance at redemption, one sacrifice she could make to try and make everything better.

Jade let the phone slip between her fingers to join the TV remote on a duvet. She searched around to find the remote and the room lit with lurid primary colours as a daytime show filled the screen. Sufficient grey light spilled from tightly closed worn curtains to warn her another day had already started. She leaned forward, pulling the pillows high to make a headrest against the wall and sat up to watch. Four women were having a spirited argument, gesticulating wildly so the cameras continually switched position to one or the other, pulling back into a panoramic shot when all four shouted at once. At least she imagined they were shouting. The TV was on mute.

Jade found the menu button and scrolled until she found the breakfast news. Cars were being swept down a street on a tide of brown water. There could have been bodies, or trees, or bits of houses. She stared disinterested at the human tragedy unfolding, not bothered whether it was Libya, Italy or anywhere really – long as it wasn't here in Glasgow. A news reporter appeared in shot, distress written on her face. Distress and fear as the water redoubled its efforts, reaching closer to the high embankment they'd selected for its view of the carnage. The camera lost focus as part of the background slipped into the water, railings and pavement joining the flood until the video feed showed the camera operator's feet running for safety.

The news switched to the body hanging from the tree and Jade's interest abruptly heightened. She leaned forward in concentration, finger pressed on the volume until the commentary filled the small bedsit.

'... man's body discovered on Friday morning has been identified as Jack Bentall, a student at the Open University. Police enquiries are ongoing, and the public are requested to get in touch if they have any information that may assist the police or if anyone saw any suspicious activity in the Rutherglen area.'

'Do we know if the woman found this morning is connected to the other two unexplained murders in Glasgow this week, Julian?'

'Police Scotland are keeping an open mind and have asked the public to remain calm and avoid parks during the hours of darkness. Additional police patrols will be on the streets at night to reassure the public.'

'And are they any closer to finding those responsible?'

'The police don't have a spokesperson available to speak to us, but until the serious crimes unit have been able to confirm that these murders are in any way linked, they prefer to keep the investigation wide open as to how many people might be involved.'

'Thank you, Julian. That's Julian Harwell reporting from the scene of the latest murder in Rutherglen, and it looks like the police are no closer to finding the killer. Now over to Will on the sports desk.'

Jade pressed mute and the TV displayed silent excerpts from a football match. She turned it off, leaving the room to be illuminated by the diffuse grey light seeping around the edges of worn curtains. A figure stirred beside her, arms reaching out and encouraging her to lie back down. She brushed hair away from the young man's face, turned towards soft lips that parted in invitation. Jade settled back into a warm embrace and let passion dispel the image of the hanging man and the guilt haunting her.

Outside the drawn curtains, Saturday morning traffic and pedestrians continued without giving much thought to the murders taking place in their city. Yet the newspaper headlines screamed from every newsagent window, lurid headlines along with blurred photographs taken with telephoto lenses of crime scenes inadequately protected. A young woman's body spread-eagled as if for crucifixion in the River Kelvin; the youth cocooned and hanging from a tree in Queen's Park; the most recent atrocity with another woman suspended upside down from the tumulus in Rutherglen. References were made to Jack the Ripper, questions asked why the police hadn't made any progress. One of the papers had christened the serial killer as The Pagan.

* * *

Lauren Martin huddled on her settee, fag in one hand and a cheap wine in the other. Face pale and unhealthy in the blue cast from a TV screen displaying twenty-four-hour news in case her daughter's face appeared. Her phone on the seat beside her, silent. She reached for her mobile for the tenth time that morning, not wanting to hear any news but feeling herself withering away to a husk in the absence of any information. She steeled herself, made the call.

'Teàrlach Paterson?' Lauren took a last hungry drag on her cigarette. 'It's Lauren. Lauren Martin. Have you found Jade?'

'We drew a blank at the church, Lauren. According to the guy I met, she left at her usual time on Thursday, mid-afternoon. We've been checking hospitals and with the police, nothing doing. Are you sure she doesn't have any friends she'd stay with, old school friends or mates she goes out with?'

Lauren collapsed in on herself. She had expected nothing

else, but the confirmation that her daughter was still missing sapped the life out of her.

'I said there's no one else. We only have each other!' The words were followed by a sob. 'What am I going to do?'

Teàrlach remained silent as her anguished words waited on an answer.

'You should contact the police, Lauren. Like I said at the start. I've tried finding Jade – we're still looking, but without any means of tracking her or some idea where she might have gone, it's like looking for a needle in a haystack.'

Now it was Teàrlach waiting for a response. Lauren wiped her nose with the back of her hand, told herself to get a grip. Reached for a wine glass and emptied the contents before answering.

'I'll contact the polis. They won't give a fuck about us, but if you're not going to be any use, you might as well fuck off as well.'

She pressed the end call button with more force than was required, throwing the phone across the room so it skittered across the worn carpet and came to a rest against the far wall.

TWENTY-EIGHT
PERJURY

Teàrlach didn't need to explain Lauren's message, she'd screamed loud enough for Dee to hear from the other side of his desk.

'Take it we're off the case, then?'

'Not sure it's as easy as that, Dee.' Teàrlach stood, awkwardly passing her in the doorway to make for the coffee machine. 'You want one?'

She nodded, watched him as he spooned beans into the machine and placed a mug under the waiting nozzle. Teàrlach officiated like a priest at a mass, the grinding of beans and sputtering of hot, fragrant coffee taking the place of officiant and response. Somehow, the ritual provided a release to the tension in the air.

'Here.' Teàrlach held out a mug. 'I don't know if we can abandon Jade and her mother at this stage.'

'Doesn't seem right, I agree,' she answered. 'Do you still think they're linked? The Martins and these deaths?'

'There's too much of a coincidence with the ropework for there *not* to be a connection. The Warmingtons next door, the journal with a map pretty much predicting where these murder victims are going to be found. Something ties them all together.'

Dee's wry smile made him regret his choice of words.

'Aye, alright. All the same, the Martins know more than they're letting on.' He sat down again behind his desk. 'And something's off with Keith Martin's murder.'

She sat down opposite him, blowing steam off her mug and watching him with an expression he couldn't read.

'How do you mean off – because he didn't defend himself against the knife?'

Teàrlach nodded. 'Exactly! Even if Logan managed to puncture his heart with the first blow, Keith would still have been able to put his arms up in self-defence.'

He frowned, remembering the prison visit and the aunt's comments about her nephew. 'If that's what killed him.'

'Thought that's not in any doubt,' Dee responded. 'Logan had the knife in his hand. Blood all over him and he made a confession.'

'Yes. It seems that way.' Teàrlach responded thoughtfully. 'And the police were quick enough to accept that's what had happened. Makes their life easier too.'

'So, what you thinking, Sherlock?' Her head tilted slightly as she regarded him.

'I'm thinking maybe Logan didn't kill him,' he answered thoughtfully. 'I'm wondering if Keith Martin was already dead by the time Logan stabbed him.'

'How's that work out?' Dee's expression made it clear she thought Teàrlach had lost the plot.

'That's the bit I haven't figured out yet, but I've a feeling that Jade and her mother can fill in the blanks.'

'Only Jade's gone missing,' Dee reminded him.

'Aye, and that's why we'll continue looking for her.'

Her mouth twisted in puzzlement. 'I see where you're going

with Keith not defending himself, I get that. But why would Logan stab his dad if he was already dead? More to the point, why is he taking the rap for a murder he may not have committed?'

Teàrlach levelled a finger at her. 'That's exactly what we need to find out, and it's why Nicole asked us to investigate in the first place.'

'Is he protecting his mum, or Jade?' Dee suggested two possible suspects for Keith Martin's murder that Logan might want to go to prison for.

'Either are possibilities. Jade had motive – well, so did her mum if she thought her husband was...' Teàrlach struggled to find an appropriate expression.

'Shagging his daughter?'

'Aye.' He sighed. 'You could put it like that.'

'So, what do we do now? Logan's not talking, and I'll be surprised if you get any sense out of his mum – and Jade's taken herself away.'

'Or been taken away,' Teàrlach added. He cleared a space on his desk, placing his coffee mug to one side. 'Let's have another look at that map, with the pentagram. See where the next two bodies should turn up.'

Dee fetched the copy from her desk, spotting the pile of photocopies Chloe had made before returning Keith Warmington's journal. She laid it down on Teàrlach's desk and they both peered intently at the last two locations.

'So, here,' Teàrlach squinted. 'This one's over by SPS Barlinnie.'

'Earth,' Dee helpfully added.

He frowned. 'Are there any monuments, ancient sites around there?'

She fetched her laptop, started a search. 'Nothing doing, least nothing showing up on this antiquities site.'

'What does Earth signify to you?'

'If I was a psycho leaving bodies wrapped in rope at the points of a pentangle?' Dee sought to clarify.

'Exactly.'

'Someone buried, I guess.'

Teàrlach nodded in confirmation. 'That would be my hunch too. And if you wanted somewhere where you could dig a hole without attracting too much suspicion?'

Dee studied the map. 'Well, I'd probably avoid digging a bloody great hole right next to Barlinnie Prison.'

'Agreed.'

'Which leaves this Seven Lochs Wetland Park. It's not too far off the pentagram, access is good. Chances are you could plant a body without anyone calling the police. Still risky, but it hasn't stopped the perpetrator before.'

'Only problem is it's a large area.'

Dee was clicking away on her laptop. 'Over nineteen square kilometres.'

'Shit! What about the other one, this point near Bishopbriggs?'

They shifted attention to the uppermost point on the pentagram, pointing directly north.

'Fire,' Dee helpfully added. 'Nothing showing up here as an ancient site. Found a few flint arrowheads over here, or there's a well over there that William Wallace is meant to have drunk from.'

Teàrlach's expression dissuaded her from looking up any other tenuous links to antiquities.

'Nothing obvious we can assume is the target for dumping a body?'

'Can't see anything. Looks like a typical suburban street to me.'

Teàrlach sighed in frustration. 'We're missing something. I know it's staring me in the face, but I can't see it.'

'But what's the point of killing a bunch of random people

and leaving them strung up around the city? It makes no sense.' Dee put a voice to the one obvious fact that bedevilled his thoughts.

'It makes sense to whoever is behind all this, and that's going to be the challenge – to think the same way as the killer. We just have to catch him before he finds his next victim.' Teàrlach stared at the map with a feeling of hopelessness.

TWENTY-NINE
PAR

Peter McKinnon wasn't having the best of days. It had started when the golf club president beckoned him over as soon as he'd set foot in the clubhouse, and instead of the expected ribald exchange, he was quietly advised that if he hadn't paid his club fees by the end of the day, he would no longer be allowed to remain a member. There was mention of waiting lists, important people with money queuing to join the club. He'd had to bluster, apologise for an oversight, assure him that he'd deal with it as soon as he went home. The exchange unsettled him so much that his game suffered terribly, so much so that he'd had to make some excuse about feeling under par and quitting before the fourth hole. The way he was hitting the ball it was just as well – there was another leader board on display in the club bar where the worst round took top position.

His ill humour only worsened after realising there was insufficient money in the bank to even cover the membership. A growing stack of manilla envelopes caught his eye, stashed ironically enough under the award for Golfer of the Year. A shiny golfer frozen mid-swing on a block of Perspex. The award had nothing to do with golfing prowess and a lot to do with donations to the upkeep of the club buildings. That was when he still had money to burn.

'Oh, you home already? Is it raining?'

Peter McKinnon didn't look up from his contemplation of the award, wondering where and when his life had taken such a downward turn. His wife was part of it, losing her youth and beauty until she reminded him each day of his own gradual dissolution.

'No. Not feeling so good this morning, thought I'd stay at home and take it easy.'

'Oh dear. What's wrong?' The back of Amanda's hand touched his forehead. 'Can I get you anything?'

'No, it's nothing to worry about. I'll just have a quiet day. Settle down to some work.'

'Well, if you're sure?' she asked hesitantly. 'I could always ask the doctor to call.'

The thought of calling anyone from the private health company made him feel worse. Their envelope was in the pile demanding payment of overdue accounts along with all the others.

He held her hand as she moved it from his forehead, turned to look at her. 'I'm all right, really. I could do with looking at some work, been letting it build up.'

Amanda regarded him from under lowered eyelashes, eyes analytic and doubtful. 'I could stay if you want. I'm only having a spa and lunch with the girls.'

He didn't want. 'I'll be fine. Seriously – you go off and enjoy your spa.' He gave her hand a pat in encouragement, seeing the relief flood her face.

'Well, you look after yourself. I don't know what I'd do without you. See you later, love.'

Her kiss fell as short as his expectations, and he returned his attention to the trophy. It had gathered dust since he'd sacked the housekeeper. He'd accused her of not doing a good enough job, letting standards slide. Easier than admitting he didn't have the cash to pay her. The girls. He could see them all in his imagination, trophy wives. He'd bedded a few of them, the thrill of the chase always exceeding the short-lived pleasure of the actual messy biological act. Now even those trophies were gathering dust.

If he didn't raise some money soon, there would be hell to pay! Peter McKinnon linked his hands on an expansive stomach and gave the problem serious thought. The house was already mortgaged to the hilt, the church as well. Subscriptions from the lodge only covered the food bills. All he had left was the £100,000 Keith Martin owed him, and the silly bugger had managed to get himself killed. His thoughts turned to the private investigator and his cute sidekick, and his humour took another downward spiral. The wife, Lauren, must have told them he was chasing her for money.

He took the opportunity of being alone to see if the Martins' house had been sold yet, searching Pritchard's Estate Agency website. There it was – and under offer! The asking price was over £120,000. Even with fees, that would leave Lauren with enough to pay him back the money her husband owed. It wasn't much but would keep him going until the other project brought in money.

How much money? Peter closed his eyes, stretched out in his chair and imagined the riches that waited. More than enough to leave all this behind – the debts, the house and Amanda. Especially Amanda. She already had her suspicions that the money was running out and as soon as that happened, she'd be off. It was the same with the other girls. Hanging in there to collect the life insurance or clean up after the will. He had no doubt they'd all shared stories of his philandering, could imagine them laughing at his lacklustre performance in bed. Could imagine the girls sharing out the husbands as a calculated ploy to keep them from seeking younger blood. The girls. He snorted in derision. Average age forty-something, reaching the point where the foundations were starting to crumble.

He deserved a new start, and this time he'd keep the money for himself. Peter reached for his mobile. It was time for another cosy chat with Lauren Martin – time to remind her that £100,000 of that money coming was due to him.

Lauren answered the call immediately. 'Jade? Is that you? Where are you?'

Peter looked at the phone in irritation. 'It's me, Peter McKinnon. I see your house is under offer and I'm reminding you that £100k of that belongs to me.'

'Oh God. I thought you were Jade.' Her sobs sounded clearly in his ear.

'No, well, I'm clearly not her.' His irritation reached new heights. He didn't have time to deal with a crying woman. 'When is the sale going to be completed? Only I need that money yesterday. I've bent over backwards to help you and your husband, delaying taking the money until you're able to pay, but I'm going to start adding interest if I don't receive the money in full in the very near future.'

Her answer came in the form of redoubled sobbing, words appearing at random intervals amongst the convulsive gasps for air.

'I don't have it. I don't know when. My daughter. Do you know where Jade is? She's gone missing!'

'Oh for God's sake!' This was getting him nowhere. 'Ask your bloody private investigator to look for her. I want my money and I want it as soon as the sale's been made. Don't fuck me around, Lauren. I'm warning you.'

He slammed the phone down, glared at it for good measure,

then stretched back in his chair and contemplated the ceiling. 'I shouldn't have told her to involve the PI,' Peter McKinnon admonished himself. Life was proving difficult enough without encouraging a private investigator to start snooping around his life, especially where Jade was concerned. Not now the project was so close to bearing fruit.

THIRTY
PHARMS

Teàrlach's phone rang, Chloe's name on the display.

'Hi, Chloe.'

'I spoke to your Welsh detective, John Jenkins.'

'How did that go?'

'Yeah, all right. He's definitely thinking I'm a New Age flake, but he's taken it on board. I sent him a copy of the map and pentagram overlay.' She paused. 'I mentioned the ropes and the symbolic meaning of the knots. Was that OK?'

'Doesn't do any harm. You didn't mention—'

Chloe cut in before he could finish. 'No. Nothing about the next-door neighbours.'

Teàrlach could see Dee visibly relax from the corner of his eye. 'Good. Did you get anything from him? Where they are with the investigation?'

'Not really. I did ask, but all he said was they were following a lead. Sorry.'

'No, it's all right. Wasn't expecting them to provide an update on their enquiry, but interesting that they're following a specific lead.'

Dee caught his eye, as her fingers started an urgent clatter on her keyboard.

'Are you working today?' Chloe asked.

'Aye. We're in the office anyway, and I'm worried that Jade Martin is still unaccounted for. There's also the fact that two points of your pentagram are waiting for bodies, and I don't have much faith in our Welsh detective solving the case fast enough.'

'Is Dee there with you?'

'Aye, she had to collect something.'

This time the pause was considerably longer. 'Do you want me to come in too?'

Teàrlach detected a hidden agenda, too well concealed for him to put a finger on it. 'No, you're OK. Thanks for the offer. I'll see you Monday – have a good weekend.'

'Yeah, OK.' Chloe sounded doubtful. 'I'm going to see my parents – with Leo. Been a while since I've seen them.'

'Oh well, good luck.' He ended the call, turned his attention back to Dee. She was deeply engrossed in reading her screen, oblivious to the conversation he'd just had with Chloe.

'Have you found anything?' he asked, more from hope than any expectation that Dee's illicit search of police files would provide anything of interest.

'Aye. This is interesting.' She continued reading to herself.

Teàrlach tried to keep the impatience out of his voice. 'What have you got?'

She raised her eyes from the screen to focus on his. Teàrlach's impatience turned to discomfort as she held his gaze for too long.

'This.' Dee swung her screen around to face him, watching as he moved closer into focus range and read the screen.

'Carfentanil? What is it, a drug like GHB?'

'Let me read up on it.' Dee retrieved her laptop, fingers hammering the keys.

'This hasn't shown up in any of the other victims' toxicology reports?'

Dee shook her head. 'They've only come up with strangulation – and those reports are hedged with caveats. No, this is from the woman they found this morning.'

'Wouldn't they check for something like this as a matter of course?'

'OK, here we are. Carfentanil found in bloods.' She caught Teàrlach's puzzled expression. 'Says here it's present in very low concentrations. I guess it's not something forensics would have spotted if they hadn't deliberately tested for it.'

'But this body was found at six thirty in the morning. Maybe the drug was still fresh enough to stand out?'

'Guess so,' Dee shrugged in response. 'She was also strung upside down so her bladder may not have completely emptied.'

Teàrlach thought it through whilst Dee carried on reading. If each victim was drugged, then they'd be easier to manoeuvre, less chance of fighting back. The relative youth of the victims also made it more likely that they were being targeted in bars or nightclubs. With the exception of the Warmingtons of course, but even there – if the old couple had been spiked, then arranging them in that macabre so-called suicide would have been easier to do. Which left Keith Martin.

'You know Keith Martin was stabbed without defending himself?'

Dee looked up again. 'Aye, so?'

Teàrlach drew his brows down in concentration. 'What if he'd been drugged and was semi-comatose? Wouldn't that slow down his ability to fight back?'

Her head tilted slightly before she answered. 'You know why they're called date rape drugs, right?'

Teàrlach was detective enough to see her eyes narrowing.

'Aye. I get your point. He'd have been helpless.'

'Exactly! You try spending every night where you have to

keep watch over everyone's drinks as well as your own. It's a fucking war zone out there for women!'

'So, we could be looking at an MO that's common to all these murders? Whoever's killing these people is drugging them senseless and then stabbing or tying them up.'

'And if the dose is too high, then they'll kill them that way anyway.'

Teàrlach started to see how that might pan out. 'So in the case of the pentagram murders, he wasn't expecting them to be found before the drugs had dissipated – or they'd been stored somewhere before wrapping them in rope. And in the case of the Warmingtons, it had been weeks since they'd been murdered. Which just leaves Keith Martin – and his body was still warm when they sent it off to the coroner.'

'Aye, but imagine you're the coroner. Corpse is brought in with so many stab wounds he leaks like a colander. Police have arrested the son holding a knife which matches the wounds. Are you going to check for obscure drugs – especially if his liver and kidneys have been turned into mincemeat?'

Teàrlach admired Dee's way with words as much as her analytical skills.

'OK. So we have something that links all these murders together, and even DI Jenkins won't be too far behind us. But how does that help with our investigation?'

Dee shrugged. 'Dunno. Any one of the family could have spiked the dad. Maybe they overdid the dose?'

Teàrlach wasn't so sure. 'If he was already dead when Logan stabbed him, I don't think there would be so much blood. Mostly because his heart wasn't beating.'

'Unless he was comatose, and they thought he was dead. Or Logan pumped his chest to try resuscitation?'

'Before or after stabbing him?'

'Only one person has the answer to that, and he's banged up in Barlinnie.' Dee frowned as she continued reading. 'You remember when the Chechens took theatre-goers hostage in Moscow, back in 2002?'

'Vaguely.' Teàrlach wondered where this was going.

'There's a report here, says Porton Down found carfentanil and remifentanil in clothing from two British survivors, and in the urine from a third after the Russians knocked the entire theatre out with some gas.'

'Tell me you've not hacked into Porton Down?'

Dee laughed at his shocked expression. 'That would be a challenge – no, Wikipedia.' She spun the screen back towards him in confirmation.

He shook his head in bewilderment.

Teàrlach stood. 'Time I paid Logan another visit, let him know his sister's missing and see if that doesn't loosen his tongue. I can check the site of the Earth pentagram point on the way, if you want to join me?'

He'd tried to sound casual. Dee's amused face told him he'd most likely failed.

'Aye, go on then. I'll wear my leather jacket in case it pisses down.'

THIRTY-ONE
PASSWORD

Teàrlach hadn't accounted for the strict visiting hours at Barlinnie. The best he could try for was a virtual meeting on the Sunday morning if Logan Martin agreed to his request.

'Guess it's a walk in the park, then?' Dee commented from the passenger seat.

'Aye. Anything but Barlinnie Prison car park.'

Seven Lochs Wetlands Park didn't even match the precise location of Chloe's pentagram overlay – that honour belonged to a section of the M8 motorway. Teàrlach drove aimlessly around until he was able to park in a residential street, opposite a footpath leading into trees and adjacent to a patch of green given over to a golf course.

'Are we wasting our time?' Dee put voice to the thought running in Teàrlach's mind.

'Probably. How large an area does this place cover?'

'Over nineteen square kilometres in total. Made up from a bunch of smaller parks and disused industrial sites. The hole in a needle in a haystack doesn't even begin to come close.'

He reached for the map, searched for anything that might offer a clue. It was hopeless. No ancient sites, no obvious landmarks. Outside the car windows the sun had finally broken through and birds responded with song as if spring was starting over. A cyclist threaded his way past the barrier put in place to prevent drivers practising their off-road skills, his purple lycra-clad body effortlessly bending and balancing without needing to unclip his feet from the pedals.

'How many vehicle entrances are there? Is there one near here?' Teàrlach watched the cyclist until the last hint of purple had been obscured by trees.

Dee bent over her phone screen. 'Can't see any. There's plenty of paths big enough to drive down, but they're all pedestrian or bike paths. Like this one.' She indicated the path the cyclist had taken.

'Might as well have a look, now we're here.' Teàrlach opened the car door, waited for Dee to follow and locked it behind them.

The path was wide enough to take a car as Dee had mentioned, only a padlocked barrier prevented anyone from attempting that route. He held the padlock anyway, checked it was secure.

'Wouldn't stop anyone who seriously wanted to drive down here,' Dee mentioned casually. 'Or maybe he has a key? Works for the parks department?'

'Could be,' Teàrlach answered. 'Or maybe there's nothing here at all.' His attention was attracted by movement on the green, a golfer driving an electric buggy in pursuit of a little white ball. It was soon joined by another. They sounded like bluebottles in the distance and the sound irritated him. He imagined flies circling for an easy meal, buried just under the ground.

'Do you think the daughter is in danger, Jade Martin?' Dee stood so close to him that he started, taking a step back. She watched him with the same intensity a lab technician observes an experiment, her eyes expressing disappointment with his reaction.

'I don't know,' Teàrlach blurted out in his sudden confusion. 'Maybe she just wants away from her mother.'

The leads they had into Keith Martin's death, the tenuous links to the recent murders, nothing substantial enough to follow with any certainty. There was a bigger picture at play here, something that connected everything together, but he was too blind to see it.

His phone rang. Teàrlach checked the display, it was Lauren.

'Hi, Lauren, I'm afraid I don't have any news for you about Jade.'

'That's what I'm calling you about.' Lauren's strained voice replied. 'I know who has her. It's that Peter McKinnon. He threatened me this morning, said he wants the money Keith owed him.'

'What did he say, exactly?'

'He wants his £100,000 as soon as our house is sold and isn't going to wait any longer. He told me not to fuck him about.'

'Did he say that he had Jade? Was he threatening to do anything to her?' Teàrlach pressed for more information.

There was a sound of a cigarette being lit, followed by a deep inhale before she answered.

'I asked him if he knew where Jade was and he said to get you to find out.' Her voice broke. 'I know he has her. He's evil. It's all the money we have.'

Teàrlach processed the conflation of Jade's loss with the money and wondered which was upsetting her the most.

'Did you contact the police, like you said?'

The silence told him all he needed to know.

'I can't involve the polis. I can't.'

'Lauren, there's very little we can do in these circumstances. If you think Peter McKinnon has kidnapped Jade, then your only option is the police. We can't break down his door and look for her.'

Dee tapped his shoulder, motioned to mute the call. 'Ask if Jade has her own bank account, credit card whatever. May be able to trace her that way.'

'There's one last thing we can try,' Teàrlach continued. 'Does Jade have any bank accounts or credit cards? We may be able to find her that way.'

'Not that I know of. She's only just left school. Wait there.' He could hear footsteps fading away and shrugged at Dee, waiting for Lauren to return.

'I've found this in her drawer. Just a string of numbers and a message of some kind, maybe it's a password?'

'Can you take a photo, send it to me as a text? If we can make any sense of it, then that might help us track her down. In the meantime, you really need to contact the police about your daughter.'

'Not happening. I'll send this to you now.' She cut the call.

'Might as well head back to the car, see whatever Lauren sends us.' Teàrlach climbed back into the car, Dee buckling up beside him as a chime announced a text. He peered at his screen short-sightedly, then passed his phone over to Dee.

'What do you make of it?'

Dee thoughtfully pursed her lips before replying. 'Could be a bank account. These numbers look like a sort code has been added to an account number. If so, then this nonsense word may be the password. I'll forward it to myself so I can have a closer look.'

Teàrlach started the car, pulled away from the kerb. 'I'll drop you at the office so you can collect your bike. If you manage to find anything, you'll let me know?'

'Sure thing.'

Teàrlach's phone rang again, a distraught woman's voice issuing from the handsfree.

'My daughter's gone missing. Can you help? The police aren't doing anything. I don't know where else I can go.' Wracking sobs sounded as if the woman had been holding back a tidal wave of emotion until that moment.

'When was this? Have you tried her friends, the usual places?' Teàrlach felt a familiar hollow pit forming in his stomach. He sensed Dee's concern, imagined her making the same connection to the recent murders.

'She went out clubbing with her friends on Thursday night. When she didn't call yesterday, I thought she must be busy, then I called her flat this morning and they said they thought she was with me. It's been almost forty hours since anyone's seen her.' Her voice broke into sobs. 'Please, you have to help.'

He exchanged a look with Dee.

'What's your daughter's name?'

'Emily Katz. She's only nineteen – she's just a child.'

'What's your address?'

They didn't speak on the way back from Seven Lochs Park, there wasn't anything to be said. At the back of both their minds was the thought that this latest missing woman might have been taken by the same serial killer. The association with Earth on the pentagram led them both to imagine the same scenario – that another body lay buried somewhere in the vicinity of the park.

THIRTY-TWO
PECULIAR

Dee sat down at her desk, opened her laptop and started work on the scrap of paper Lauren Martin had found in Jade's bedroom. The numbers soon resolved into a sort code and account number as she had expected, then she tried logging on as Jade Martin. Not recognised. Whatever username Jade had, it wasn't her actual name, and without any social media to harvest, this was going to be a difficult nut to crack.

Dee made herself a fresh brew, searching the Glasgow rooftops for inspiration whilst the coffee machine managed a fair impersonation of someone being throttled to death beside her. So far, there wasn't any obvious link between any of the murder victims placed on Chloe's pentagram. All young, male and female – yet old enough that their absence didn't trigger the police into immediate action. This might be deliberate, Dee thought. Ensuring any police activity was delayed until any vestige of drugs had left the body. Yet the bodies had been carefully placed where they were going to be found: suspended from trees in public places; in the River Kelvin near a major bridge. Only the last body had been discovered early enough that traces of drugs still remained in the young woman's system.

The coffee machine gasped its last breath, and Dee took a full mug back to her desk. If the serial killer wanted each of his victims found, then there should be some obvious sign of a body at each site. The problem was, these pentagram points were approximations at best – based on a sketch Chloe had overlayed on a map of Glasgow. The bodies discovered so far did equate to the symbols used on the pentagram: Water; Spirit; Air. That only left Earth and Fire. Assuming the Pagan was working his or her way methodically around the pentagram, then it made sense that the next body would symbolise Earth. But if the body had been buried, how was anyone going to find it?

Dee sipped thoughtfully, trying to imagine what the killer was trying to accomplish by ritual killings. If he was after notoriety, then that box was ticked – every news broadcast and newspaper had some article about the most recent murder victim and speculation was already running wild. It was only a matter of time before someone let slip about the pentagram and then the conspiracy theorists would be out in force.

The murders exhibited an almost religious care in how they'd been bound and presented. It took care and forethought for the victims to be selected, drugged and presented in the way they had without the perpetrator being spotted. How could anyone be taken from a crowded bar or nightclub, almost certainly drugged or appearing to be close to passing out, without attracting the notice of friends or staff?

Dee's fingers hovered over the keyboard. She could break into Jade's bank account, but it would take hours and would expose her to a degree of risk. There were still the encrypted files belonging to Peter McKinnon waiting to be viewed in detail, and she hadn't checked the police reports for the latest updates. She decided to start with the police investigation, carefully picking her way through the secure server without setting off any alarms.

Each of the victims had been identified, their names and

backgrounds, family and history outlined in sparce detail. Dee read on, searching for anything that might lead them to Jade or this new woman, Emily Katz. At the back of her mind was the thought that either might be the latest victim, and Dee couldn't bear the thought of them being left to die without doing everything she could. It was Emily's police report that gave her the first real lead. A friend's witness statement said she'd taken ill at the Le Parisian nightclub, and they'd called for an Uber to take her home. Subsequent investigation with Uber discovered that the allocated driver waited five minutes, then took another fare. His alibi had been confirmed, in which case – what happened to Emily after Le Parisian? There was a mention of video footage from outside the club, but Emily had woven a drunken path out of shot.

Something had happened to her in the time between exiting the club and the arrival of the Uber some ten minutes after the initial call. The taxi had parked outside the club and in full view of the camera after Emily had walked out of sight, so unless the driver collected her further down the road after waiting five minutes, someone else must have taken her off the street. Dee continued reading the witness statement. Her friends had checked up on her, seen she'd declined the Uber, then switched off her mobile. The girl giving the statement said she'd looked outside the club for Emily, but she was nowhere to be seen and assumed she'd just taken another taxi home.

'Some friend,' Dee muttered under her breath. Leaving a friend to travel home alone when she was either drunk or drugged was an abdication of responsibility – and Emily might have paid the ultimate price.

Dee dug deeper into the police files, looking into the circumstances of each recent murder associated with the serial killings. The first young woman, found in the Kelvin, had been walking home and never completed the short journey from work to her parents' house. The police were working on the assumption that she'd been abducted sometime between 7 p.m. and 8 p.m., focussing their enquiries on the route she regularly walked. No witness reports were available. Dee was at least able to put a name to the woman left in the Kelvin – Julie Simpson.

The young man found suspended from a tree had been identified as Jack Bentall, a student at an open university course. He'd been to a gig, leaving the venue after 11 p.m. and went missing in the walk back to his halls of residence. The police had identified him before any of his fellow students had realised Jack was no longer in his room or turning up for lectures. They had security footage of his arriving and then leaving the venue on his own. Like the other victim, he had simply vanished off the street.

Dee opened the file for the next murder, Bryony Knight. She'd taken a bus to Sauchiehall Street to do some shopping, and the police had matched credit card receipts to the shops she visited. Some time that afternoon Bryony used her credit card for the last time and disappeared from sight until a night worker spotted her hanging upside down on his way home.

Now Dee had names to put to each victim, they became all the more real, no longer anonymous but people with lives and dreams for their future cruelly cut short. In each case the police had made no progress. No witnesses had come forward, no reports of abductions or unusual behaviour, no CCTV or mobile phones to track.

She frowned at her screen. Three of these people had been taken off the street – in the case of Bryony Knight taken in broad daylight from one of Glasgow's busiest shopping streets. That one stood out as the only daytime disappearance, all the others that they knew about had gone missing at night. Bryony was also the only one found with traces of carfentanil in her system, thanks to the night shift worker spotting her in the early hours and forensics specifically testing for it. Had the killer made a mistake, grown overconfident in their ability to snatch people without being seen?

Dee decided on a course of action. Whoever the murderer was, and the likelihood was they were looking for a man, he'd picked a street that was covered in CCTV cameras. One of those must have caught the moment Bryony disappeared. She bent over her keyboard. It was going to be a long afternoon.

THIRTY-THREE
PAIN

The street was close to Glasgow Royal Infirmary. The houses here were a mixture of small flats and even smaller terraces, the road surface paved with bricks laid out in a herringbone pattern in a nod to gentrification. This was an area favoured by those bravely reaching out towards the lowest rung of the property ladder. Unremarkable was the thought crossing Teàrlach's mind – not the first place anyone would associate with abduction or murder. People move to places like this because they're meant to be safe, far enough away from deprivation, drugs and violence to pretend such things don't exist. Except of course, they do.

Emily Katz's mother opened the door. She looked as if she hadn't slept for days, a bewildered expression crossing her face when she failed to identify him. Her partner stood in the hallway behind her, looking lost in his own home.

'I'm Teàrlach Paterson. You called me, about your missing daughter?'

'Oh, thank God! Come in, come in.' She pulled the door fully open, pressing herself against the wall. 'I'm Sandra, this is Niklas.'

'Come into the garden room,' her partner spoke in the precise way Germans often do. He led the way to a conservatory at the back of the house, indicating a bamboo seat that Teàrlach doubted would take his weight. He lowered himself gingerly into the creaking embrace of the furniture as Emily's parents settled themselves on a similar seat built for two. They stared at him with the same anticipation an audience might expect of a conjurer when he reaches inside his hat for the first time, but he had no rabbit to offer.

'What can you tell me about your daughter, Emily?' he opened.

Sandra spoke. It was almost always the woman. Niklas remained mute, fixing Teàrlach in the hope there was more to be seen than a first impression would indicate.

'Emily works at the Royal Infirmary, it's only a thirty-minute walk along the A8 from here. She sometimes pops in to see us – she lives with another nurse in a shared flat further up the road.'

Teàrlach noted the present tense, pulling out his notebook and writing brief notes as she spoke.

'She sometimes stays over with us. Emily's always been a home girl – we keep her room for her with her soft toys and...' Her voice cracked with sudden emotion, and she buried her head deep within her hands, shaking convulsively. Her partner stretched out a protective arm, drew her in close. He mimed an apology as if breaking down in tears was in some way an incorrect way to behave when a daughter goes missing.

'Is that why her flatmate took so long before she noticed Emily had gone missing?'

Niklas looked hopefully at his partner who remained buried in her hands, then spoke on her behalf.

'She came round to see us this morning. Wondered why Emily missed her shift. Thought she might be ill. There's still a lot of Covid around.' He added this as if it might in some way explain his daughter's disappearance,

'Can you give me Emily's flat address, and the name of her flatmate?'

'It's 12b Wallace View, over in Cranhill. She shares it with another nurse, Ashleigh McIntyre. They've been friends since college.' He stopped like a man who had just worked out the solution to a particularly difficult problem. 'You will be able to find her, won't you?'

Teàrlach engaged with the hope written across his face, then with Sandra newly resurfaced from her hands, eyes moist with tears.

'I'll do my best,' he answered. 'The police will be working on the case; chances are they'll find her in a few days.'

Niklas paled, reading more into Teàrlach's words than he'd said.

'You don't think it's anything to do with this Pagan on the news?'

Teàrlach hadn't heard the term, but it was exactly the name the press would come up with. Ritualised killings, bound in rope. *Just wait until the pentagram is mentioned.* He thought it was likely their daughter was a potential victim, but he wasn't going to put either parent through that at this early stage.

'No. Chances are she's taken herself off somewhere for a few days. Was she happy at work, no boyfriend problems or anything worrying her?'

Sandra took heart from Teàrlach's lie, and attempted a smile which fell short of a grimace.

'Emily wasn't interested in boys,' Sandra said decisively. 'She loved her job. I can't understand how she could just go off and not tell us?' Her voice quavered, fresh tears rolling down each cheek. She sniffed, rummaged around for a handkerchief, and pressed it against each eye in turn.

'Talk to Ashleigh,' Niklas intoned, each word efficiently

clipped and separated from its neighbours. 'She was the last one to see her.'

Teàrlach nodded, wondering what message Niklas was trying to impart. 'Do you have a recent photograph, her phone number, any places or people she might have gone to visit?'

'I'll get it.' Niklas removed his arm and left them both alone. He gave the impression of being relieved to have some task to do, one that wasn't impossible.

'You will find my girl, won't you?' Sandra implored. Her wet eyes held his in desperation. 'She's my little girl. I can't...' The tears began afresh, leaving Teàrlach helplessly voicing platitudes he didn't believe.

Niklas returned, handing over a photograph of a young woman smiling shyly, dressed in a nurse's uniform.

'This is her mobile...' An additional sheet of paper was handed over. 'And these are friends she's stayed with in the past. I've called them all several times – none of them have seen her.'

'Thanks. This nightclub – Le Parisian. Did she go there regularly?'

Niklas gave the same lost look that he had when Teàrlach first saw him.

'I don't know. I've never heard her mention it.'

'Does she go off anywhere, to friends or travelling, without letting either of you know she's likely to be away for a few days?'

'No. Never!' Sandra had raised her head from her hands to make the emphatic comment. 'She knew that I'd worry myself sick – she always told me before going anywhere.'

Teàrlach stood.

'I'll do my best to find your daughter, I can promise you that.'

Sandra gave him a fleeting smile, then buried her face in her handkerchief.

'Can you call her flatmate, tell her to expect me in the next few minutes?'

Sandra raised her head to give a quick nod, then wiped her eyes free of tears.

'I'll show you out.' Niklas offered, leading the short distance back to the front door. He stood on the step as Teàrlach passed, catching hold of his arm and pulling him in close.

'If someone's taken her, I promise you I'll kill the bastard.' His words were for Teàrlach only, and all the more menacing for being quietly spoken.

Teàrlach nodded and Niklas let go of his arm. He remained rooted on the doorstep as Teàrlach drove away, his figure staring at the car in the rear-view mirror until lost from sight.

Niklas's response was one he'd seen before. A need to lash out, to fix the unfixable. To bring retribution that the judiciary and courts were unable to provide. If Emily was going to be another victim of the Glasgow serial killer, Niklas would be looking to exact a price for the pain that would cause.

Number 12b Wallace View was one of a 1950s housing scheme of four-storey tenements. Identical, severe buildings that wouldn't have looked out of place in East Germany before the Iron Curtain was demolished. They faced a sloping scrub wasteland, the embankment high enough to effectively conceal the view of yet more tenements replicating brutalist architecture until the public funding finally gave out. The residents kept the place tidy, rectangular patches of fenced-in grass kept mowed, streets clear of litter. The windows on this street all faced due north, permanently in shadow. Teàrlach parked easily enough – not many of the residents could afford cars.

He pressed the door intercom, a woman's voice responded.

'Who is it?'

'My name's Teàrlach Paterson. I've been asked to look for Emily Katz. Her parents told me you were the last person to see her. Can I come in?'

He waited for five long seconds before the door answered with a rasping electronic buzz. A flight of concrete steps led upwards to a shared first floor landing. The door on his left opened as far as a security chain allowed, dark brown eyes observed him through the crack.

'What do you want? I've already told the police everything I can.' She sounded anxious.

'I know you both went to the Le Parisian nightclub on Thursday, and Emily left on her own. Was it you who called the Uber for her?'

'How do I know you're the detective?'

Teàrlach handed her a business card through the gap in the door, delicate fingers snatching it from his. The door closed. He could hear the sound of a security chain jangling through the wood, then she opened the door wide.

'You'd better come in.'

Teàrlach stepped into a wide entrance hall, waiting for Ashleigh to close the door behind him. She was early twenties, olive skin and elfin face framing the brown eyes he'd seen through the gap in the door. Her hand automatically went to her jet-black hair, brushing it back with a distracted air. She led him into a sitting room, inviting him to sit whilst she fidgeted from foot to foot.

'Do you want a tea or coffee?'

'No, thanks.' Teàrlach produced a notebook from his pocket, opened it at the first blank page and retrieved a biro. 'Can you take me through the evening you spent with Emily, places you went, anything you can remember?'

She reluctantly sat down, fixed her attention on the worn carpet. 'We were celebrating John's birthday – it was his twenty-fourth. Had a few drinks in the Last Hope and then went to the Parisian for a bit of a dance. It wasn't a heavy night, we all had work the next day.'

'How many of you were there?'

'Just me and Emily, John and Rupert. We've been mates since college, hang out as a foursome sometimes.'

Teàrlach's biro scratched as he made notes. 'And John and Rupert – did either of them have any romantic involvement with Emily?'

Ashleigh's attention switched from carpet to Teàrlach with an incredulous expression.

'What? No, of course not!' He could see the light of understanding dawn as she realised he didn't know any of these people.

'Le Parisian's a gay club,' she explained. 'John and Rupert have been an item for years.'

Teàrlach processed the part Ashleigh hadn't mentioned.

'And you and Emily?'

Her interest returned to the floor. 'Her parents don't want to know about it. They prefer to think of us as flatmates.'

'So, you and Emily are together?'

'We were.' He noticed Ashleigh's hands starting to curl and uncurl at her sides. She reminded him of a cat. 'We'd had an argument that night, nothing serious. That's why I stayed instead of going home with her... I didn't know she'd go missing.'

Ashleigh's hands stopped their curling and went to her face, wiping tears away from her eyes. Teàrlach could see the wet trails they left on each cheek as she faced him again.

'I thought she'd gone back to her mum. I didn't know something had happened to her. It's all my fault...'

She broke down weeping, leaving Teàrlach feeling useless. He produced his handkerchief, waved it in her direction like a flag of surrender. It took her a while before she noticed, shaking her head and reaching for a box of tissues instead. She blew her nose, wiped it clean and engaged with him once more.

'I don't know where she is. I've tried calling, but her phone goes straight to voicemail and with these murders...'

Teàrlach waited for the tears to subside.

'Can you tell me how she was when she left?'

Ashleigh sniffed an affirmative, wiping her eyes with another tissue. Teàrlach could see a small mound of discarded tissues growing by her feet.

'She started acting weird, like she was really drunk. I thought she was pretending because we'd had the same amount to drink – it wasn't enough to make her that drunk.'

'Could her drink have been spiked?'

'No way.' Ashleigh shook her head in denial. 'We all watch for each other's drinks, the boys as well.'

'But you said Emily was acting weird, like she was really drunk?'

'Yeah but, she was putting it on to make us leave. That's why I called the Uber, to call her bluff.'

'What if she wasn't putting it on?' Teàrlach asked gently.

Ashleigh had no answer for him except for the guilt written in her brown eyes.

'Can I see the Uber details?'

She swiped her phone, handed it over for Teàrlach to copy the booking details. The ride had been booked for 11:40, cancelled at 11:45. He sent the pertinent details to Dee, asked her to prioritise the search for Emily.

'OK. Thanks.' He stood to leave. 'I'll let you know as soon as we hear anything – can you call me if Emily gets in touch?'

Ashleigh nodded once before her face crumpled.

'I'll let myself out.'

THIRTY-FOUR
PARISIAN

Le Parisian nightclub entrance was situated down a side street in the East End of Glasgow, an area of small family businesses, quirky coffee shops and trendy bars. The club may have once been a small warehouse, perhaps a cinema in a previous life. Now the only sign that the building wasn't disused was the garish addition of a French tri-colour plastic canopy and Le Parisian in red neon lettering over the side entrance.

Teàrlach pulled up outside the door, spotting a CCTV camera anchored to red brick. He parked, found a doorbell set far enough away from the entrance to make it difficult to find and waited. The main road he'd just turned off was the same route to the Royal Infirmary that Emily and Ashleigh would take every day from their shared flat, and only fifteen minutes or so from Emily's parents' house. Further down the side road, beyond two dilapidated lock-up garages leaning onto the club for support, were four-storey flats dating from the Victorian era.

According to Ashleigh's Uber booking, Emily's ride had been cancelled. Teàrlach concluded she must have started walking home, either to the shared flat or her parents' house. That route would have been busy even at midnight, so how was she taken off the street without alerting anyone to her abduction? Teàrlach stared up at the CCTV in the hope that someone would come and open the door, but the club remained silent. The place gave every indication of being deserted.

The sound of bolts being drawn back alerted him to the fact that someone was inside the building. A woman blinked in the daylight, emerging from the dark recess of the doorway like a nocturnal creature out of its comfort zone. Her belligerent face was prematurely lined with worry and age, fixing Teàrlach with a look that expressed her annoyance at being disturbed.

'What do you want?' She looked him up and down in a clear effort to categorise him – not delivery; not police; not anyone she recognised. Her expression settled on trouble.

Teàrlach handed over a business card.

'My name's Teàrlach Paterson. I'm a private investigator looking for a young missing woman, last seen here on Thursday night.' He helpfully pointed to the CCTV camera.

'What do you expect me to do about it?'

Teàrlach aimed for a winning smile. He realised he must have missed as the woman's head pulled back into the club so much like an alarmed tortoise that his smile became more natural.

'I was hoping I could look at the CCTV footage. For Thursday night? You have cameras inside the club as well, right?'

'How do I know? I just clean the place. You'll have to come back when they open. Six o'clock.'

The brief conversation ended with the door shutting. The sound of bolts being drawn back into place underlined the abrupt termination. He returned to his car, made for the office. Ashleigh was obviously upset at Emily's disappearance – her parents had confirmed that it was out of character for her to go off without first letting them know and all her friends had claimed no contact. She'd been missing for two days. If there were red flags associated with someone's disappearance, then Emily was collecting the full set.

Teàrlach thought as he drove, starting with Nicole Martin's appearance at his office just five days ago on Monday. She believed without doubt that her brother had been murdered by anyone other than her nephew, Logan. She'd all but implicated Lauren and Jade, both of whom she'd described as monsters, although from what he'd seen of the two women he was inclined to put that down to deep-seated animosity. The circumstantial evidence against Logan was overwhelming, plus he'd admitted to stabbing his father to death. Yet Teàrlach wasn't convinced of his guilt. There was the puzzling lack of self-defence wounds to Keith Martin's arms and hands for one thing, then Logan's strange comment about Keith being a sacrifice. Jade and her mother were hiding something, he was sure of that, but Lauren was genuinely frightened for Jade since she'd been missing.

Now not only was he searching for Jade Martin, but this latest young woman, Emily Katz, had vanished without trace. Had the serial killer already filled the last two points on the pentagram and how were these bizarre, ritualistic murders connected to the Martins' next-door neighbours? Teàrlach had little doubt these incidents were related – the coincidence of rope featuring in each death made that conclusion all but inevitable. The detectives working the case had made no arrests. Whoever had placed the victims in full view had managed to do so without anyone witnessing the act. The woman in the river, and two bodies left in trees at archaeological sites would not have been easy to place – much less hoisted up into the branches.

Teàrlach shivered, despite the heat of the day. He couldn't escape the thought that these murders were ritualistic, and there was something deeply unnatural at play here beyond the actions of a crazed individual. Something unworldly. The only suspects he had in play were both connected with the breakaway Freemason lodge – Peter McKinnon who Lauren had accused of kidnapping her daughter, and the guy he'd seen at the re-purposed church on Crow Road where Jade worked part-time.

He arrived back at the office as the five o'clock news came on the car radio. Although the police had made no further progress in identifying the serial murderer, he was relieved that no more bodies had been reported. At least there was still hope for finding Jade and Emily alive.

Dee was still bent over her laptop as Teàrlach entered the office, a fresh cup of coffee by her side.

'You still here? Thought you were collecting your bike and going home. It's a Saturday,' Teàrlach added.

Dee spared him a disparaging glance from over the top of her screen.

'There's at least two women missing that we know about, and until we find them – or the bastard responsible for these murders – I'm not going to feel good partying away the weekend.'

'Fair comment.'

'How did you get on, with the girl's parents?' She switched her attention away from the screen and watched him carefully for his reaction.

'They're worried – with good reason. She never returned from the nightclub she went to on Thursday night with her girlfriend – The Parisian in the East End. They'd had some sort of break-up, her partner called her an Uber as she was acting drunk, but the driver cancelled when she didn't show.'

'Think she'd been spiked?'

Teàrlach nodded. 'Her partner claims it was impossible – they were in a group of four and all watched each other's drinks, but she also claimed Emily hadn't had enough to drink to be as drunk as she made out.'

'CCTV from the club?' Dee asked.

'Aye. Tried that, but there was only an uncommunicative cleaner that answered the door. It opens in an hour.' He collapsed behind his desk, frowning at the window view across to the Clyde. 'How about you? You found anything that can help us find these girls?'

Dee carried her battered laptop through to his office, swivelled the screen around for him to view.

'Found this,' she answered.

THIRTY-FIVE
PODGY AND DODGY

The video footage running on Dee's laptop was of such poor quality that Teàrlach would have struggled even if he did wear the glasses he needed. The image eventually resolved into a grainy night-time street view, headlights and streetlights flaring portions of the screen into incoherence. Dee's finger alerted him to the blurred figure of a woman staggering along the pavement and his interest quickened.

'What are we looking at?'

'I pulled this from a traffic camera. The resolution is crap, the camera must be at least ten years old. I think they use it to assess traffic flow, so image quality isn't important. This is looking along the A8 eastbound, just after the turnoff to Le Parisian.'

Teàrlach searched for a date, squinting at white numerals on the upper left corner of the screen.

'Thursday 20th, 11:48 p.m. Is this Emily Katz?' No amount of squinting would help bring the woman's outline into focus.

'She's in the right place at the right time – or not,' Dee added darkly. 'I've had to hack into so many cameras, and this is the only possible contender.'

A bus headed towards them, headlights catching the lens and occluding the image in white noise.

'There!' Dee stretched across and hit the spacebar, freezing the picture as it reappeared on the screen. A car had pulled into the kerb, the solitary woman caught in the act of climbing into the back. Even with the picture clarity being as bad as it was, Teàrlach could make out the unmistakable glow of a taxi light on the roof.

'Any way of seeing the numberplate?' he asked, more in hope than in any expectation of Dee miraculously sharpening the image.

'No,' Dee replied emphatically. 'And I've spent hours searching for this car on other video feeds. The original quality is so piss poor I can't even make out the make or colour.'

'And we can't even be sure this is Emily we're looking at.' Teàrlach's frustration was clear in his voice.

'It wasn't an Uber at any rate. Not with a taxi sign on the roof.'

'If that roof sign says taxi. Private hires are allowed to put their telephone numbers and advertising up as long as they're not masquerading as a taxi.' He leaned back in his chair, rubbed the strain out of his eyes. 'Even then, it's not exactly difficult to put something like that on top of a car roof. They sell magnetic mounts online.'

Dee pictured herself in the place of the woman frozen on the screen: drunk or drugged, barely able to control her legs, unable to think clearly beyond a need to get home.

'I'd probably trust a taxi, in that state.' She spoke quietly. 'And so would any of the other people this bastard has taken – even the woman taken in broad daylight from Sauchiehall Street.'

'Sorry, who's that?'

Dee updated him with the latest from the police files, putting names to the bodies.

'We need to let the police know they're looking for a taxi driver.' Teàrlach reached for his mobile. Dee placed her hand on his before he had a chance to dial out. It stayed there for longer than was needed.

'Can't,' Dee said softly. 'I hacked the camera.'

Teàrlach cursed under his breath, reluctantly removing his hand away from his mobile and the warmth of Dee's hand.

'There's something else I found,' Dee continued. 'Those numbers in Jade Martin's bedside drawer – they're for a bank account.'

'Any recent transactions?'

Dee shook her head. 'Haven't managed to get into it. I really need to phish my way into back office and make out I'm internal before I'd get anywhere – and it's the weekend.'

Teàrlach wasn't entirely sure he knew what she was talking about but followed the gist.

'There's something been going on with Lauren and Jade. I'm beginning to think Nicole Martin may have been right all along.'

'That Logan didn't kill his dad?'

Teàrlach shook his head in frustration. 'I don't know. There's something off about it – the lack of any defensive marks on his dad's arms or hands. You don't stand there passively when someone's repeatedly stabbing into your chest. It makes no sense.'

'What if he was drugged like you thought?'

Teàrlach started to dispute her theory. 'No way. Police forensics would have caught anything like that in his bloods.'

'Except most of his blood was soaking into the hall by the time they collected his body and cause of death was staring them in the face.'

'Alleged cause of death,' Teàrlach added thoughtfully. 'And if that's the case, then we've found a link between the Martins and the Pagan murders.'

'What about the neighbours? Think someone spiked them and acted out some perverse fantasy, then left them to die like that?'

'Christ knows. Their bodies were found so late any trace would have gone by the time forensics had them.'

'What's going on here, Teàrlach? What possible connection is there to the Martins and this serial killer?'

'I don't know. If there is a connection, then it's drugs – but that doesn't explain tying victims up in fancy ropework and leaving them on the points of a pentagram.' He stared out over the city, catching the play of sun and shadows as a prevailing westerly dragged puffy cumulous clouds over the sky. 'Whatever this is, the catalyst was the murder of Keith Martin.'

'More like the Warmingtons,' Dee countered. 'They died almost a year ago, remember? And they're the first murder victims tied up in rope.'

He acquiesced, nodding slowly to himself. 'Maybe they were a trial run. They don't fit on Chloe's pentagram, yet it's too much of a coincidence for there not to be a link to this Pagan character.'

'And they lived next door to the Martins,' Dee added. 'And we still haven't worked out what the Freemasons have to do with it all.'

'I'm beginning to think Jade Martin has taken herself out of circulation rather than anything else. I passed on that message from her brother, and she looked scared.' Teàrlach stroked an imaginary beard as he thought. 'Freemasons like their symbols and geometry. This Pagan serial killer is using the same MO as whoever killed the Warmingtons. What if they had to die because they had become a threat – or knew too much?'

'Something to do with the Martins next door?'

'Aye – except William Warmington was at pains to protect Jade from someone, or something – according to his journals.'

'Well, it can't be her brother cos he's banged up in Barlinnie, and the dad's out of the picture.' Dee stated the facts succinctly.

'That leaves Lauren, who doesn't exactly fit my expectations of either a serial killer or a drugs baron, and Jade.'

'There's still the characters at this breakaway lodge on Crow Road.'

'Aye.' Teàrlach pictured the rotund golfer, Peter McKinnon, and the pale individual inside the church. 'Podgy and Dodgy. There's always them.'

He checked the time – coming up for seven. 'It's late. There's nothing more we can do tonight. We'll make a fresh start tomorrow – if you don't mind losing the whole weekend?'

Dee locked eyes with him, holding Teàrlach frozen in place and wondering what telepathic message she was attempting to convey.

'Fine. I'll see you tomorrow, then.' Dee picked up her laptop and walked out of his office, collecting her backpack and helmet as she went.

He watched her don her leathers and leave in silence. Teàrlach couldn't help but feel he'd just been tested and found lacking.

THIRTY-SIX
PUSHER

Jade entered Le Parisian, skirt so high that the bouncers had trouble focussing on the contents of her clutch bag. Her boyfriend tagged along, jealous of the wandering eyes but worried about the contents of Jade's bag. If she was searched...

'C'mon. Let's get a drink.' Jade walked confidently to the bar, not even considering that the staff might want to check her false ID. Since she'd shaved her hair to within centimetres of her scalp, the world had treated her like an adult. Losing those flowing locks had added years to her age – and at sixteen having years added to your age is something to be wished for. Having a boyfriend three years older helped.

'Can we just deal and get out?' He spoke directly into her ear, relying on the incessant beat to drown out his words for anyone else to hear.

'Relax.' Jade rolled her painted eyes in despair. She wanted a man but had hooked a pretty boy. No matter – he'd do for the moment. Long enough for her to shift the last samples she had tucked inside the lining of her bag. This stuff was so strong a single tab was sufficient to send the user into a zombie state. She just had to sell what she had left and then she'd have enough to leave Glasgow – and sooner rather than later. Once Peter McKinnon realised she was no longer working for him, he'd send someone after her. The same guy who killed her dad.

For the moment though, she was safe. So was Logan – or as safe as he could be locked up in Barlinnie. Her mum was OK as long as the money from the house sale was still in play, and everything should come together before their home managed to be sold.

Her boyfriend ordered at the bar whilst Jade checked out the clientele. She'd already made eye contact with a few who knew she dealt. With a bit of luck, she'd shift the whole lot tonight, then she'd make them pay!

She let herself think about her dad, seeing him slumped against the wall as Logan repeatedly stabbed him again and again – long after he was already dead. There should be an emotional response attached to that memory, but all she had was numbness. Jade couldn't understand why she couldn't grieve for her father. She knew without doubt that she loved him, despite his refusal to believe she wasn't his little girl any longer. They had fought almost every day over stupid things – getting piercings, staying out late, going to concerts. He was only trying to protect her, she knew. When she watched him being killed, she was frozen to the spot, not believing anything she was seeing was real.

In her bedroom, half a tab in her system and the world had turned into an agreeable multi-dimensional space devoid of care. She hadn't been out of it so much that she didn't hear the screaming – floating out onto the landing and seeing her dad squealing like a stuck pig. His face staring up at her with the understanding that he was going to die there, in the hall.

She still hadn't processed what had happened to her dad. It could have been a nightmare except for the recording on her stolen iPhone – the one she used for dealing. Deep inside she knew she couldn't deal with the reality of his murder, or she'd revert to being that little girl – lost, alone and helpless. She knew how that would turn out once they started looking for her.

She had been beyond caring about anything at the time and had watched the events unfolding on her screen. Saw Logan running in from the back garden to help, held back with one hand, then the words hissed into his face.

'Say anything and Jade dies. You understand?'

The bloodied knife held too close to his eyes. Then forced into Logan's hand.

'You do it. You stab him.'

'I can't. I won't.' Logan sounded so weak. Crying impotently in the face of death.

His hands were gripped from behind, his body pushed to where his dad slowly slumped down a bloodstained wall. The knife plunged in, spraying blood over Logan's face as the heart was pierced.

'There. You've killed him. You've killed your dad.'

Logan's hand forced again and again to plunge the knife, hitting against ribcage, sinking wetly into stomach.

The hands released him.

'You do it. You do it or I'll kill you and then your sister.'

Logan's face crumpled into tears and fright.

'And then I'll kill your mother as soon as she comes through that door. Your choice.'

Logan's pathetic stab at his father's dying body.

'Harder! Do it harder.'

Logan sobbing as he stuck the knife in.

'Good boy.' His tormentor's voice now kind and encouraging. 'You tell the police you did it. Don't try saying anything else because I'm a cop and I'll know. Who do you think they'll believe?'

Logan half-heartedly making another stab into red meat.

'Harder! Do it harder or I'll fucking kill you now!'

Her brother, mad with fear and stabbing again and again with blood spraying the walls and staining the carpet.

'Don't stop. Tell the police it was you or I'll kill them all.'

Then it was just Logan, his arm going backwards and forwards leaving arcs of red in the air. She'd gone back in her room, shut the door, stood inside the pentagram and waited for her mother to come home.

She felt the first tears form since her dad had died, blinked them away angrily before anyone could notice. There would be time enough to grieve for everything soon. She just had to keep her head straight and not think about it. Jade took the drink from her boyfriend, felt the heat from the vodka and the sweetness from the coke. Her father's murder could have been nothing but a dream – except for the video on her mobile. She had a plan. A plan to pay back the man who killed her dad and take care of Logan and her mum. If she could stay alive long enough to put it into action.

THIRTY-SEVEN
IGNIS

The man lay comatose in the back of the cab. He might have already died for all she cared. It was all going wrong – the Water sacrifice had surfaced and been found; teenagers had seen the Spirit offering high up in the trees; the Air tribute had slipped its knots and dropped down so the first passer-by couldn't miss seeing it. Only Earth remained undiscovered, buried where she was unlikely to be found – and hers would be a slow death. Everything was meant to remain hidden until the full moon. After that, none of this would matter anymore. She operated the remote for the rear windows, flushed out the deadly aerosol before reaching the industrial unit.

She walked the pentagram with less fervour this last time, spoke the words with a worry they no longer held any feeling.

'Offero ignem, ut omnia emundes.'

At the triangle symbol, she knelt down, lit a candle and prayed for forgiveness to the old gods. This sacrifice would require strength.

'I walk through fire and shall not be burned, and the flame shall not consume me.'

There was one last offering to be made. Blood from fire and then the resurrection would come. Tonight.

THIRTY-EIGHT

FIRE

Bill McAdam crossed the Castlecary viaduct at well under the speed limit his Freightliner goods train was subject to. He enjoyed the sensation of gliding above the M80, seeing the few vehicles passing underneath him at this ungodly hour. He imagined the steam trains that had passed this way when the viaduct was first built, almost two hundred years ago. Driving a train gave him time to think, often about those who'd travelled down these same tracks before him. Perhaps it was a function of staring at those twin metal rails, forever trying to meet in the distance. They stretched away like an unfulfilled promise to tomorrow, leaving nothing but memories behind them. At times like this, with the darkness pressing in from his cab windows and the world asleep, he often felt disconnected from reality.

In the dark, the world took on a completely different aspect. Rails appeared as if by magic, lit by the powerful lights mounted in the front of the electric locomotive as it pulled rattling freight cars through the night. It was a pity they'd all but stopped using the sleek electric locomotives – operating costs came before environmental concerns. Now he was more likely to be driving an older diesel engine, complete with the noise and smell. It didn't bother Bill that much; at least the diesel was an honest, workmanlike engine that sounded alive. These electrics always felt like upscaled model railways. Sometimes, he questioned whether he existed in a model trainset himself and had to laugh at his own existential dread in case he was proven right.

Train driving did that to you. Not so much the passenger trains – the regular stops and announcements kept that connection with the rest of humanity. But the overnight freights, that was different. He had dreamt of emigrating to the US or Canada, maybe even Australia when he was still young. Riding steel rails over impossible distances for days on end, seeing vast prairies, giant mountains, forgotten towns where people lived their lives unnoticed. Watching herds of buffalo or seeing the ghosts of Blackfoot, Crow or Dakota riding free through an innocent land before the white man poisoned and imprisoned it all.

Croy Station sailed past, deserted except for platform lights illuminating the scene in sterile LED illumination like a film set awaiting actors. He'd slipped into that state where the rails mesmerised the mind, sat static in his cab whilst the world moved towards him, then pulled away behind him. Bill blinked hard, removing the illusion so he again was back in control, guiding the freight on towards Glasgow.

Lenzie Station came and went, and Bill checked the time: 2:17 a.m. It was mostly urban now, heading through Bishopbriggs. Less danger of deer crossing the rails. Now he had to look out for more purposeful trespassers – the drunk taking a short-cut, the debris left deliberately on the rails. At least he didn't have to worry too much about young lads throwing breeze blocks off the bridges at this time of morning.

As if on cue, something large was manhandled off the bridge directly in front of him, dropping down towards the rails. He slammed on the brakes, instinctively covering his face with his forearm and waiting for the inevitable impact and flying glass. The lights went off, the engine died and the train shuddered to a halt some distance down the track as the combined mass of freight reluctantly lost inertia. Bill stared at the controls in confusion, digital displays coming back to life as on-board batteries took over. He opened the cab door, looked back down the track and saw the overhead power lines erupting into flame. Still breathless from the imagined impact, the phone shook in his hand as he waited for someone to answer.

* * *

The first railway workers on the scene smelled it before they saw it, that lingering aroma of burned pork which pre-warned the experienced hands of another suicide. Only this was no suicide. The body remained caught in the overhead power lines, blackened beyond any hope of identification except by dental records. They'd had to wait for the all-clear before approaching, engineers taking precautions to discharge any latent voltage before letting the crew anywhere near the lines. Police and ambulance cars lined the bridge, flashing blue lights joining the glare of spotlights to cast the scene in lurid detail.

Word had spread before they were able to cut the corpse free of the cables, and a bleary-eyed film crew joined a freelance photographer on the bridge.

'Don't cut any more than you have to and handle the body as little as possible.' The detective giving the instructions stood beside them on the embankment, holding onto a metal fence to stop himself slipping down through the brambles and bushes lining the railway.

White helmeted railway workers ignored him, watching as a hastily arranged diesel shunted a working platform closer to the body. This was dirty and unpleasant work, made all the more difficult by the metal harness the body had been placed in.

Whoever the lunatic was who'd pushed the body off the bridge, he'd managed to fuse the power lines to the harness. At least that made releasing the body that much easier. A few quick blasts from an angle grinder and the overhead powerlines parted, dropping their contents unceremoniously onto the tracks.

'It's all yours,' one of the orange-clad railway workers shouted up to the policeman.

'How do we get down to recover the body?' the policeman responded.

'We can't piss about waiting for you. This section needs replacing, otherwise the entire network will be thrown into chaos. We'll bring it up.'

'No! We'll come down. We need the forensics.'

'That way.' One of the railway team pointed down the tracks. 'You can get down to the tracks. Drive down that road you're on for fifty metres. We'll open the service gate.'

White-clad forensics suits appeared like ghosts in the night, rolling the blackened and still smoking remains onto a stretcher before carrying their burden out of the floodlights. Down at the scene, railway workers tried to forget the image seared in their memories and prayed for the lingering smell to be drowned in diesel fumes. New cables arrived down the track, additional workers climbed gantries and began the business of splicing powerlines together. They took comfort from the noise and activity around them, focussing on the job in hand rather than watch the private ambulance depart into the night. Forensics officers scraped the bridge parapet in search of clues, shone torches over the road above and rails below.

The film crew and reporters lost interest, faded away like bloodthirsty vampires as dawn touched the eastern sky and the city slept. Down on the tracks the last traces of the night's drama were repaired, overhead power lines were tested and a small army of orange-clad workers climbed into a minibus. A diesel locomotive carried the last of the equipment and workers back to the local depot. A replacement driver was given the go-ahead to take Bill's freight train onward to its destination before the morning commuter trains started their work.

On the mortuary slab, a forensics expert began the laborious process of removing wire from the burned remains of what had once been a human body. It was only when the first fragment of rope appeared, tied in a complex knot and by some miracle left untouched by the fireball that had engulfed the victim did he realise the Pagan had struck again.

THIRTY-NINE
PENANCE

Teàrlach grimly read the online news, short in detail this early on a Sunday morning yet too detailed for him to face having anything other than coffee for breakfast. The accompanying photograph was of a railway line taken from a road bridge, workers in hi-vis and white helmets looking up at an object suspended in cables above their heads. The floodlights caught whisps of white smoke curling heavenwards from an indistinct blackened object caught on the powerlines.

He had a premonition, the geographical location confirmed it. The 'suicide' that the reporter used to describe the death was positioned as close as made no odds to the final pentagram point, the one Chloe had marked as Fire. Was this going to be the missing woman, Emily Katz?

Teàrlach had woken from a troubled sleep – fire had played a part in his dreams as well. A replay of the deliberate and sadistic immolation of his mother and younger brother in their 'safe' flat. He had the role of onlooker, unable to raise a hand to help or shout a warning as the petrol poured through the letter-box. The flame exploding along the corridor and trapping them, screaming for help. There was no comfort for him knowing he was too young to help, too far away living with his aunt on the Isle of Mull. All that he had been left was a visceral hatred of his father that he'd take to his grave.

Last evening hadn't gone well. Dee had left him at the office without a word. Somehow, he'd upset her, and he'd rerun their last few conversations in his mind searching fruitlessly for any offence. There'd been a message in her eyes when he'd asked her if she didn't mind working the weekend, and he'd failed to understand whatever she was trying to say. Unsettled by Dee's reaction, he'd called in at his local before hitting the sack, and Mags had been uncharacteristically quiet behind the bar. Even her husband had picked up on it. He'd caught them having quiet words in between serving the busy Saturday night crowd, seen her husband's face crease with worry whenever he looked her way. Teàrlach knew she was dying, and same as in his dream could do nothing about it. The only colour in her cheeks had been hastily applied with a brush, red blotches doing little but emphasise how white her skin had become, how thin and stretched over the bones of her skull. When it was time to leave, her goodbye sounded terminal to his ears.

When he reached home, the answering machine had blinked a welcome. A message from the care home asking him to visit his father again, claiming he was 'near the end'. Teàrlach had been in no fit state to drive even if he'd wanted to. He didn't. The only possible reason for going would have been to cheer the bastard over the finishing line, with a side-helping of sorrow that his end had been made more painless than it should. No wonder he'd had that same dream last night.

Teàrlach finished skimming the news in case any further details had been added. Nothing apart from an anodyne statement to the effect that trains were now running normally. He needed to know if this was Emily's body callously dropped onto the high voltage lines –or was it Jade's? Two mothers were waiting on him to reassure them that this wasn't their child, charred and burned beyond recognition. Two mothers waiting to see their daughters again, fearful that would never happen.

He felt powerless, unable to do anything other than mouth platitudes to mothers desperate for him to find their missing children. All they had to go on was Chloe's pentagram, a possible connection to a taxi driver and a breakaway Freemason sect run by a bankrupt millionaire.

He smashed his hand down on the table in frustration. At least four deaths could now be attributed to the so-called Pagan killer and neither he nor the police were any closer to finding the culprit. Somehow, there was a link to the Warmingtons, whose peculiar double death started a chain of events that he was sure led to Keith Martin's frenzied knife attack.

It was 8:30 a.m., too early for his video call with Logan Martin in Barlinnie Prison. Dee would be able to view the active police investigation, see if either missing woman had been identified as the victim. His hand hovered over the mobile. There was a contact number on his phone, a sarcastic member of Glasgow's serious crime squad who'd interviewed him last winter. Teàrlach pressed the call button.

'DI Johnson. What do you want?'

Teàrlach smiled, despite everything.

'Good morning, detective. I was hoping we might be able to help one another.'

'I sincerely doubt that, Mr Paterson. You do realise it's not even nine on a bleeding Sunday?'

'Aye, I'm aware of the sanctity of the day. Are you investigating these serial killings?'

'Why do you ask?'

'Because I'm looking for two young women who've recently gone missing.'

'You said we could help each other. What do you know?'

'This last event, on the railway. My PA Chloe sent your people a map recently, with a pentagram drawn on it.'

'I've seen it. She's lucky I'm not charging her with wasting police time.' DI Johnson spoke brusquely. 'We're in the middle of a complex investigation, Mr Paterson. I'd advise you to tell your staff to keep their black magic theories to themselves.'

'Look at that map again, Inspector, and tell me where the point marked Fire is.'

The detective's exasperation sounded as an explosion of air. 'Wait. If this is a wind-up, I'll have your arse.'

Teàrlach waited until he heard the detective's footsteps returning.

'Well?' he asked.

'What the fuck is this?'

'We both tried to tell you the bodies have been placed on the points of a pentangle. The drawing came from the journal of William Warmington who lived next door to Keith Martin.'

'Why are you involved with the Warmingtons?' the detective snapped.

'We're working with a solicitor looking for next of kin. It's just a coincidence we had his journal and Chloe made the link to these murders.'

'Coincidence?' The detective shared Teàrlach's view of coincidence – at least they had that one thing in common.

'That's right. If anything else comes to light, I'll be the first to let you know.'

'So, what do you want from me?'

'Who died last night? I need to know if it's one of the women I'm searching for.' Teàrlach waited on a response.

'It wasn't a woman. There was enough of the body left to tell you that.'

'Thanks.' Teàrlach spoke from the heart. He couldn't face telling another mother her daughter was dead – not today. 'There's still a location marked Earth to visit on the map – you may want to look at that area in case someone's been buried.'

'I'll be in touch.' DI Johnson ended the call.

FORTY
PLANTED

Dee stretched out in bed, opening her eyes to another sunny August day, and ran through the conversation she'd had with Teàrlach a couple of nights ago. He'd opened up more about his life than she'd expected – taking her into his confidence in a way that made her feel they had grown closer as the evening progressed. With a personal history like that, he'd actually come out of it fairly well. That made two of them.

Like Teàrlach, she watched the same online news as she drank her morning coffee, made the same connection to Chloe's map, pictured Emily or Jade's body where a burned figure lay entangled in the overhead power lines.

Dee hated herself for investing so much in Teàrlach. He'd made it clear the first time they'd met that he wasn't interested in any sort of relationship apart from their professional one. Was it merely her imagination that read so much into shared moments, catching his eyes on her, that kiss? Why did she even need a relationship? She'd managed perfectly well without any emotional attachment up to now.

This landscape was alien to her. A life spent in care taught self-reliance above everything or anyone else. She'd let down her guard, let an easy friendship turn into something far more dangerous.

'Get a grip,' Dee advised herself. Her computer screens waited on her, an instant refuge from the complications of life. She still had to search through Peter McKinnon's encrypted files and now she had the key to do so. Then the police files may contain something of use since last night's murder. She could call Teàrlach, see what he wanted her to focus on?

That last thought decided her. Every other minute the PI was intruding into her consciousness one way or another. She was behaving like a lovesick teenager and that needed to stop. Chloe's map lay next to her laptop, the pentangle points labelled from Water through to Fire. Her focus took her anti-clockwise around the pentangle, associating each point with a murder victim. The killer had placed the bodies sequentially, following a widdershins course around the symbol. That figured – any student of the occult would know that travelling anti-clockwise, in opposition to the natural course of the sun in the northern hemisphere, following a left-hand or sinister path is the supposed route to another world. Is that what the Pagan was after, access to an otherworld?

If she was right, then they were on the right track investigating the point marked Earth yesterday. Whoever had been buried there had now been underground for at least three days and the serial killer had made his last sacrifice – Fire. That decided her, she had to have a closer look around Seven Lochs Park, large as it was.

The golf course was quiet when Dee parked her bike at the golf club, close to where Chloe's pentagram point coincided with the underlying map. At this time of day only the truly fanatic golfers were out, a few motorized golf carts already halfway around the circuit. She'd attracted a few interested looks from the mostly middle-aged men arriving at the pavilion as she climbed off her bike. Stomachs drew in, chests puffed out until Argyle pattern jumpers protested at the unusual posture. Dee ignored them all, stuffing her helmet into a backpack and striking off towards the pentangle apex.

Her path took her towards where she and Teàrlach had parked yesterday afternoon, following a line of trees bordering the smooth, green sward of the golf course. Dee paid scant attention to the course or the few golfers, apart from keeping a wary eye out for stray balls. Digging a bloody great hole in the middle of the green would have been a difficult enough feat to manage at night unnoticed, and even more difficult for it to remain undetected during the day. Instead, Dee focussed her attention on the scrub bounding the course, searching for any signs of fresh digging. The same doubts that had assailed her yesterday came back. How could a body be transported this far out in an area without vehicular access – unless the Pagan had a key to the road barriers?

Another golfcart whined into view, carrying its burden of geriatrics with golf bags strapped on the back. The occupants exchanged morning greetings, the cart momentarily veering off course as a gloved hand rose in welcome. Dee watched through narrowed eyes as they came to a halt, selecting clubs and adopting a stance in readiness for the next driving shot down the green. They were aware of her standing by the trees, watching, and took more care than usual in lining up their shots.

Dee had no interest in their golfing prowess, she was more interested in how two large golf bags strapped onto the back of the cart and the space available for a passenger in the front seat. Or a dead body. In fact, given the sparsity of people on the course, their average age and visual acuity, a dead body could be taken around the course in full daylight and chances were no one would even realise.

She continued searching the edge of the course with new determination now the logistics of transporting a body had been resolved, at least to her own satisfaction. The thought that a young woman lay under the soil within metres of where Dee stood made her feel physically sick. The likelihood of still being alive after a few days underground was not even worth hoping for. Dee just hoped that Emily or Jade had been dead before being interred and hadn't suffered the nightmare of being drugged and woken to find themselves buried alive. What sort of madman were they dealing with here? Leaving bodies in the Kelvin, suspended from trees and dropped onto railway power lines. What was the symbolism of the ropes and knots? Somehow, this was connected to the Freemasons – it was the only link that made any sense. From the Warmingtons through to Keith Martin and then the bound victims placed on the pentagram, they all shared a common origin. Was Teàrlach talking to Logan Martin now, on video link to Barlinnie Prison?

Dee scuffed the ground angrily with her boot. She focussed her anger where it would be more usefully applied, concentrating instead on the serial killer responsible for these deaths.

The sound of approaching sirens attracted her attention, tearing her focus away from a detailed sweep of the ground ahead to see two police cars park beside her bike. Dee turned back to the job in hand, her heart catching in her throat as she spied freshly dug earth a few metres ahead. She ran towards it, disappointed when it turned out to be nothing more than a newly planted tree, the patch of freshly disturbed soil too small to conceal a body. A white plastic tube protected the young tree from becoming a tasty snack for wild deer. A label had been attached, describing the genus as *Quercus Petrea* and in smaller print the words *Sessile Oak*.

Dee frowned, then took a step closer. It wasn't the unusualness of finding an oak tree planted on the edge of a golf course that had attracted her attention, more the elaborate string knot used to secure the label to the tree. She pulled out her mobile, took a close-up shot and beckoned to the line of police beginning their sweep of the course back at the car park. Whatever the Pagan had planned for the pentagram point marked Earth, Dee hoped that this time it didn't involve a body.

FORTY-ONE
PRE-ARRANGED

It was 11:30 a.m. Teàrlach sat waiting at his computer for the prison to allow him onto a pre-arranged video call with Logan Martin. He wasn't even sure if Logan had accepted his request for a meet, but Barlinnie Prison had sent him a link and now he sat staring at a screen advising him the moderator knew he was there. Contacting Logan was a last-ditch attempt to obtain any sense out of the Martin family. The mother, Lauren, was hiding something he was certain, and now that she was out of her mind with worry for her daughter, he stood even less chance of getting anything of sense from her. Jade had vanished into thin air – he worried she might be a potential victim, but his sixth sense told him she was acting on her own volition. The change of appearance from schoolgirl to skinhead and discovery of a secret bank account were enough to reassure him that she was probably hiding on purpose.

His screen remained obstinately blank. Maybe Logan didn't want to speak to him after all. His aunt, Nicole, had been convinced of Logan's innocence. Convinced enough to have paid a second instalment into the company bank account despite him being banged up with a full confession on record.

Teàrlach tapped his foot impatiently as he waited. If he had to give an opinion on Logan's guilt, then it would come back as innocent. The most unlikely people can be killers – driven by anger, or fear, or love, or just plain evil. Logan didn't fit neatly into any of these categories. He gave the impression of being a gentle soul, even from within the confines of one of Scotland's toughest prisons.

If Logan didn't kill his father – and the blood-spattered knife in his hand gave lie to that hypothesis – then who did? There were only two other people in the house at the time of Keith Martin's death, as far as the official record went. Jade Martin and her mother, Lauren. Lauren's alibi was based on her arriving after her husband had already been stabbed to death; Jade's alibi was less secure with her allegedly listening to music in her bedroom and missing it all, a version of events that must have stretched credulity at the time. What if there was another person involved? One who never appeared in the official record? Teàrlach had a strong suspicion Jade knew more than she had claimed.

Logan's face appearing on the screen put paid to any further conjecture.

'What do you want?' Logan managed to avoid making eye contact, preferring instead to look at a point over Teàrlach's left shoulder. There was bruising evident on his cheek. Logan's right eye was angled away from the camera, but Teàrlach couldn't fail to notice the bruising and the eye half-closed.

'Has someone been hurting you?'

Logan shook his head. 'I'm fine. Just an accident.'

Teàrlach didn't press him. The biggest error Logan could make in prison was to grass on any other inmate – or guard. At least he knew enough to avoid putting himself in the crosshairs for further beatings.

'OK. I just wanted to let you know Jade's disappeared and

your mum is out of her head with worry. Wondered if you might have any idea where she is?'

Now he had his attention. Logan faced the camera straight on, any attempt to conceal his beating forgotten.

'When did this happen?'

'She never returned home on Thursday afternoon. She was last seen working at the church on Crow Road. Nobody's seen her since.'

Teàrlach watched Logan as he processed the information.

'You gave her my warning? Told her to keep away from them and leave Glasgow if she had to?'

'Aye, I told her. Like you asked.'

Logan visibly relaxed.

'Then she's taken herself off somewhere.' He leaned back in his chair, bored eyes focussing back on something out of Teàrlach's view.

'Do you know where that somewhere is? Your mother is sick with worry – especially with these serial killings happening around town.'

'Jade can look after herself.'

Teàrlach decided to attempt a different tack. 'Your mother told me a character called Peter McKinnon was threatening her – is this the same man Jade needed to keep away from? What do you know about him?'

Logan looked directly at the camera.

'No comment.'

Now he had Teàrlach's interest. Logan could have said almost anything in response to that question, but to use the standard response for any suspect under caution told him Peter McKinnon was very much on Logan's radar.

'I don't think you killed your dad,' Teàrlach spoke quietly. 'You're covering for someone, aren't you?'

Logan's eyes widened and he stood, taking himself out of camera.

'I've nothing else to say. Finish the call.'

The connection closed, leaving Teàrlach staring at his own reflection in the screen. That last comment had hit the mark. Logan had almost run from the video call, so desperate was he to avoid any further questioning along those lines. What was it about Peter McKinnon that struck so much fear into the Martins? Even Logan could put up a good fight against the podgy middle-aged golfer. It couldn't be the man's wealth – by Dee's reckoning he was mortgaged up to the hilt and facing bankruptcy. That at least explained why he was leaning heavily on Lauren to sell her house and pay back whatever her husband owed as a gambling debt.

There were two things that bothered Teàrlach following that brief conversation. The first was Logan's immediate close-down on the mention of Peter McKinnon's name. That would tend to imply that the man had some influence on the inside, or with the screws who'd be listening in to their exchange. Sufficient to have Logan threatened?

The second thing that bothered Teàrlach was Logan's offhand statement that Jade could look after herself. How did he expect his young sister who should by rights still be at school to fend for herself, especially if faced with violence? And why the change from pleading with him on his first visit to find Jade and protect her to now dismissing any concerns regarding her safety?

The only conclusion Teàrlach had come to following his investigation into Keith Martin's murder was that he now accepted Nicole Martin's allegation that her nephew was innocent.

FORTY-TWO
PIPE

Dee called Chloe as soon as she finished speaking to the police. They'd kept her there on the golf course for an hour, waiting for some detective to make an appearance and give her the third degree. He knew about the pentagram, so Chloe must have reached someone in the force who'd listen to her. He also knew Teàrlach, which was just as well, otherwise she'd be awaiting questioning in some Glasgow nick. The guy had been an arse – one of those detectives who use sarcasm to cover their own personal inadequacies. If he was in charge of the Pagan murders, then the police didn't stand a chance of finding him. She'd had to prevent them cutting the label off the tree, explaining the knot used was as much a clue as anything. He'd looked at her like she was an idiot and she'd had to explain the significance of the rope knots used in the previous murders – remembering to omit the Warmingtons from her list.

'Chloe, sorry to call on a Sunday. Can your brother help with another knot, I'm sending the photo now.' A chime sent the snap on its way.

'This another body? I've not seen anything since the railway this morning?'

'No. This time it's a label tied to an oak tree, at the location marked Earth.'

Chloe took a moment to process the information. 'So, the Pagan's gone from being a serial killer to a guerrilla gardener? That's quite the radical change of career.'

Dee laughed, despite the seriousness of the call. 'Aye, right enough. If it *is* him.'

'I'll send the photo off to Leo, see what he has to say. You with Teàrlach?'

She detected more than a casual interest in Chloe's voice and responded in an offhand manner.

'No. He had that video call with Logan this morning. I've not seen him. I was just having a look around the Seven Lochs just in case one of the girls' bodies was here. Didn't feel like I could just sit around and do nothing.'

'No. I know. I've been going through my copy of the journals again, seeing if anything gives a clue as to what the Pagan is trying to accomplish. Trouble is most of it is weird, drugged up stuff. Willie keeps mentioning the moon, describes how Glasgow means Moon Deity and mentions some ancient lunar temple built on the site of St Mungo's miracle – whatever that means. That page is so heavily marked with comments I can scarcely read what's underneath.'

'You think he was out of his head, suffering from carbon monoxide poisoning or whatever?' Dee held her mobile squashed against her shoulder as she pulled on leather gloves.

'Don't know when these journals were written, they look as if he's had them a while. Whatever the truth of it, the Pagan must have had access to some of this material himself, otherwise he wouldn't be following the same pentagram placement. Could be they both discussed this stuff, especially if they were both Freemasons.'

'Aye. This Freemason connection is key to the whole thing. I'm sure of it. I'll wait to hear from you, or your brother. Going to give Teàrlach an update in case it helps us find Jade or Emily.'

Dee pulled on her helmet, spraying gravel as she accelerated out of the golf course car park. She needed to see Teàrlach, if only to understand how he felt about them both. Maybe that kiss had been nothing more than a drunken impulse, God knows she had plenty of experience in that. Her entire adult life had followed the trajectory of that spinning bottle. So much so she had seriously considered joining alcoholics anonymous except to do so would be admitting she had a problem, that she couldn't cope. Dee had looked after herself for as long as she could remember – the orphanages with predatory staff, the schools where the stigma of being an orphan attracted hate instead of compassion. Was this why Teàrlach's kiss had such an impact, or was she reading far too much into one transitory moment?

The Glasgow streets were quieter at lunchtime on a Sunday, giving her the space to open up the throttle and play dodgems with the speed cameras. Going at speed also pushed disturbing thoughts to the back of her mind, made her concentrate on the present, on being alive and staying that way.

Teàrlach's flat was a first-floor apartment close to Glasgow University. She'd not seen it before, except on street view when first researching his background. He lived in a leafy suburb, three-storey red-brick Edwardian tenement facing a shared strip of parkland. Dee parked her bike, tucked her gloves into her helmet and stood at the shared entrance feeling uncharacteristically nervous. The nerves turned as quickly to anger, berating herself for getting into such a state over one shared drunken kiss. She rang his doorbell and waited.

Teàrlach opened the door himself, rather than relying on the intercom. The look of surprise was real.

'Dee! Wasn't expecting you. Do you want to come in?'

She nodded, quietly pleased to see the confusion written on his face.

'A coffee would be good,' she quipped as she stepped past him into a shared entrance hall. The close had been recently cleaned, and the floor tiles almost sparkled in the sunshine let in by the door. A rack of three wooden post boxes were fixed to the wall – they looked as if they'd been there since the place had been built back in the early 1900s.

'Come on up.' Teàrlach led the way up a sweeping staircase to the first floor. A door stood open, sounds of mellow jazz coming from inside.

'Take a seat, I'll be with you in a second.' He pulled shut a door leading to a bedroom, unmade bed suddenly lost from view.

She settled into a settee facing the windows, branches from the park trees stretching towards her. Teàrlach was busy in a kitchen, plates being collected and dumped in a dishwasher, kettle filled and switched on. Dee looked around her, noting the sparse furniture and belongings so like her own living space. A bookshelf dominated one wall, old leather-bound books taking the top shelf, more recent paperbacks occupying the lower shelves. She spotted the book he'd been given by the Glasgow gangster, Tony Masterton, minutes before he'd been killed – *The Wasteland* by T.S. Eliot. Two men, both so different and yet they shared the same love of poetry. A shiver ran down her spine as she thought of the loch he'd fallen into, the dark water lapping at the foundations of his house.

'You cold?'

Teàrlach's voice made her jump.

'No.' She reached for the mug of coffee, smiled a thanks and received a tight smile in return. He cast around for somewhere to sit and she realised she'd taken his seat. There was plenty of room to share the settee, but he made for an armchair by the window, moving a book before settling down.

'Did you manage to talk to Logan?' Dee took refuge in work to defuse the awkwardness of their encounter.

'Aye. He's not giving anything away – except he doesn't appear too concerned about his sister going missing. Says she's taken herself off after I'd passed on his warning and that she can look after herself.'

Dee raised an eyebrow in response.

'She's only just turned sixteen!'

Teàrlach shrugged, took an appreciative sip from his mug as if her comment didn't require an answer.

Dee pressed for more information. 'What about his dad's murder – is he still taking the rap?'

'Aye. He's also wary of Peter McKinnon. I told him he was pressurising his mum for money, and he basically clammed up. Then I told him I didn't believe he killed his dad, and he closed down the call.'

'Do you think he's innocent?' Dee asked.

'I'm almost convinced of it, despite all the evidence to the contrary. He doesn't strike me as being a killer, I'm with his aunt on that.'

Dee sipped her coffee, staring at his profile as he turned to look out of the window. What was going on underneath that mop of unruly hair? There was a photograph on the wall beside his chair, a woman and a young teenager stood on a beach and self-consciously smiling at the camera.

'Is that you?'

Teàrlach turned at the sound of her voice, followed her pointing finger to the photograph.

'Aye, that's me and my aunt. Taken on Calgary Bay. I'd have been twelve or thereabouts.'

'Thought Calgary was in Canada.'

He studied her thoughtfully.

'It is. This is the name of a bay on Mull. There's an old pink stone jetty further out, you can just about see it in the photo.'

Teàrlach stared at his younger self in contemplation. 'That's the last thing they touched before being shipped out to Canada.'

'Clearances?' Dee made the connection.

'Aye. They took what they could with them – few belongings, the language and culture. And the placenames.'

He let out a long-drawn breath.

'What did you want to see me about?'

Dee lied with practised ease.

'I found Earth – or what's buried there at any rate.' She selected the photo on her phone, stretched an arm out for him to take it in his hand. 'Someone has planted an oak tree at the final pentagram point, tied the label with a fancy knot. I've asked Chloe to get her brother to ID it.'

'No body?'

'Doesn't look like it. Just a freshly dug area with a tree wrapped in one of those plastic pipes.'

She saw Teàrlach's eyes squinting in concentration and bit back the comment about him needing glasses.

'Where is this, exactly?'

FORTY-THREE
PACT

Dee's phone rang and Teàrlach passed it back to her, a frown etched on his forehead.

'Hi, Chloe.'

'Hey. Leo's identified the knot for you. He said it's a Dara knot.'

'Any significance to it? Anything to do with the pentagram?'

'He said it's the strongest knot and associated with strength and oak trees. According to what I found online, the ancient celts associated the Dara knot with wisdom, leadership and destiny. It's also known as the dark knot, but he's no idea why.'

'What are we meant to make of that?' Dee asked.

'I'm no detective, but it looks like you've found the last pentagram point.'

'Yeah, thanks, Chloe – and thank Leo for me.'

Teàrlach had listened in to the conversation, his frown showing no sign of leaving.

'It's just a tree he's planted?' Chloe queried.

'Looked like it to me. The police turned up at the same time I did, so I didn't have much of a chance to investigate.'

'Thank God for that! See you tomorrow.'

Teàrlach waited until Dee's call with Chloe had finished before speaking.

'Can you access the police report – see what they say?'

'I'll need my laptop, it's in the top box. Won't be a minute.'

She returned, the laptop already open in one arm and fingers tapping an urgent rhythm on the keyboard.

'Do you need my wi-fi password?' Teàrlach offered.

She shot him a disparaging glance from over the top of her screen. 'I don't think that would be a bright idea. I use a wireless dongle, with a few precautions so I can't be traced. Hang on...' Dee's lips pursed in concentration. 'OK. I don't think we're going to find much; they've only been there a couple of hours.'

Teàrlach watched her as she bent over the keyboard in concentration, eyes sweeping across the screen. He hoped to hell that this was only a newly planted tree – not the fresh grave of the killer's latest victim.

'Nothing in the report, but they've called in forensics.'

The worry gnawing in the pit of his stomach intensified. 'OK. They'd do that in case there's any evidence left at the scene – hair samples, fibres, fingerprints. Doesn't necessarily mean they've found a body.' Teàrlach's reasoned explanation did nothing to allay his fears.

'What do *you* think's going on? With the pentagram and the quasi-religious pagan stuff? And why randomly kill people to leave them at each point?' Dee's question hung in the air.

Teàrlach held her eyes and his frown melted.

'We follow the facts. There's no doubt now that Willie Warmington's journal is the basis for these murders. The pentagram, the location of each body, even the knots used to bind each victim. Then the Warmingtons themselves – whoever killed them used exactly the same methodology as these other victims.'

'What about Keith Martin? Where's he fit into all this?'

Teàrlach paused, took another sip of coffee. 'He's connected to the Warmingtons through the Freemasons. I don't think the serial killer was his murderer, there's nothing ritualistic about his death, but I'm fairly sure they've locked the wrong person up in Barlinnie.'

'Then there's the use of drugs. They found traces on Bryony Knight's body.'

'Aye. And the video of Emily Katz you found getting into a taxi – she could hardly walk.'

'So, where do we go from here?' Dee closed her laptop in frustration.

'We only have two lines of enquiry that hold out any hope of working out who's behind this. There's the Martin family and whatever their connection is in all this, and there's the Freemasons. Specifically, the breakaway sect or whatever you want to call it that Peter McKinnon has set up.' He stood up, took his mug through to the small kitchen space off the living room.

'Did you get anywhere with McKinnon's files?' Teàrlach called through the open doorway, above the splash of water hitting a sink.

Dee stood up as well, handing him her mug as he came back into the room. Teàrlach quickly washed it, placing it next to his on the draining board. She had regained her composure when he faced her once more.

'I've downloaded the encryption key so I can read them. Had a brief look but nothing stood out. He mentions some project that's nearing completion.'

'Does it say what the project is?' Teàrlach pressed for more information.

'Not that I saw. There's certainly nothing about sacrificing young bodies on a pentagram.'

'We need to have a closer look at this Peter McKinnon – and the rest of his coven.'

'Lodge,' Dee corrected.

'Aye, whatever.'

Dee's phone rang again, Chloe's face on the screen.

'Have you seen the news?' Chloe's words sounded breathless on the speakerphone.

Teàrlach's gut tightened with anxiety. 'What have you heard?'

'They've found a coffin, underneath the tree. TV presenter caught the shout on the live microphone before they set up a perimeter and were able to push the news crews back.'

It was the news he'd been expecting, and with it went the one small hope he'd clung onto.

FORTY-FOUR
PICK

Teàrlach and Dee drove in silence to the Crow Road, parking in a side street close to the lodge. The streets were quiet this time on a Sunday, devoid of traffic wardens and the usual press of pedestrians. The late August sun still held heat, warming the pavements and tarmac, so the slight breeze brought welcome relief. The church appeared deserted, solid door locked.

'What next?' Dee asked. 'I couldn't see any other way in.'

She watched as Teàrlach dug around in his jacket pocket, pulling out a leather wallet. He opened it in front of her, but instead of bank cards and crisp banknotes, it revealed a selection of slim metal tools.

'Picks,' he explained before crouching down in front of the antique lock. 'Stand behind me so I'm not so obvious from the road.'

Dee positioned herself between Teàrlach and the path leading to the main road, switching her attention between passing traffic and his fingers working the picks inside the lock. A solid click announced success and he stood, opening the church door so they could enter, then closing it behind them.

They stood in the same entrance foyer Teàrlach recognised from his first visit, the same cobwebs, the same business cards and flyers advertising services. They listened intently for sounds of movement beyond the dividing door, then Teàrlach pushed it open.

Dee looked around her. The stained-glass windows were encrusted with decades of city grime, turning the vast interior into a mottled palette of blues and reds as sunbeams made reluctant progress through thick glass. Her first impression was of being underwater, until the smell of ancient dust confirmed they were inside what was once a church. The building still retained a grasp on its heritage – angels held court in the windows, saints' halos catching the afternoon sun. Then her gaze was drawn to the altar, or the stage that now held that focus. Flags draped listlessly from wooden poles, depicting geometric symbols she recognised from Warmington's journals and reminding her of crass displays from fascist rallies or government announcements. In the centre of the stage a pentagram took pride of place – an exact copy of the one she'd seen on Jade's bedroom wall.

'Was that here when you looked around earlier?' She kept her voice low, although she was fairly certain they were alone.

Teàrlach was staring at the same thing and something in his expression told her this was new to him.

'No,' he confirmed. He moved towards the stage for a closer inspection. 'I only saw the flags and paintings by the entrance last time I was here. This is recent.' He reached towards the pentagram. 'I'd say the paint is fresh, maybe a few days old.'

His fingers came away from the point marked Fire. He held them up for Dee to see the red staining his fingertips.'

'If this is paint,' he added. 'Have a look around, I don't know how long we have. I'll look in the vestry, that's the only place I saw last time I was here.'

He took himself through a narrow archway, leaving Dee alone. She took another look at the pentagram, grabbed a photo with her phone, then began searching the church. The rest of the interior didn't look as if it had been touched. Serried rows of severe wooden benches faced what was once the altar, now devoid of hymnals and prayerbooks. Only the front two rows showed evidence of recent occupation, all the latter rows retained a cover of dust, thick enough to write in. Substantial stone walls kept the interior feeling cold, despite the August sun outside. Traffic noise only intruded when large lorries or buses passed by, their bass notes felt as vibrations from the floor rather than heard. There were no doors, no passages leading off apart from the one Teàrlach had entered. She followed after him once she'd confirmed there was nothing of interest in the nave.

Teàrlach had been busy with his picks. They lay on a flagstone by his feet, the previously locked door to a small cupboard now wide open with shelves of cleaning equipment on display.

'Found anything?' She peered over his shoulder, saw nothing of interest.

'Seems to be just a cupboard,' Teàrlach responded doubtfully. 'The guy who was here opened it up for me, said it's where Jade accessed the cleaning stuff. It just seems off – keeping a cupboard like this locked.'

She left him rummaging around in the bottles and tins and inspected the small room they stood in. This must have been where the priest prepared before a service, there was a toilet off through an open door, small, tarnished mirror on the wall, ancient PA system occupying a few shelves. A cabinet under the shelves attracted her interest. She tried it only to find it was locked.

'Could do with your safecracking skills here, Teàrlach.'

He reluctantly emerged from the cupboard with a puzzled expression.

'I don't get it. Locking a cleaning cupboard.' He turned his attention to the cabinet. 'Let's have a look at this.'

Teàrlach made short work of the lock, opening the cupboard and revealing the same old leatherbound book that he had seen before hidden from view under a cloth. He placed it on the table and Dee searched around for a light switch, a bare bulb lit up.

'What is it, a bible?' Dee stared at what was obviously an antique. Metal clasps held it shut, the leather so worn with age and handling that no lettering had survived on the cover. When Teàrlach released the clasps and opened it, they were faced with the inspiration for Willie Warmington's arcane drawings.

Teàrlach was immediately put in mind of the Book of Kells, that illuminated Celtic manuscript from the first century depicting biblical scenes in stunning visual detail. But it was clear this was no bible. The Celtic symbolism was similar, with knots and symbols adding ornamental designs to the text and drawings, but the content owed nothing to the Christian religion.

The title page was in Latin and meant nothing to either of them, but the drawing underneath depicted the phases of the moon arranged in a circle. Full moon at the top, then moving anti-clockwise through waning to new moon, then back through waxing to full. A pentagram was held confined within the circle, but it was the centre of the page that held their attention.

Depicted in gold leaf, exquisitely rendered, was a unicorn. One hoof was raised as in a greeting, its head thrown back and central horn spiralling up to point at the full moon. It stood in a pool of ruby red blood, spilt from a golden chalice lying on the ground under its hooves.

'Those look like the knots that were used on the bodies.' Dee pointed to the Celtic ornamentation forming a frame around the page.

Teàrlach nodded in agreement. 'And whatever's behind these murders, this book is part of it.'

'I'll take a shot of each page,' Dee volunteered.

'Aye. There's too much going on here to make head or tail of it in the next few minutes. I'll carry on exploring – there must be access to the belltower or crypt or something. This can't be all there is in a building this size.'

FORTY-FIVE
PRECURSOR

Whilst Teàrlach rummaged around in the cleaner's cupboard, Dee laboriously photographed each page of the manuscript. The pages were thick vellum, every spare surface covered with ornate writing and illustrations, the margins full of Celtic knots and ornamentation. She could see a few parallels to the bible – one scene depicted the Garden of Eden with a snake's body wrapped around a tree, yet the two figures depicting Adam and Eve laid proprietary hands on the snake's head as if they were fondling some exotic pet. Many pages concerned themselves with a study of the stars and phases of the moon, position of the planets and seasons. There must have been ten pages, and she worked quickly to finish photographing them all. The last page showed a river flowing through a forest, passing a settlement on its way to the sea. Dee studied the picture, wondering what she found familiar about the map.

'Hey, Teàrlach. Come and look at this – does this look like the Clyde to you?'

There was a muffled thump and curse as Teàrlach quickly straightened up from crouching in the cupboard, followed by the sound of tins falling off a shelf onto the stone floor.

'Shit! Just hit my head on a shelf.'

He rubbed the top of his head, shooting her an accusative stare for causing the accident and began replacing the tins.

'Hang on. What's this?'

Dee could see him stretching towards the back of the cupboard and reaching for something. Whatever it was, there was a click and Teàrlach managed the unusual trick of fitting himself into a cupboard that didn't have space for him. He backed out, giving Dee a broad smile as he did so.

'I knew there was more to it.' He beckoned her over, and she craned to peer around his shoulder.

The back of the cupboard had swung inwards on hinges, the pots and tins still residing on the shelves, but now they were suspended above a spiral stone staircase that led down into darkness.

'Think I've found something,' Teàrlach said.

'What's down there?' Dee asked.

'Let's find out, shall we?'

Dee shut the leatherbound book, snapped the catches closed and replaced it where Teàrlach had found it, shutting the cupboard for good measure.

'Lead on, Macduff,' Dee encouraged.

'You know the line is "Lay on, Macduff", don't you?' He appeared genuinely upset at her misquote.

'Happy to lay on him if he's fit enough,' she quipped.

Teàrlach's expression was indecipherable as he pulled a flashlight from a pocket and shone the beam down into the darkness.

'Come on, then. Don't want to spend too long in here. Breaking and entering is still a crime as far as I know.'

They followed a single turn of the stairs and reached a stone floor. The flashlight revealed a space the size of the nave above.

'Must be the crypt,' Teàrlach spoke hesitantly. He spotted a light switch on the wall, clicked it and fluorescent lights creaked into action.

A line of new tables occupied the centre of the space, laboratory glassware arranged in a business-like manner. Small packets of chemicals occupied shelving against one of the stone walls and a corrugated silver pipe wound its way from a fume cabinet towards an outside wall. Dee was reminded of the snake illustration from the manuscript. A white suit complete with face mask and air supply hung on a hook. She immediately thought of Porton Down.

'This doesn't look much like Freemasonry.' Dee's voice echoed inside the cavernous space.

'No, this reminds me more of a drug manufacturing place I once saw in India,' Teàrlach spoke thoughtfully. He took out his phone, took close-ups of the packets of chemicals. Chinese characters offered a clue as to the origin, labels identified the contents in English.

'4-AP, Norfentanyl.' He started reading the labels out loud.

'They're not making fentanyl, are they?' Dee asked.

Teàrlach rapidly backed away from the shelves.

'Think we ought to leave. God knows what's in the air down here.'

He covered his face with a handkerchief, making his way swiftly to the stone stairs. Dee was already climbing back up, holding her breath until she exited back into the vestry.

'Fuck's sake, Teàrlach,' she gasped. 'We can't let them set up a fentanyl factory in the middle of Glasgow!'

He carefully closed the concealed door behind him and locked it with his picks.

'We're going to leave here as quietly as we came. Is the book back where we found it?'

'Aye. Just need to lock the cupboard.'

Teàrlach made swift work of the lock.

'Let's go. Freemasons are one thing; drug manufacturing is something else. I don't want to be here when they return.'

They left the church as they found it, Teàrlach locking the old church door behind him.

'I'll have to give the drugs squad an anonymous tip-off – can't let on we've been inside the place. You feeling OK?' He directed the question at Dee as they hurried back to the car.

'Aye, I'm fine.' She gave him an encouraging smile, saw his look of relief. 'Why do you ask?'

'You're just being quiet – for you. Thought you might have inhaled some of that stuff in the crypt.'

'No. Soon as I saw there were bags of chemicals there, I held my breath. Used to do it for fun when I was younger. I can hold my breath for almost three minutes – same as a Navy Seal.'

Teàrlach shook his head in response.

'No. The reason I was quiet is because I took this out of the entrance foyer.' She held a postcard up for him.

'Local taxi service.' He dutifully read.

'Aye, now the address,' Dee prompted.

Teàrlach squinted to read the smaller writing underneath a mobile phone number.

'*Fifteen Seaview Drive.*' The import clearly struck him as he said the words, going by his expression. It was two doors down from the Martins.

FORTY-SIX
PHOTOGRAPHS

'When are you going to find yourself a nice young man?'

Chloe exchanged a swift side-eye with Leo, but not subtle enough for her mother not to have noticed.

'And that job of yours, playing at detectives with that unsavoury T-shirt character.'

'Teàrlach, Mum, his name's Teàrlach.'

'Shylock then. You're not getting any younger. I'd had the both of you by the time I was your age.'

'I'm not even sure I want a kid.'

Silence fell over the dining table as Chloe's words proved indigestible to her parents, necessitating some serious chewing before they could be swallowed.

'You'll feel differently when you're older,' her mother announced into the silence. 'Life's too important to be wasted.'

Chloe didn't have a ready answer, so cleared her plate instead.

'How's the job going, Leo?' Her father attempted a conciliatory approach, dialling down the rising tension.

'Yeah, fine, Dad. Beats fishing at any rate.'

Chloe stood, carried her plate over to the sink.

'Leave that, Chloe. I'll do the washing. You can make us all a cuppa if you want to be useful.' Her mother frowned and Chloe instinctively pulled her scarf higher up.

'Everyone want tea?' She spoke lightly, worried that her neck scar had been spotted. Her mother had spent her life being useful. Chloe had squandered her youth on drugs and would have died if it wasn't for Teàrlach. Being useful was all she had to give him.

Chloe took an Uber home at six o'clock, kissing both parents and being hugged so hard by her brother she feared for her ribs. The afternoon had passed without incident, but she couldn't shake off the impression that she was a disappointment to both parents. They wanted nothing more than for her to return to the church, meet a nice, Christian boy and produce nice, Christian babies. Her brother viewed her with confusion, observant enough to realise his young sister had changed in the time since he'd been away from home, unknowing of how close she'd come to ending it all. Some skeletons are best left undisturbed.

Chloe had focussed on her mobile on the journey back to her flat, making it obvious to the driver by her monosyllabic responses that she wasn't in the mood for a chat. The online news reported a body being recovered from the grave, and the small hope Chloe nurtured of this one victim being found alive faded. Putting the phone back in her jacket pocket, Chloe watched the city streets slide past. The taxi dropped her outside her flat, impatient for her to leave so he could catch the next fare. Chloe's phone pinged as she climbed the common close stairway and entered within her home router range. It was a message from Dee.

> Hey, Chloe, found this old book at the Freemason lodge. Took pictures in case you can make anything out. Looks like it's where Warmington's journals found their inspiration. Off with Teàrlach to track down a taxi driver. See you Monday.

The photos had been uploaded to the cloud. She entered her flat, kicked off her shoes and grabbed her laptop before collapsing into her favourite chair. Her interest quickened as the first picture revealed itself. There was the same pentagram symbol that had first caught her eye except now there was a direct correlation to the moon. She struggled to link the sacrificial deaths to the moon's phases, but it made no sense. Each body had been discovered over a period of a few days – too short a time for any correlation to the lunar cycle. Yet there had to be a connection, this first drawing alone was evidence enough that the moon played an important role in the rituals. Her eye kept being drawn to the golden unicorn at the centre of the pentagram, a chalice spilling wine or blood underneath its raised hoof.

If the murders weren't being arranged according to the lunar cycles, then why were they being positioned at the points of the pentangle? Was the geometry more important than the timings? Chloe scanned the other pages in bewilderment – there was too much information here to make any intuitive guess. Even the margins were full of Celtic designs, including representations of the knots Leo had named for them. She stared out of her windows, catching other lives being lived through glimpses into other flats. Down at ground level, the streets were still busy with traffic, the pavements thronged with people making full use of the weekend before Monday spoilt it all. Above her head, clouds parted to reveal blue sky, then the moon appeared as a faded, yellow button hanging in space.

Chloe stared up, surprised how visible the moon was in

daytime. She quickly went back to her laptop, entered a search for the moon's phases. Tonight was a full moon – named the cold moon, the long night moon or the oak moon. That couldn't be a coincidence. The oak tree planted on the final corpse. The Dara knot associated with oak trees. But what did it all mean?

She looked again at the unicorn taking central place in the pentagram. Suddenly struck with a thought, Chloe grabbed her Glasgow map with the pentagram overlay. There, in the centre of the pentagram! She'd been so focussed on the pentagram points that she'd not even considered where they all radiated out from. The exact centre lay on top of Glasgow's Necropolis. Whatever the reason for these murders, whoever was behind them, everything literally pointed to the Necropolis and to tonight.

FORTY-SEVEN
PARENTS

Whilst Chloe was experiencing an uncomfortable tea with her family, Teàrlach and Dee parked close to the unassuming terraced house where Keith Martin had breathed his last breath.

'How do you want to play this?' Dee asked.

Teàrlach dragged his eyes away from the drunken For Sale sign still hanging on outside number seventeen.

'If we have the right guy, we don't want to scare him off,' Teàrlach replied. 'I wonder how easy it is for someone to move through the back gardens?'

'Did you not have a good look when you explored the house?'

Teàrlach shook his head. 'I was more interested in searching the inside, looking at the pentagram on Jade's floor – didn't really look at the garden. Although I had a good view of the neighbours' gardens from Logan's bedroom window so the fences couldn't have been high.'

'You think this taxi driver could have entered the Martins' house and left without anyone noticing?'

'If he's the one we're looking for, then yes. And he could be responsible for sabotaging the Warmingtons' gas flue.

Remember in his journal Willie mentioned someone standing in his garden?'

'Aye. Didn't he say it wasn't human?'

They exchanged a look.

'Takes human fingers to tie those knots.' Teàrlach's expression was grim.

'But we haven't any solid evidence against him,' Dee countered. 'Nothing we can take to the police – except a nascent drug manufacturing facility in the church basement which may not even be connected to all this.'

'You're right. All we have is some grainy footage from a traffic camera showing Emily Katz staggering along the road and a taxi picking her up.' He smacked his hand on the steering wheel in frustration. 'If that's Emily's body they've found...'

Dee had no comfort to offer. Outside the car windows, life continued as usual on Seaview Drive, the terraced houses thrown into shadow by the high-rises opposite. An ice-cream van chimed in the distance, maybe the same one that had provided rubbernecking residents with refreshments as Keith Martin's body was carried away in an ambulance, his son dispatched in a squad car. Whatever had set these events into motion, they were parked in the eye of the storm.

'There's no taxi outside number fifteen,' Dee stated the obvious. 'I could call the number on the card; say I'm wanting a lift?'

'Too dangerous.'

'Not if you're following. I could talk to him. Sound him out?'

'And what if it is the Pagan or whatever his name really is? I only have to lose him in the traffic, and you'd be on your own,' Teàrlach reacted angrily. 'I can't risk it.'

'It's me taking the risk,' Dee corrected quietly.

'Aye, and I don't want anything happening to you.'

Dee pulled out her phone, swiped the screen and tapped.

'There, you can track me – on Find My.' Dee selected an icon, opening a map with them both placed in Seaview Drive. 'It's not the most accurate, but you can see where I am within three metres. With a good signal,' she added.

Teàrlach studied the two overlapping circles with their faces superimposed on top. He turned towards her, forehead creased with concern.

'No. It's too much of a risk. What if he drugged you like he did the others? You wouldn't stand a chance.'

'Look. He's already managed a full house on the pentagram. Chances are he's finished his killing spree and will just go back to driving taxis and will never be caught. Besides, I want to catch this bastard as much as you do. We can't just sit here and do nothing.'

Teàrlach started the car, accelerated away from the kerb so fast the wheels spun on loose gravel.

'The answer's still no!' he said emphatically. 'I'm not putting anyone at risk. We'll catch him some other way.'

Dee saw he wasn't going to change his mind. 'So, what do we do?'

'We go back to my place so you can collect your bike, and then I'm going to see if that's Emily's body they dug up this morning. Either way, I have to see her parents.'

They drove for a while in silence, each preoccupied with their own thoughts.

'We can at least let the police know about the lab in the church basement,' Dee eventually prompted. 'If you're worried about any more people dying, then a fentanyl lab in the centre of Glasgow will be responsible for a lot more deaths than this lunatic.'

'Aye, you're right. Trouble is, we can't let on that we broke into the place. Can you raise an anonymous report, make it so they can't trace where it came from?'

Dee shared a pitying expression with him.

'What do you think?'

'Sorry. Of course you can. You never know, that might be enough to throw a spanner in the works and make the Pagan break cover. It's worth a shot.'

Teàrlach pulled up outside his flat. 'You might as well go home, raise that tip-off about the lab. I'm going to talk to a detective I know from the Major Investigations Team, see what the story is before I visit Emily's family.'

'I'll see you tomorrow.' Dee waited longer than was necessary in case there was anything more.

'See you tomorrow,' Teàrlach echoed. He barely looked her way as she climbed out of the car, distractedly checking his phone before returning it to the dashboard.

She stood at the side of the road, watching until his car had turned the corner. She knew he was preoccupied with the latest find, concerned that he would have to face Emily's family with the worst news a parent can ever hear. In a few more hours, the clubs would be open, and Dee had a plan – one which Teàrlach wouldn't approve of.

FORTY-EIGHT
PARALYTIC

Dee had raised the anonymous tip-off as soon as she'd returned to her apartment. It was safer to send it from there as the IP masking was already in place, although whether the police would raid a Freemason lodge was a moot point. She'd seen the news – they were confirming a body had been found but no further detail. A quick look at the police server revealed it had been a young woman's body – the last entry mentioned requesting formal identification from Emily Katz's parents.

She spared a thought for Teàrlach, knowing he'd find out as soon as the ID had been confirmed, but saved her compassion for Emily's parents. Dee couldn't imagine the pain of seeing your own child laid out on the slab, knowing she'd have spent her last hours trapped underground with no way out but death. Hopefully, her killer had enough empathy to have killed her quickly, not allow her to be buried alive. Somehow, Dee doubted that would be true.

This was all connected to the book she'd found at the lodge; she was certain of it. This wouldn't be the first time an ancient manuscript had been responsible for causing innocent deaths, you just had to look at the bible for the most obvious example.

None of this was getting them any closer to finding who the Pagan really was. Dee was certain it had to be the taxi driver who was last seen picking up Emily, and like Teàrlach, she didn't believe it was a mere coincidence that a taxi service advertised in the lodge. The same lodge with a connection to Seaview Drive and the murders committed there.

She checked the time; it was 8:45 p.m. and the nightclubs would be opening in a few hours. Plenty of time for a shower and makeup. If she was going to attract a serial killer, she'd have to prepare. Dee slammed a ready meal in the microwave, sat down at her computer and wrote a message for Teàrlach. She scheduled it so he'd receive it before 11 p.m., early enough for him to still be up and about but too late to stop her. She copied a bespoke app she'd designed for her phone, added it to a second message in case the evening didn't go to plan, and sent it to her mobile.

The microwave announced her meal was ready. There was one last thing she needed to do just in case she was separated from her phone. The tracker she selected from the drawer under her desk was small enough to conceal in her clothing. Dee mulled over her plan as she forked an unappetising pasta into her mouth, only too aware of its shortcomings. It relied on the Pagan being the taxi driver; on him needing another victim when the five pentagram points were already taken; on him selecting Dee as the next victim. It also relied on Teàrlach managing to rescue her if she needed rescuing. The pepper spray concealed in her clothing was illegal enough to make that requirement unlikely. Satisfied that she'd covered all eventualities, she headed for the bathroom.

Pirates Club was a seedy joint near the General Hospital. Dee had selected it as being in the same general area where the other victims had last been seen – in the Pagan's catchment zone she thought mirthlessly. The club was full enough, techno blasting at a level that thankfully made any of the chat-up lines coming her way unintelligible. Whoever designed the place had over-done the pirate vibe – half an MDF prow jutted out from behind the DJ with a buxom figurehead looming overhead; staff wore striped blue and white T-shirts with red bandanas wrapped around their heads. Fishing nets draped across the ceiling holding coloured glass floats picked out in the flashing lights. Dee gave it an hour, drank enough shots to blend in but not so many that she risked losing her edge. It was eleven o'clock. She called the taxi number from the club foyer, letting the remorseless beats set the scene for her.

'Seaview Taxis.'

'I just want a lift from Pirates Club back to my flat in Hyndland.' Dee took care to slur her words. 'Can you fit me in?'

She'd chosen Teàrlach's address in case she needed him nearby.

There was a considered pause. 'How many of you are there?'

'Only me.'

'I'll have a driver with you in ten. Be outside, they won't hang around for you.'

'Thanks.' Dee felt a hit of adrenaline in her stomach. If the taxi driver was the serial killer, she'd just volunteered to be his next victim. She checked her phone, and found a string of calls from Teàrlach starting minutes ago. At least he cared about her. Deft fingers opened the iPhone settings and a single stab set her concealed tracker live on Teàrlach's mobile so he could follow her movements. A second stab set the custom app Dee had designed into action – as long as she interacted with her mobile within two-minute intervals it remained in a dormant state.

The taxi stopped far enough away from the club to avoid the CCTV cameras outside the entrance. It might have been the same car that had picked up Emily Katz, the video quality from the traffic camera wasn't good enough for a positive ID. Dee walked up to the driver's window, bent down to have a good look. Her first reaction was shock – they'd sent a woman driver. She kept her face averted yet Dee's first observation was how pale her skin was – long blond hair, vivid red lipstick and a face that didn't see much of the sun. When the driver turned to look at her, she focussed on the palest blue eyes she'd ever seen.

'Taxi to Hyndland?' The Glasgow accent explained the lack of a tan.

'Aye. Thanks.' Dee listened to herself critically as she slurred her words. That sounded more Sean Connery than the man himself. She staggered slightly as she opened the back door, sank into the seat and fumbled for the seatbelt.

'That you for the night?' The driver fixed Dee in her rear-view mirror, waiting until she'd finished strapping in.

'Aye. Got to work tomorrow. Think I started too early.' She offered her a smile as the seatbelt finally engaged.

'You're not going to be sick in the back of my car, are you, hen?' Her eyes hadn't left the rear-view mirror.

'I'll be sure to let you know,' Dee countered.

The driver looked as if she was about to add a comment, gave her one last glance in the mirror and started driving.

'You have someone waiting for you – case you need a hand?' A judgemental tone had entered the driver's voice.

'No. I don't need anyone else,' she answered combatively, daring her to disagree. The irony of her comment wasn't wasted on her, keying her phone volume control in her pocket to activate her version of the dead man's switch. She needed Teàrlach as her backup, and it suddenly occurred to her that maybe she should have pre-arranged this with him beforehand. As long as she pressed the volume control every two minutes, then nothing much would happen on the app she'd designed. If she missed pressing it, then Teàrlach and Chloe's phones should go off like a siren and display her location with a help message. Sitting in the back of the taxi, Dee stopped worrying that this wasn't sufficient protection. She had hoped to snare the Pagan, not this frumpy pale woman with weird eyes. She wondered if they were contact lenses.

'Where to in Hyndland, love?'

She gave Teàrlach's address. They were heading in the right direction. The driver now spent more time looking at the road ahead than checking her out in the mirror and Dee began to relax. This was a madcap scheme in the first place, putting herself out as bait for a potential serial killer. What had made her risk it? The answer wasn't forthcoming. She wanted to find out who the Pagan was before anyone else was killed, that was true. She wanted Teàrlach to see her for what she was – not just some hacker that had been foisted on him by his previous client. She wanted him to care about her.

'Fuck's sake,' she whispered to herself. This was a recurring theme in her life – the orphaned girl desperate for love and willing to destroy everything to achieve that impossible goal. This time she'd gone too far and put her own life up as collateral. The volume control received another vicious prod. What if this weirdo was driving her to the Pagan? Was she capable of fighting two people?

She was thinking of Teàrlach again. It was like a sickness in her mind. She watched Glasgow streets slide past, the sky stained with the last vestige of sunset even this late in the day, turning dark velvet before the night. She glimpsed a full moon as they turned at a junction, briefly showing itself between the urban canyon walls until another turn hid it from view again.

The sight made her wonder if she had been affected by the moon. Lunatics, lunacy – they all shared that name for a good reason. Were women more connected to the moon because they, too, followed the same cycle? Would this fixation on Teàrlach wane with the passing of the days? She stabbed the volume button again, taking several attempts before her fingers engaged.

Dee felt more drunk than when she'd left the club. The motion of the taxi was making her feel ill. Her vision began to swim. She opened her mouth to warn the taxi driver that she'd better stop before she was sick only to see her eyes fixed on her again. The taxi stopped and Dee slumped against her seatbelt. She tried to speak but had lost the use of her vocal chords. Outside the taxi window, the moon hung motionless in the sky. It was the last thing Dee saw.

FORTY-NINE
PARTY

Teàrlach met with Detective Johnson from the Major Investigations Team in The Renfield, a pub in the city centre frequented by Glasgow's police community. The detective was sat at a table facing the door like a gunslinger, observing Teàrlach over a pint glass clamped to his lips. Teàrlach felt an immediate sense of relief – he was there on his own. If he had company, then he wouldn't have been free to talk.

'Can I get you one?' Teàrlach called from the bar, ordering a pint for himself.

'Not for me. Make it quick – I've a lot on. What did you want to see me about?'

Teàrlach pulled up a chair to join him at the table. 'I'm working for Emily Katz's parents. Their daughter, Emily, has gone missing.'

Detective Johnson's expression remained neutral, but his eyes left Teàrlach to focus on his half-empty glass. 'It will be on the news soon anyway.' He lifted his pint glass and emptied the remaining contents down his throat, replacing the empty glass on the table without any sign of having enjoyed it.

'What will be on the news?' A prescient hollow filled Teàrlach's chest as hope for finding Emily alive evaporated.

'That's their girl we found today, parents confirmed it a few hours ago.'

The admission still stung even though he was expecting it. 'Are you any closer to finding him?'

'Why do you think I'd share a live investigation with you?' The detective spoke quietly enough not to risk being overheard above the background noise.

'Because we told you where to look.'

The detective glared at him from over the table. 'If you're holding back on me Teàrlach, I'll make your life so bloody miserable you'll wish you'd never been born.' The detective's voice sounded loud and clear in the Glasgow bar.

Heads turned towards their table, a momentary lapse of conversation expanding from the epicentre of the detective's angry outburst. Teàrlach waited until noise levels returned to normal.

'We've given you all we have. Willie Warmington's journal had the map and pentagram; whoever the Pagan is, he's using the same information to place his bodies – any more than that we're as much in the dark as you are. Whatever this is all about, it's connected to the journal.'

The detective gave him the benefit of the doubt. 'The bastard buried her alive. He'd even given her an air supply hidden inside the tree guard – we found a hosepipe going into the coffin so she didn't asphyxiate straight away.'

He raised his head to look directly into Teàrlach's eyes. 'I need to catch him. He's made it personal.'

'You and me both.' Teàrlach left his pint untouched. 'I'm going to see her parents. I told them she'd be alright.'

The detective nodded, his eyes held an understanding of what that felt like. 'Call me if you hear anything. Doesn't matter how unlikely – anything you can give me to help catch this bastard.'

Teàrlach paused. 'We think there's a connection to the Freemason lodge in Crow Road.'

DI Johnson's head jerked up in recognition. It was apparent he'd seen the anonymous report Dee said she was going to send.

'And there's a taxi operating out of number fifteen Seaview Drive, close to the house Keith Martin was murdered in. Worth forensics having a look at it.'

Teàrlach left with the detective's command to come back ringing in his ears.

Niklas Katz opened the door, silently beckoned Teàrlach inside. Emily's mother was curled up in a foetal position on a chair, silently rocking backwards and forwards.

'You said she was going to be all right. You said you were going to find her!' Sandra Katz unwound like a striking snake, shooting venom towards Teàrlach.

'I'm sorry. We found where she was – only we were too late.'

'You'll find who did this to her? You'll kill him for me?' Sandra demanded.

'I'll kill him if you won't.' Niklas repeated the threat he'd issued on their first meeting.

'We're working closely with the police. I'm going to find who did this to your daughter, I can promise you that.'

'I want him dead!' Sandra spoke in a more measured way. 'I don't want him locked up for a few years, then let out on good behaviour. I want him dead so he can never hurt anyone again.'

There was a part of him that agreed, a part of him that wanted the murderer to suffer a slow agonising death. Teàrlach pushed the thought away.

'I'll find who is responsible for Emily's murder, and I'll make sure he can't hurt anyone ever again.'

Sandra's wet eyes interrogated his, suddenly wide with shock.

'Is she dead?' Her voice sounded muffled from her hands.

Teàrlach couldn't understand what she meant. Hadn't they both just returned from identifying the body? 'I'm sorry?'

It was Niklas who made sense of Teàrlach's confusion. 'Emily is still alive. They brought her out alive. She's in a coma.'

Teàrlach suddenly realised the detective had only mentioned finding Emily and having the parents identify her. He'd automatically assumed the girl was dead and had ignored the detective's calls to come back. An overwhelming sense of relief washed over him, tempered with an equally strong sense of embarrassment at making such a basic error.

'I'm sorry. I thought – when I heard. She's not been able to say who it was?' He heard himself floundering.

They both looked at him in confusion.

'She's in a coma,' Niklas repeated more slowly. 'She hasn't had anything to drink for almost three days. We left her in intensive care, but the doctor said she'd pull through.'

'Thank God for that!' Teàrlach's words were heartfelt.

'No. Thank *you* for finding her. Any later...' Niklas faltered.

'I'm sorry.' Teàrlach realised he was repeating himself as he directed the apology towards Emily's mother. 'I didn't mean to worry you any more than you have been. I'm glad you have her back.'

Sandra attempted a weak smile.

'I'll see you out.' Niklas indicated the door. The visit was over.

'You find him, and if you can't kill him, I'll do it.' Niklas stood on his front door, quietly spoken but quivering with his need for vengeance.

'I'll keep in touch,' Teàrlach offered as a parting remark.

The job was difficult enough without having homicidal parents on his heels.

He drove home with the relief still flooding his veins. He'd been convinced Emily had been found dead; first the mention of a coffin and then the detective saying the parents had positively identified the girl. Intensive care and likely to pull through – this was the first positive break he'd had all week. He'd put his foot in it with her parents, though; he'd almost given Sandra Katz a heart attack when he inadvertently spoke of her daughter's murder.

He'd been putting in too many hours, chasing around the city from dawn to dusk. Teàrlach decided to relax when he reached his flat, putting his feet up on the settee and settling down for a quiet night. That was until he received Dee's text.

He was frantically chasing Dee's signal through Glasgow's dark streets when his phone went off like a siren.

> If you're seeing this, the Pagan's got me. Follow the tracker signal and be quick.

FIFTY
PRESSURE

Detective Johnson studied his empty pint following Teàrlach's brief visit. He'd seen the anonymous report stating there was an illegal drug factory hidden in the basement of the Freemason lodge on the Crow Road. It had been received with some hilarity at the station, tempered with unease as the rumour was that the assistant chief constable was known to be a member of that particular lodge. There was no way in hell that any officer was going out on a limb and requesting a search warrant – not for such an obvious wind-up. Now Teàrlach had point blank stated there was a direct link to the Pagan, he had to take it seriously. If Teàrlach was wrong, then he'd likely be waving goodbye to a police career and tidy pension.

It wasn't a difficult decision to make. The search for the Pagan had taken precedence over every other investigation they faced. The publicity alone was making the entire police force look inept and the chief constable had made her frustration clear. 'No matter what it takes,' she'd said.

Detective Johnson made the call, arranging for a search warrant to be raised immediately. He spared a moment's thought for the poor bastard having to disturb a sheriff or Justice of the Peace at this hour for authorisation, then just as quickly turned his attention to the other piece of information Teàrlach had given him.

Teàrlach suggesting they investigate the Martins' near neighbour was the first lead they'd had in finding the Pagan. The PI and his team had been on the money with the pentagram – bizarre though it had sounded at the time, and they knew more than they liked to admit about the ropework connecting all these deaths. Every death except for Keith Martin's.

The PI had suggested a taxi was involved, working from fifteen Seaview Drive. Detective Johnson had already considered a rogue taxi driver as fitting the Pagan's MO. Being able to take victims off the street – sometimes in broad daylight.

He considered the most recent case, that of the young woman Emily Katz. Her partner had given them a statement saying she'd called for a taxi to take her home from the club. A taxi that had never arrived – or so they thought. Each of the Pagan's victims might have conceivably taken a taxi immediately before they went missing. He mentally listed them, the young men and women walking home from work or about their normal activities. Bryony Knight – she'd been shopping in Sauchiehall Street and disappeared in broad daylight. The detective had nothing to lose. If the raid on the Crow Road lodge came back with nothing, then his neck was already on the chopping block – and he'd make sure he took Teàrlach Paterson down with him.

He made a quick call. 'I need an armed response team, dog handler and at least a couple of squad cars ready in the next ten minutes – oh, and you'd better raise another search warrant. This one for fifteen Seaview Drive. Find out who's at that address, I need a name and any previous – and now!'

Two men gathered around the detective's table as he finished requesting backup.

'What's going down?'

The detective pocketed his phone, standing up but still a head shorter than the two men flanking him.

'Think we may have a lead on the Pagan.'

The words rippled around the bar leaving a palpable silence in their wake.

'What do you want us to do?' the second giant asked.

'Meet me at fifteen Seaview Drive, near to where Keith Martin was stabbed a few months back. I've asked for a warrant, so keep low until the armed response team arrive.'

'Is this for real? He's at that address?' The first man's eagerness was infectious.

'It's a tip-off from someone I trust. If he's not there, then I hope to hell we find something that leads us to him, or I'm finished.'

FIFTY-ONE
PAGODA

Teàrlach drove like a man possessed, following the moving dot on the map which he prayed would lead him to Dee. She was close, less than a mile away. Chloe had called him just after the alarm had sounded, in a panic and preparing to drive off in pursuit. He'd told her he was near to Dee's location and she was better staying put and acting as point of contact. It was bad enough having Dee in danger, never mind Chloe risking her life as well.

He cursed, sick at the thought that this was his fault. Dee had suggested putting herself out there as bait, but he'd told her not to. Teàrlach knew Dee only too well to have guessed she'd ignore him and do things her own way, no matter what he said. If only he hadn't been so worried about meeting Emily's parents – facing them in the full knowledge that he'd promised their daughter would be found safe and well and there was nothing for them to worry about. Instead, she'd almost died alone, buried alive and only found at the last minute. Now Dee might face an even worse fate.

The dot had stopped moving and Teàrlach accelerated in the hope that he'd find her before losing contact. The signal abruptly disappeared off his screen, her last position on the A82 heading towards Hyndland. Had she been trying to reach his flat? He risked a closer look at the map only to realise her signal had vanished on the Kelvin Bridge. The image of the woman found in the Kelvin River came to him, Dee's red hair washing over her lifeless face. He was only a few minutes away. If she'd been pushed over the bridge, he still had time to save her.

Teàrlach came to a screeching halt on the bridge, flung open the car door and leaned over the green metal parapet, anxiously scanning for a body in the water. There was nothing to be seen. He ran across the road, looking downstream in case she was caught in the current. His heart hammered in his chest. There was no easy way down and Dee's body could have drifted out of sight by now. He reached for his phone to call the emergency services, remembered he'd left it on the dash and cursed for the lost seconds as he ran back over the road to his car. Teàrlach heard his phone before he made the car, reached inside to grab it. It was Chloe.

'Can't talk now, Chloe. I think Dee's been thrown off the Kelvin Bridge. I need to call the police, ambulance.' He realised he was in a panic, forced himself to take slow breaths.

'Wait!' Chloe shouted. 'Dee's signal has come back on. She said in her text she had a tracker and to use that, not follow her phone. I think I know where he's taking her.'

Teàrlach had been about to cut Chloe off.

'What do you mean? Where?'

'It's been staring us in the face the whole time. The centre of the pentangle. He's taking her to the Necropolis. That's where her tracker is heading for now.'

Teàrlach's heart sank with sudden realisation. 'He still has another sacrifice to make.'

Chloe couldn't bring herself to answer.

His mind raced. The Necropolis was a ten-minute drive

from where he was, and Dee could only be a few minutes ahead of him. He still had time to save her.

'I'm going there now. Call the police, tell them the Pagan has kidnapped Dee and is taking her to the Necropolis.' Teàrlach started the car, swung across the lanes in a U-turn. 'You'd better tell them to call an ambulance as well,' he added grimly.

'I'm on it.'

Teàrlach cut the call, saw a new dot had started moving across the map on his screen.

'Clever girl.' He pushed the car as fast as he dared, thankful the late Sunday traffic was light. 'I'm coming for you, Dee.' His fingers tightened on the steering wheel, knuckles turning white with the pressure. Whoever the Pagan was, he was coming for him too. Teàrlach didn't allow himself to think that Dee might already be dead, that he might already be too late. He joined the M8, pushing the car towards a hundred as he accelerated towards Cathedral Square. Other drivers expressed their anger at his speed by deliberately slowing down in front of him, brake-checking so he was forced into changing lanes. He held his temper in check, the last thing he needed now was to be involved in a collision. The turn-off was just ahead, traffic slowing to a more moderate pace. Teàrlach saw a taxi up front, attempted overtaking a bus and almost hit a guy staggering off the pavement. He wrenched the steering wheel, somehow managed to avoid both the bus and the pedestrian. Dee's signal had come to a halt at the Necropolis. Whoever was in the taxi ahead of him, it wasn't her. The traffic in front stopped at red lights. Teàrlach drummed his fingers on the steering wheel in frustration, wondering whether to ditch the car and run the rest of the way. There was no chance of overtaking, a double-decker bus took up the other lane. After what seemed like an eternity, the lights changed to green and the traffic moved forward at a snail's pace.

Teàrlach saw a taxi parked up on Wishart Street, next to

one of the pedestrian accesses to the Necropolis. Dee's signal faded as he pulled up behind the car, her last known position somewhere up on the dark cemetery hill. The taxi was empty of occupants, woman's clothing left scattered on the passenger seat. Teàrlach speed-dialled Chloe as he started running up into the Necropolis, making for the top of the hill and the dark tombs ahead.

'Have you found her?' Chloe's hopeful voice answered immediately.

'Not yet. I'm at the Necropolis. Her signal's gone.' He spoke in short, urgent sentences. Teàrlach's breath was needed for the run up the winding path, ears attuned for any sound that could lead him to Dee.

'Any idea where he's going?' Teàrlach spoke more quietly now, not wanting to warn the Pagan that he was being followed. The area covered over thirty acres, full of tombs built in the style of Egyptian needles, gothic temples and thousands of tombstones, any one of which could conceal the Pagan or Dee in the darkness.

'The whole place is full of Freemason symbols. From the research I've done, the Necropolis has been laid out according to some secret Freemason plan. The Warmington journals make no mention of it, so I don't know where he's headed. I thought maybe he'd head for a mausoleum – somewhere he could stay out of sight until he...' Chloe's voice faded out.

'He's not going to do anything to her. I promise you,' Teàrlach countered. He spoke with more conviction than he felt. The Necropolis covered a huge area, it was almost midnight, and he may have been alone in the world. Without Dee's tracker signal, finding her was going to be an impossible task. If only he had the book Dee was studying at the lodge – maybe that held a clue. Teàrlach stopped to take a breath. The city lights lay all around him, the spire of Glasgow cathedral piercing the night sky. Clouds parted above, allowing a full moon to cast a silver spotlight over the cemetery. He couldn't see or hear anyone in the vicinity. There was only one way someone could drag Dee all this way from the road against her will and that was with her drugged or unconscious. He knew her, she'd fight every step of the way and scream blue murder – but he only heard owls patrolling, faint rustling as small creatures explored around him.

'Wait! I think I have something.' Chloe's voice sounded metallic and loud in the silence. 'Dee uploaded pictures from the manuscript she found at Crow Road. There was a pentagram with the picture of a gold unicorn at the centre. I think it's something to do with a unicorn!'

Teàrlach waited impatiently for Chloe to give him something useful. Every second he spent waiting on this path, Dee was in greater danger.

'What have you got, Chloe? I need something. They could be anywhere.' His eyes swept around the monuments and carved stones, searching for anything that could lead him to Dee.

'There's only one reference I can find. There's a mausoleum at the top of the Necropolis – a large, circular building. It's the grave of Samuel Forge, he was something to do with the original planning of the whole site in the 1800s. According to this reference in Wikipedia, the mausoleum door hasn't been unlocked for years as the key had been lost and get this – carved unicorns surround the doorway. I'm sending you a picture, should be easy to find even at night.'

Teàrlach muted his phone just in time to avoid the chime announcing his presence to the night. The picture of a stone pagoda filled his screen – the same building that lay illuminated by the full moon at the top of the path in front of him.

'I see it! Are the police on their way?'

Sirens sounded from somewhere far off. It was such a

normal soundtrack to city life they may have had nothing to do with Teàrlach's search.

'I'll chase them up again, and tell them to make for the Forge mausoleum.'

Teàrlach ended the call, started running up to the top of the hill with the stone building now firmly set in his sights. Dee had to be there. If he couldn't find her in the next few minutes, there was no knowing what the Pagan would do to her – might have already done.

FIFTY-TWO
PLANS

Peter McKinnon arrived at Crow Road in time to see the police forcing their way into the lodge building. He'd had a tip-off from Detective John Jenkins and had hoped to arrive before the police – clear the basement shelves of a few incriminating substances and be there to make up a cock and bull story to explain the chemical lab paraphernalia. Something along the lines of preserving the stonework or inserting a damp-proof course.

Instead, he was faced with a fait accompli – unless they didn't discover the entrance to the basement level. That one hope lay in ruins as a forensics officer carried out parcels he recognised. There was no innocent explanation for storing norfentanyl on the premises, not when the equipment required for making batches of fentanyl lay in full view. He didn't have much time before they came for him. The assistant chief constable wouldn't be able to make this disappear, not like his previous indiscretions with speeding tickets and drink-driving. Now the ACC would have some serious questions to answer himself.

The fact that the ACC didn't have a clue what was in the

basement wouldn't be much of a defence – no one would seriously believe any lodge members wouldn't know what was going on underneath their feet. Not that he gave a thought about the membership – that had just worked as a convenient cover. Someone had talked, someone who knew what was going on.

Peter McKinnon sat in his car feeling the rage building inside him. This was his last gamble to regain his fortune, setting up a drugs factory at huge personal expense and risk here in the centre of Glasgow. A ready-made customer base on the doorstep. Starting small, testing the market and the process before attracting the interest of the big guys. He never wanted to sell on the streets, there was too much of a risk of the drugs squad tracing the source that way. No, the plan was to perfect the process and become a supplier to the county lines gangs. Having the raw materials shipped in and distributing the pure drug from the lab – maximum profit, minimum risk. Only now someone had shopped him, and a prison sentence was a formality once they caught up with him.

He watched as the carefully bought raw ingredients were packed into a forensics van by white-garbed technicians, looking more like spacemen with breathing apparatus and full-face masks. His Chinese suppliers didn't know him or this address – everything had been shipped via third parties to a holding unit on the outskirts of town to test how secure and dependable the supply chain was.

There were only a few people who knew about the lab, apart from himself. Keith Martin, who'd built the concealed entrance disguised as a cupboard and then had the audacity to threaten him with the police unless he cancelled his gambling debt. Then Willie Warmington and his pathetic loyalty to the Freemasons. He'd turned up at the church to persuade them not to set up a breakaway lodge at the same time the first delivery of lab equipment arrived. He was a true believer in

Freemasonry, took it more seriously than anyone else he knew. Talked about the broken pillar, going against the instructions of higher-level masons. He didn't understand what the lab was for, accepted Peter's word that it was for treating woodworm in the joists and rafters. The old fool was losing the plot anyway, actually believed all the mumbo-jumbo instead of treating it like a glorified social networking club with strange costumes and even stranger rituals. Trouble was Willie Warmington wasn't that stupid – eventually he was going to work out what was going on – and he had a loose mouth. One that needed closing.

The dead hadn't talked, which left two possibilities. Donald Ritchie had been his friend since school. A brilliant mind, an erratic, if not dangerous personality. He'd studied chemistry at university but had been thrown out for substance abuse – substances he'd created in the university labs. You had to be careful around Don. Peter McKinnon knew that he was a vicious little bastard who derived enjoyment from seeing other creatures suffer. That had become apparent all those years ago when he'd killed his pet cat. They'd been eight years old, and Don had this great idea of tying the cat up so it couldn't fight back. It still managed to land a good few scratches when it realised what they intended – what Don intended. It had been the newest member of their gang, the Welsh boy John Jenkins, who'd grabbed the knife off Don and efficiently finished the animal off, proving himself to be worthy of their friendship. 'Used to live on a farm,' he'd explained in his sing-song accent as he wiped the blade clean on the cat's fur.

No, it wouldn't be Don. He might be psychotic, but he had a healthy sense of self-preservation and stood to gain financially from the project. He'd only be putting himself at risk of imprisonment by letting the police know about the lab. Detective John Jenkins had too much to lose if they connected him to the lab so that left Jade Martin. She would never have been involved but for her father's debt – volunteering to work it off and sell Don's samples in the clubs.

He cursed Don Ritchie under his breath. The Warmingtons had been disposed of without attracting any interest – tampering with the gas boiler flue and making it look like they died of carbon monoxide poisoning had been the plan. It was only later he heard about the bizarre discovery of finding them roped up in bed. They'd been lucky John Jenkins was the senior officer on the scene and had somehow managed to make it look like an accidental death.

Peter started the car, moved away from the kerb and put distance between himself and the lodge. He could put the blame for the drugs manufacturing onto Don, say he personally never had cause to go into the basement. It would be Don's fingerprints and DNA all over the equipment – and he was the only one with the expertise, plus previous which the university could be enticed to share with the police. The police wouldn't buy his own innocent plea, but they wouldn't have enough evidence to prosecute him. It would be his word against that of a man with a history of illicit drug manufacturing.

The only problem he had left was Jade Martin. She knew about the drugs, knew he knew. She was selling them on the street for him, testing both the product and the market whilst working off her father's gambling debt. If she was arrested, then he couldn't guarantee her silence – and she almost certainly suspected that he'd had her dad killed. The issue was that Jade had gone to ground. He needed to find her before the police did, or more accurately, John Jenkins needed to find her and dispose of her. That would kill two birds with one stone. If the police were able to pin Jade's murder on John, then he'd be in the frame for Keith Martin's death as well. The hastily developed plan took firmer shape as Peter considered Jade's brother, doing time for a murder he didn't commit to protect his young sister. If she met an unfortunate end, then her brother had no reason to continue taking the rap for his father's death. It was only the threat of having the rest of the family killed that kept him inside in the first place, and he'd confirm John Jenkins as his father's murderer.

The police would be looking to have him arrested. They might even be at his home now. Peter McKinnon made for Lauren Martin's shabby flat on the Crow Road. She must have an idea where Jade was. He called Don's number from a burner phone as he drove. It rang out to answerphone. He didn't leave a message.

FIFTY-THREE
PURGATORY

Peter McKinnon rang Lauren Martin's flat bell for the seventh time, letting his fat finger rest on the button for a good minute. Still no answer. She was in there, he could see her lights were on from over the road. Keeping low in the hope that whoever it was would eventually give up and leave. He stood on the doorstep, Sunday night revellers barely giving him a glance as they staggered down Crow Road, their attention fixed on the hypnotic flashing blue lights further down where the drugs squad were combing the lodge. His lodge!

'Fuck's sake!' The profanity was a prayer, fervently spoken to the warm, summer night. Peter wasn't expecting the universe to answer, although even a gambler on a losing streak has that small sliver of hope that the odds must move in their direction eventually. The blue strobes mocked him, his last, desperate attempt to regain his fortune lay under the analytical eye of the police.

'Lost yer key, mate?'

Peter spun around in shock, expecting to feel the heavy hand of an arresting officer land on his shoulder. The words were accompanied by stale breath, unpleasantly scented with cigarettes and beer. A middle-aged man was standing patiently behind him with the air of someone whose journey through life hadn't been kind. He had a premature stoop, a body worn down by the effort of living. His eyes were kind, though, recognising something in Peter that spoke of a shared suffering.

'Aye. My girlfriend's on the top floor. Doorbell's fucked.' Peter extemporised, focussed on a key held ready for the lock. He stood to one side, allowing access to the front door. The answer came as a nod, a philosophical acceptance that everything and everyone eventually meets the same fate as the doorbell.

'Landlord never fixes anything.' He held the door until Peter had entered, then selected another key to a ground floor flat and left Peter standing next to the mailboxes in the shared entrance hallway. Timed lights illuminated a staircase leading to the next floors.

Peter climbed the stairs with the same hope that those on Jacob's ladder held in their hearts. Absolution, an escape from Hell. Only Jade had the power to cast him down. She'd played her card, now she had to die.

He knocked gently on Lauren's door, heard uncertain steps approach.

'Who is it?' Her nervousness was evident.

'Peter McKinnon. If you ever want to see Jade alive again, you'd better let me in.' He smiled to himself, twisting the logic behind the purpose of his visit in the knowledge that this would make her open the door. Only Jade held the key to her mother's heart.

He pushed the door as soon as it began to open, forcing Lauren backwards into the mean little hall.

'Tell me where your daughter is.'

Lauren backed away from him with her hands covering her mouth as if that would stop any words from escaping. He pushed her so violently she almost flew into the sitting room, staggering off balance and collapsing into the nearest chair to avoid falling to the floor.

'I don't know where she is...'

A violent slap stopped her words more effectively.

'I haven't time, Lauren. And I haven't anything to lose. You either tell me where she is or I'm going to beat it out of you.' His thin lips curled into a malicious smile. 'Now where is she?'

Lauren's frightened eyes begged him not to strike her again. Her hand touched her cheek, feeling the tears falling.

'I really don't know. I've been trying to find her. There's a PI looking for her.'

Peter McKinnon dropped his arm before it completed the swing towards her head.

'What PI?' The memory of the two characters who'd turned up on his doorstep came back into focus.

'Teàrlach. Teàrlach Paterson. He said he'd find her for me.' The words came between sobs. 'I just want my girl back.'

Peter regarded her without compassion. The PI nosing around was potentially a problem bigger than Jade Martin. He was inclined to believe her. Lauren Martin didn't have the mental capacity to come up with an excuse like this under duress. He considered killing her, wrapping the flex from the standard lamp around her neck and pulling with all his strength. It would make him feel better, but given the way everything was going wrong for him, it may just mean a longer prison sentence – and he needed to avoid prison. Other people were sent down – the poor, the immigrants. Not people like him. He was meant to be immune.

'You've no idea where she's gone?'

Lauren shook her head so hard that tears flew across the floor.

'I've not been here. You understand?'

Lauren looked at him with the first glimmer of hope that she might survive this encounter.

'No. I've not seen you. I promise.'

He felt sick looking at her hopeful, tear-stained face, aged with cigarettes and worry.

'Fuck's sake!' He slammed the door behind him. The sound of her sobs diminished by the time he was down a flight. *That much closer to hell,* came the unwelcome thought.

Peter McKinnon stood on the doorstep and pulled the door shut, leaving hope behind him in the stale shared hallway and sagging mailboxes. The Crow Road was indifferent to the approaching midnight, to the vultures circling around his head. His eyes were drawn upwards to the night sky, to a full moon dressed in tattered clouds. He hardly ever looked skywards and found the novelty of moon and stars a welcome diversion to a consideration of bankruptcy and imprisonment.

He was running out of options. If Jade couldn't be found, then she could testify that he was behind the drugs factory and his fate was sealed. This troublesome PI might have already dug up incriminating evidence. He'd need to kill the lot of them or have Don kill them. But Don wasn't answering his phone.

The thought occurred to him that Don might have already been arrested; he might even be in the interview room now cutting a deal.

Peter needed to run, but all he had was his car and maxed-out credit cards. He returned to his car, sat uselessly in the driving seat until a squad car cruised past. It was only a matter of time – sixteen years to life imprisonment. He'd not survive prison. There was only one option left.

FIFTY-FOUR
PURSUIT

Jade let the video of her father's murder play on her phone for the umpteenth time, watching as he put up no resistance to the blade sliding into his chest. He might as well have welcomed death for all the reaction he gave. He'd been drugged, she could see that clearly now. He had the same slack, expressionless face other users displayed after taking one of Peter's tiny pills. The large, thickset man doing the stabbing was unknown to her. He never looked up the stairs, otherwise she knew she would have died on that day too.

She had a second video, one she'd recorded covertly in the basement of the church when Peter McKinnon and Donald Ritchie gave her another bag of fifty tabs to distribute.

'That's to work off the interest your dad owes me,' Peter had said. 'Sell them at a tenner each. That's £500 you have to make.'

She'd sold them for a lot more, carefully building up a nest egg of her own in case things went bad. Then he'd had her dad murdered and things couldn't have gone any worse. Jade knew Peter had had him killed. It was there in the video – her dad just about capable of standing up, eyes closed as he lived in some drugged dreamworld, the telltale slack features and lack of interest even in his own death. Until the end when he'd opened his eyes and seen her. Only Donald Ritchie had those drugs; Jade sure as hell hadn't left any for her dad to find.

She stood on the Crow Road, seeing the flashing blue lights of the police cars raiding the lodge. Someone had beaten her to it. Peter McKinnon, her dad's murderer and the chemist, Don, would be behind bars soon enough. She still had the evidence of them both in the crypt on her phone, and evidence to clear her brother's name. She dialled the emergency services, asked for the police.

'My name's Jade Martin. I've got evidence linking a man called Peter McKinnon to a drug factory on the Crow Road.'

The operator took it all down without emotion. Asked her where she was, told her to stay there until the police picked her up for her own safety.

'And I've a video of the man who stabbed my dad. It wasn't my brother. He needs to be let out of Barlinnie.'

Jade felt a weight lift off her shoulders. She'd done it. Peter McKinnon and his gang wouldn't be able to touch her or her family now they were locked up, and Logan would be let go. She had proof she had been coerced into selling the drugs for them. Testers, Don had said. Like they were nothing but harmless pills – but she'd seen the state of people after they'd taken them. Zombies looked more human, more alive. And they were as addictive as fuck. She couldn't go back to the clubs she'd already sold them at, otherwise she'd have been mobbed by those wanting a second fix. There was also the danger of another pusher catching her to find out where she'd obtained them – Don had enjoyed explaining how that might turn out for her.

One of the police cars peeled off from the queue parked haphazardly outside the lodge, made for her location and drew up beside her. A window slid down to reveal a solitary plain-clothes cop.

'You Jade Martin?'

She nodded, took a step towards the car.

'Hold on, I'll open the back. You'll be safe there until I take you to the station.'

He climbed out from the driver seat, held open a back door on the pavement side.

'What is it you've got? Control said something about evidence. About your father's death?'

Jade played the video, saw the copper's eyes open wide as the reel unfolded.

'That's enough.' He reached for her phone, and she quickly tucked it into her jacket pocket. Heavy eyebrows drew down in irritation, his eyes swept the vicinity where a few late-night pedestrians took unwelcome interest in what was happening.

He had a strange accent, not entirely Glaswegian. She'd heard something like it before.

'You're Logan's sister, right?'

She felt her throat beginning to tighten.

'Yes.' Her voice came as a squeak.

'You saw your dad being murdered?'

Jade put a memory to the voice, the same as in the video.

'I wasn't. It's not something I remember well. I can't say.' Her words made slow progress through a mouth that had dried and lips that refused to function.

His gaze held hers. He knew she recognised him.

'Get in the back. I'll take you to the station.'

Jade understood only too well what he wanted to do with her, and her phone. She made towards the open door, saw the quiet satisfaction in his face as he reached a hand out to guide her head down. Jade only had the one chance. She kicked the door edge with all her strength, the Doc Martens footwear adding impetus and flinging the door back into the policeman's legs. A solid crack announced the impact of metal against patella, a softer impact followed by a low groan as the door edge caught his groin.

She ran as he doubled up, risking a look behind her and seeing him start to chase after her with a face like thunder. His easy stride collapsed into a hobble as his knee refused to function.

'Fuck!' His voice followed her down the road. She took a side turning, attempting to lose him in the maze of streets heading towards Victoria Park. She couldn't trust the police – not with one of them being her dad's murderer. Jade stopped running and caught her breath. There was no sign of pursuit, yet she knew he'd be searching the streets in his car soon enough. What could she do? Her great plan was to give the evidence to the police, have Peter McKinnon and Don locked safely away and prove Logan's innocence. That plan lay in ruins now her dad's killer was a policeman. She fetched her phone out of her jacket pocket, felt Teàrlach's business card.

It was almost midnight. She didn't dare go home to her mum's and her boyfriend's flat was too far to walk without being seen by the police. She called the number on the card.

'Who is this?' Chloe's panicked voice answered.

'My name's Jade Martin. You have to help me – the polis are looking for me.'

There was a moment of disbelief at the other end of the phone. 'Look, I can't help you right now. Go home to your mum. I have to clear the line – there's an emergency.'

'No! Don't go!' Jade begged. 'I know who killed my dad. It was a policeman. I've got it on video and he's after me. I can't call the polis, or go home – he'll find me.'

* * *

Chloe made a swift calculation. There was nothing more she

could do for Teàrlach and Dee and Jade needed her help. 'Where are you exactly?'

'I don't know. Hang on.' Chloe heard Jade walking a few steps before reading a street name out loud.

'Hide in a front garden or somewhere and look out for me. I'll be in a purple Clio. I'll be there in fifteen minutes.'

Chloe ran out of her flat seconds later, her phone held tightly in one hand in case Teàrlach or Dee tried to make contact. Jade couldn't have picked a worse time to call for help.

FIFTY-FIVE
PAGAN

Teàrlach crept the last few metres towards the mausoleum, alert for any indication that the building was occupied. Silence draped the high point of the Necropolis like a thick shroud, deadening even the continual background hum of the city. He placed a hand on the door to the tomb, strangely comforted to find the surface hard and unyielding when the rest of the world had turned so liminal. If there was a gateway between the worlds of the living and the dead, he was poised at the threshold.

The moon cast its silver light on the Victorian stonework, picking out gothic details carved by stonemasons long since dead. There were the unicorns Chloe had mentioned, rearing each side of the doorway, hooves raised in anger or defiance. An iron ring was set into the oaken door, Teàrlach's hand found it, turned it as gently as he could, pushed against the solid wood with his shoulder and the door opened noiselessly under his weight.

He had been prepared for anything, or so he thought. He entered into a pentangular chamber, moonlight spilling towards the centre of the tomb from five open slits carved into the vaulted ceiling. Dee was held captive in the light, her lifeless body painted white by the cold moon. Five ropes held her upright, tied to gargoyles whose sightless eyes stared from their niches in the walls, malevolent features twisted into evil snarls. Dee's head rested on her chest, red hair spread across her shoulders which he mistook for newly shed blood in the moon's light. Teàrlach's heart stopped at the sight.

'Dee!' Her name caught in his throat. He took faltering steps towards her, eyes fixated on the sight. As his arms reached for her, he saw movement in the shadows. A woman, face hidden in darkness, stepped from behind Dee's upright body. She was dressed strangely – an embroidered cloak hung down to scrape the floor, gold thread weaving geometric patterns. A white apron was fixed to her waist, long, blond hair concealing her features. Her hand stretched in front of her, revealing a vicious long blade caught in the moon's light.

'You profane the holy of holies.'

Teàrlach took an involuntary step back as a man's voice filled the space, his attention fixed on the blade and its closeness to Dee's exposed neck. He swiftly calculated the distance between them, made to lunge forward only for the blade to reach towards her throat.

'Stay where you are!' Teàrlach froze at the command. His eyes tried to pierce the recesses of the tomb where Dee's assailant remained concealed in impenetrable darkness. The moonlight held Dee in its spotlight, shining on the whiteness of her skin. She remained motionless, her head tilted to one side and her red hair spilling over her shoulders. He needed to know if she was alive.

'Have you hurt her? I swear to God I'll kill you if you have.' Teàrlach's threat echoed emptily around the stone walls.

'He can't do anything. Look – it's almost time.'

Teàrlach struggled to see who the Pagan was speaking to,

his attention switching back and forth from the shadows to the knife.

A woman's voice came weakly from the dark. 'I'm here, Donald. I'm ready to join you. Come to your mother.'

'Not yet. It has to be at the right time. Wait for the shadows.'

Teàrlach searched in vain for the other woman, his eyes slowly adjusting to the light. What shadows was he talking about? The knife stayed poised close to Dee's throat, the hand holding it not wavering. He couldn't risk jumping the guy – not with another accomplice hiding nearby. Teàrlach risked a quick look around him.

Dee had been positioned in the centre of a pentagram etched in stone on the tomb floor. He recognised the symbols at each point of the design as being the same as in Willie Warmington's journal. The moon was almost directly overhead, picking the design out in a silver spotlight. With an awful premonition, Teàrlach realised the moonlight shining through the slits in the roof were aligning with the pattern on the floor. Shadows crept inexorably forward with the moon's progress across the sky, leading to the moment when he knew the Pagan would strike.

'Don't do it. She's not done anything to you – you don't need to harm her.' Teàrlach tried reasoning with him, hearing the desperation and pleading in his voice.

'She has to die so Mother can live.' The reply was issued from the shadows. 'This is the final one. My last sacrifice.' His voice was calm, and one Teàrlach remembered from the Freemason lodge.

His eyes searched the dark recesses of the tomb for the other woman. As far as he could make out, there were just the three of them there, caught like actors in a silver spotlight with the clock ticking towards the end.

'Don't pay him any attention, darling,' the softly spoken

woman spoke again. 'I'm almost ready to be made alive once more.'

Teàrlach's suspicions were confirmed as the man moved forward. He saw his lips moving in synchronisation with the woman's voice. He'd had experience in dealing with cold-blooded killers, but this was new. This time he was having to guess the next moves of a psychotic.

Now that the figure had stepped into the moonlight, he could see what he was facing. Even through the wig he could recognise the Freemason he'd met at the Crow Road lodge, his face twisted with insanity. Teàrlach kept his attention focussed on the blade as it drew closer to Dee's neck.

'Don't come any closer or I'll slit her throat.' The blade made contact, leaving a red line across Dee's throat in confirmation of his threat.

Teàrlach held his palms up to show he had no weapon, even as his eyes explored the space to rectify that omission.

'You don't have to hurt her.' Teàrlach spoke gently in an effort to calm the situation. 'Just let her go with me, and I'll not try to stop you.'

'She has to die. Hers is the final sacrifice – the one that brings resurrection.' His eyes flicked upwards to view the moon's progress. 'Only seconds to go.'

Teàrlach took a tentative step closer whilst his adversary was distracted. His foot knocked over a large flask concealed in shadow, the resulting impact on the flagstones sounding loud in the confined space.

The Freemason froze in horror. 'Pick her up. Put her back where she was!' The knife danced erratically around Dee's throat. 'Do it!'

Teàrlach bent down to pick up the container. It was heavy, maybe four kilos or so, and made of china. He realised he was picking up someone's ashes. Was that what this was all about – bringing his mother back from the dead?

'Put her back exactly where she was. There, on top of the pentagram.'

The knife lowered from Dee's throat to point at the patterns carved into the flagstones. Teàrlach risked another look at Dee – her eyes had fluttered open. She was alive! Her captor took a step to the side so he could watch Teàrlach position the urn in the correct location. Teàrlach only had one chance and launched the urn at his opponent's head. His target instinctively ducked, the urn catching him a glancing blow to the temple and knocking him to one side before smashing to pieces against the stone wall. White dust billowed into the moonlight as the contents spread themselves around the confined space.

The Freemason staggered off balance, and Teàrlach sprang from his crouched position headfirst into the man's apron. He heard the blade clatter to the floor as his opponent's head hit the wall with a sickeningly hollow thud. Teàrlach felt the man go limp, making a grab for the knife before he had a chance to recover, and whirled around to face whatever threat he offered. Reassured his opponent wasn't likely to be offering any trouble for a few minutes at least, Teàrlach cut the ropes holding Dee upright and took her weight as she collapsed into his arms.

'I thought you were dead.' He started carrying her towards the door, her head flopping around like a rag doll.

'Don't die that easily.' Dee's voice sounded slurred in his ear. She tried to walk, but her legs had no strength. She coughed as dust filled her nose and throat.

Teàrlach struggled with the door whilst taking Dee's weight. He let the knife fall to the floor so he could hold Dee more easily.

'Hold on. I'll just have to pull this open, and we'll be out.' Teàrlach tugged the iron ring set in the door and felt it pull towards him. Fresh air entered the stone cell, moonlight reflected off stone monuments to the dead. He took a step forward just as he felt a blade pierce his side.

'No! She has to die tonight!' The Pagan crouched, knife now red with Teàrlach's blood.

Teàrlach spun around, pushing Dee out of the mausoleum and onto the path outside. His hand automatically went to his side, felt blood pulsing from a wound. He stood, leaning in the doorway and blocking the Freemason from reaching Dee.

'You're never going to have her.' Teàrlach faced a madman. His unnaturally light eyes catching the moon and reflecting it back from a pale, white face dripping in blood.

'Then you will be the sacrifice.' A hand stretched out to drag him back into the stone cell.

Teàrlach used the last of his strength to pull the hand towards him, lowering his head to butt his opponent hard in the face. He felt a nose break just as a crippling pain caught him in his side. Teàrlach staggered backwards, reaching for the iron ring to pull the door shut, but his hand was slick with blood and slipped off, throwing him off-balance, so he landed heavily outside. He searched desperately for Dee so he could protect her from the malevolent creature coming out of the mausoleum, knife dripping with blood and murder in his eyes. Where was she?

They both saw her at the same time, holding onto the mausoleum wall for support as she dragged herself upright.

'I thought it was me you wanted?' She hardly had the strength to speak.

'Don't go near her!' Teàrlach's threat was ignored. He tried to lever himself off the ground, but his wound opened wider and blood started to soak his clothes. He could feel the world closing in on him and watched powerless as the Freemason made a grab for Dee.

She raised her hand to ward him off, and he laughed in triumph.

'We haven't time for games. Come here, it will be quick, I promise.'

Dee pushed her finger down on the small cylinder she held in her fist, releasing a stream of pepper spray directly into his face. She kept it there long after the spray had finished and he'd blindly felt his way back into the building, screaming in pain.

Teàrlach heard the unmistakable sound of people running up the gravel path towards them. He hoped to hell it was the police. The police and ambulance, he corrected himself before he spiralled into oblivion.

Teàrlach resurfaced, eyes ungluing and then instinctively narrowing against bright lights. His head pounded like the inside of a drum, each beat causing his eyes to involuntarily clench closed against the pain. His stomach reminded him he'd been stabbed, severe cramps competing with his headache for dominance. He struggled to make sense of where he was. His body was being thrown around like a toy in a washing machine, an urgent siren repeated the same klaxon call repeatedly. He couldn't understand why the noise didn't fade away on a doppler shift into the distance where it wouldn't add to his headache.

'You're with us, then?'

Teàrlach forced his eyes open, despite the bright light and the pain. Dee leaned over him, removing an oxygen mask covering her mouth.

'What...?' He only managed the one word before the world turned dark again.

When he next opened his eyes, he knew where he was. There's something instantly recognisable about a hospital – from the hard, white sheets and solid pillows to the comforting regular beeps from monitoring equipment and pervasive smell of disinfectants.

'Hello handsome.' Dee's face swam into focus. The blood had been washed away. Her neck sported a plaster, which she attempted to scratch before gently brushing his hair away from his face.

'What happened?' Teàrlach heard his voice sounding thick and slurred, but at least he managed more than one word.

Dee looked down at him with a thoughtful expression.

'Well, the exciting bit all happened when you decided to take a nap on the ground.'

She waited for a smile and shrugged when it didn't materialise.

'The police came to the rescue,' she answered. 'Took their sweet time about it. Any later and I wouldn't be here.' Dee paused, a rare serious expression flitting across her face as she replayed the events. 'Donald Ritchie took the bait and picked me up. I thought he was a woman, didn't say much and all I saw was the back of her...' She paused, corrected herself. 'His head.'

Dee shook her own head at her stupidity. 'I still set my fail-safe, needed me to touch my screen every two minutes. I thought I was wasting my time with the driver being a woman – what could go wrong?'

Teàrlach remained silent. His free hand explored his midriff, met a bandage where the knife had entered. Out of the corner of his eye, he saw a drip entering his other arm and realised why his movements had been restricted.

'Turned out he had customised his cab. Couple of gas dispensers in the back, hermetically sealed from the driver's side. Door locks that couldn't be overridden. I passed out in less than a minute – took me thirty seconds to realise it wasn't the drink that was slowing me down, but by then it was too late. I came around when he stabbed you. I tried to help, but the gas he used had paralysed me. It was all I could do to pull myself upright.'

She shuddered as she relived the memory.

'When he came for me, I thought, this is it. All I had was a small pepper spray. Just as well it was more potent than the stuff you're allowed to buy.'

'Are you alright?' Teàrlach managed to ask with a tongue that felt double the normal size.

'Me?' Dee indicated herself with surprise. 'Well, apart from being strung up as a sacrificial lamb, inhaling most of his dead mother's ashes and with this cut to my neck, yes. Everything's fine and dandy thank you.'

A nurse bustled in, gave Dee a forbidding look for disturbing her patient and asked Teàrlach how was he feeling.

He made a non-committal remark as she checked his saline drip, frowned again at Dee and warned her she could have two more minutes.

'I'm discharging myself,' she announced. 'They kept me in for observation, but I've been observed enough. Your head's fine by the way, despite the white bandage around it.'

'I know. Nothing in there anyway.' Teàrlach attempted a joke through the pain.

'Quite,' Dee agreed. 'And he managed to slice up your intestines but no major organs. He's dead, by the way.' She looked into his eyes from a short distance away. 'Had something more powerful than the knockout gas in there with him and used it when the police arrived.'

'Right! He needs to be left in peace. I have to ask you to leave.' The nurse had returned, armed with a new bottle of saline.

'I've brought you a present.' Dee left a book on his bedside table. 'Blake's rarer poetry.' She kissed him gently on his cheek, then turned away.

Teàrlach's smile remained for so long after she'd left that he wondered if some of that paralysing gas still remained on her breath.

FIFTY-SIX
PENULTIMATE

Chloe slowed down once she reached the street where Jade had said she was hiding, eyes scanning both sides of the road for any sign of the girl. There'd been no more contact from Teàrlach or Dee since the last panicked conversation, and she was desperate to drive to the Necropolis – but first she had to make sure Jade was safe. She couldn't even call the police without knowing how many of them were involved with Peter McKinnon. The city was quiet this time of morning, holding its breath for the day to come.

She pulled into the side of the road when she had driven the entire length, parking under a streetlight so Jade could see she was on her own. A close-shaven head raised cautiously from behind a privet hedge and made towards the car.

Chloe wound down her window, beckoned her urgently to join her. 'It's me, Chloe.'

Jade's frightened expression turned into one of relief and she ran to the car.

'Thank fuck! The bastard was chasing me. We have to get away from here.'

Chloe checked the girl next to her for any injuries, she

seemed to be all right. There still hadn't been anything from Teàrlach and Dee.

'Where can I take you?'

Jade bit her lip, glanced anxiously at Chloe. 'I can't go home – it's the first place they'll look.'

'OK. I'm driving to the Necropolis. My friends are in trouble, and there should be a load of police there.' She saw Jade's shocked expression, interrupted her before she could object. 'They aren't all going to be working for Peter McKinnon. I'll make sure you're safe.'

Jade didn't look convinced, but there was nothing else for it.

'Who is it that's after you?' Chloe kept her talking as she drove, the main roads thankfully free of traffic.

'I don't know his name. I filmed him killing my dad – forcing Logan to knife him as well. He said he was a cop and would kill us all if Logan didn't say he killed Dad.'

'Why didn't you tell the truth? If you had it on your camera, Logan wouldn't have had to go to prison.'

Jade sniffed, wiping her eyes with the back of her hand. 'I didn't know I had it on my camera until after. Then it was too late. They had Logan locked up and I couldn't protect him.'

Chloe concentrated on the route, joining the same roads Teàrlach had followed almost two hours ago.

'Why didn't you know? You filmed it, right?'

Another sniff answered her. 'I tried one of the tablets I was selling for them. Half a tablet,' she corrected. 'I was spaced out – didn't know what was happening. I don't even remember having my phone. If he'd looked up and seen me...'

Chloe joined the motorway, floored it so the Clio speedometer made slow progress towards seventy.

'You could still have gone to the police when you found the video.' She checked her phone, still no contact.

'Yeah, but I wanted them all locked up so me and my mum

were safe. That's why I offered to work for them so I could get evidence. I've got enough to put them all away.'

The Necropolis was surrounded by flashing blue lights as they approached; traffic cops signalling for them to take another road.

'I'm working for Teàrlach Paterson. He's up there trying to rescue Dee Fairlie. Are they all right?' Chloe realised she sounded panicky.

'Wait here.' The cop spoke to someone on the radio, beckoned them to pull into a cordoned-off area. Jade looked like she was about to run for it.

'You're OK. I'm here with you.' Chloe attempted to sound calm when every fibre in her was stretched to breaking.

A plainclothes cop tapped on the window making Chloe jump out of her seat. 'Who are you?'

Chloe explained, telling them that Jade had filmed her father's murder and then Peter McKinnon in his drugs factory. The cop demanded to see the video, his eyes widening as the clips played.

'We're taking you to the station. I'll need a full statement from you both.' He pulled open Chloe's door, motioned for a traffic cop to come over.

'I'm not going anywhere until I know what's happened to Teàrlach and Dee.' Chloe sat resolutely in the driving seat, refusing to budge.

'He's your boss, right?'

Chloe didn't trust her voice so nodded.

'They're both in hospital. Your man's been stabbed, the redhead's been drugged, but they're going to make it.'

Chloe gave thanks to a god she no longer believed in. 'OK, we're staying together, though.'

. . .

By midday, the police had all they needed. Chloe and Jade were escorted to the station car park where her purple Clio sat amongst a sea of patrol cars.

'I'll take you home.'

Lauren and Jade clasped each other so tightly they might have been one person. Jade's mum was waiting on the pavement as they arrived, pulling Jade towards her and crying with relief at the return of her daughter.

'I thought he'd killed you,' she managed eventually. 'I never thought I'd see you again.'

'I'm sorry, Mum. For everything. It's my fault.'

'Don't be daft, lass. How can any of this be your fault?' Lauren turned a tear-streaked face towards Chloe. 'Thanks so much for finding her and bringing her home. I can't ever thank you enough. And the police said Logan will be released. It's a miracle.'

Jade's wet eyes met with Chloe's. 'Thanks,' she managed.

Chloe shrugged with embarrassment. 'All part of the job.' She saw the guilt in Jade's eyes, tried not to read anything into it.

'I'll be off, then. Have to visit Teàrlach in hospital.'

They were still holding onto each other as Chloe made her way back to the car, turned the wheel towards the hospital. She hadn't driven for more than a few minutes when her phone rang, unknown caller displayed on the car hands-free screen.

'Hi, Chloe, it's me. Can you pick me up from the hospital?'

FIFTY-SEVEN
POSTSCRIPT

'You be careful now!' Mags admonished from behind the bar, her face full of concern as she caught Teàrlach holding his side.

'I will,' he answered. Teàrlach saw through the makeup, her skin an unhealthy shade of grey, the pain evident in her eyes. He didn't know what else to say. Mags was near the end. It showed in the way she held onto the bar for support, collapsed onto a bar stool at every opportunity, her shortness of breath. How could no one else see she was dying?

'You look after yourself too.' His words sounded empty.

She arched an eyebrow at him, gave a thin smile of dismissal.

Teàrlach carried a tray of drinks back to his table, ignoring the sharp pain from his side and fixing his sights on the redhead with her back to him. The pub was unnaturally quiet, even the TVs had been muted.

'I could have fetched the drinks!' Chloe scolded. 'You're not meant to be doing any lifting.'

'I can manage a tray of drinks.' He slowly sat down, holding his breath to avoid the telltale intake of air as the pain stabbed in his side like a replay.

'Here's to us.' Dee held up her glass.

They joined in the toast, Chloe deliberately keeping her glass low off the table, so Teàrlach didn't have to stretch. The glasses met with a dulled chime, and they sipped their drinks, each lost in contemplation.

'I never thanked you, Chloe.' Dee's face held an uncharacteristically serious expression. 'If you hadn't worked out where I was, I don't think either of us would be here.'

'Don't be daft!' Chloe shot back.

'No, she's right.' Teàrlach raised his eyes from a contemplation of his pint. 'We both owe you.'

'All part of the job.' Chloe spoke quietly, clearly embarrassed. 'If anything, I should have been there instead of staying safely at home.'

'Then Jade would have been killed that night as well.' He switched his attention to Dee. 'You could have been killed.'

'I wasn't!' she shot back. 'And we took that homicidal maniac off the streets.'

'So, all of those murders were to bring back his dead mother?' Chloe asked.

'It worked for St Mungo according to the illustrated manuscript they kept at the lodge.' Teàrlach lifted his pint glass, took another sip. He used his left hand, his right hand lying clenched on the tabletop.

'Although that was a robin, this was more ambitious,' Teàrlach continued. 'All I know is that no one's sad he's dead.'

'His mum,' Dee volunteered.

'Aye. Maybe,' Teàrlach reluctantly acknowledged.

'I think he was trying to raise the old gods,' Dee said. 'That medieval manuscript described the gods people worshipped before Christianity. He was offering sacrifices to them all, finishing with the moon goddess.'

Silence followed her pronouncement.

'Is Logan going to be released?' Chloe kept the conversation going.

Teàrlach shrugged. 'He should be. Jade's video evidence was clear enough.'

'I still don't understand why she didn't go to the police in the first place, or why the detective killed Logan's dad.' Chloe frowned as she spoke.

Teàrlach sipped his beer, wondered when the pain would ease in his side. The tablets he'd been given only numbed it, didn't take it away. He thought of Jade and the fentanyl tablets she sold; he could have done with a few himself.

'She couldn't go to the police. Not straight away. She knew it was a policeman who murdered her dad, so how could she trust them? Added to that, she was as high as a kite on the drugs she was selling when it all happened.'

'And she wanted to put Peter McKinnon away so he couldn't threaten them anymore, and she needed evidence for that. Except we told the police before she did,' Dee added.

'Hope they put him away for a long time,' Chloe said bitterly. 'They will, won't they?' She directed this at Teàrlach.

Teàrlach reached for his side, noticed both women watching him keenly and replaced his hand on the table. 'He'll go for plea bargaining. There's enough incriminating evidence on his hard drive to pin the lot on him. I think he'll call Donald Ritchie out for the murders of the Warmingtons and John Jenkins for Keith's murder as well if it shaves a few years off his sentence.'

'It's a bit Agatha Christie, isn't it? Having a policeman kill Keith Martin?' Chloe made the observation without humour.

'He was on the list of breakaway Freemasons, and another member of Peter McKinnon's childhood gang. I think he was in on the drugs manufacture, kept an eye out for them so they could operate safely.'

'Aye, but why not have Don kill Keith?' Chloe pursued her

line of questioning. 'He'd drugged him, he lived a few doors down. Why risk bringing someone else in?'

Dee jumped in to answer. 'Simple – because Donald would have wrapped him up in rope like he did with the Warmingtons. He'd have brought too much attention if there was even a hint of a connection between the two neighbours – and Peter McKinnon needed him to manufacture the fentanyl. Besides, John Jenkins was already involved since he'd covered up the full details about the Warmingtons' deaths and Peter knew he was a sadistic killer. If Keith had gone to the police like he threatened, then John Jenkins would have been under investigation.'

'Why didn't Jenkins run instead of sitting in his car until they found him?' Chloe worried at the case like a dog with a bone.

'He knew the game was up once he'd lost Jade. She had the evidence, and he probably knew Peter McKinnon would throw them all under the bus to try and save himself. Shame he didn't have the guts to kill himself.' Dee downed her drink in one.

'You can't be sure he was intending to do that.' Teàrlach lifted his pint with his right hand, grimaced and replaced it back on the table. 'Just because they found him parked at the docks – doesn't mean he was thinking of driving off the quayside.'

Dee exchanged a look with Chloe.

'Well, at least Jade's back with her mum,' Chloe said brightly. 'And Lauren gets to keep the money from the house sale. So it's not all bad news.'

'And Nicole Martin's happy with the file we gave her. Logan's been exonerated as far as she's concerned,' Dee added. 'She's given us all free vouchers for a week's boarding at the kennels.'

'Not much use as none of us have a bloody dog,' Teàrlach's tone darkened.

Chloe had another attempt to lighten the mood. 'I heard the illustrated manuscript they found at the Crow Road lodge is going to the National Museum. Meant to be the first ten pages from the Book of Kells – been missing since forever. Some expert on the news says it's the first written record of Scottish religious beliefs predating Christianity. They think they were deliberately torn out by monks as blasphemous. God knows how they ended up with Peter McKinnon, passed down through generations of Freemasons, I guess. Apparently, it's worth a tidy sum – more than he would have made from his drug manufacturing by all accounts. They're talking millions.'

'Aye, and because the stupid bastard set up a drugs factory in the crypt, the police can take it all as proceeds of crime. He could have cleared all of his debts and had plenty left over to start again.' Teàrlach shook his head in disbelief.

'So that's it? Case closed?' Chloe asked expectantly.

'Aye. Case closed,' Teàrlach responded without enthusiasm.

Chloe stood. 'My round.' She took the tray off to the bar.

* * *

'I thought we'd lost you.' Dee had waited until Chloe was out of earshot, staring deep into Teàrlach's eyes. They were sitting so close together that she could see the bruising on his forehead underneath the tousled hair.

'I thought we'd lost *you*,' he repeated. 'I couldn't have lived with another death on my conscience.'

His left hand sought hers, held her in a grip so tight she wanted to pull her hand away or cry out in pain – except she squeezed back with all her might.

'Ahem.' Chloe coughed discreetly. 'Here's your drinks.'

They moved apart from each other, both embarrassed to have been caught. Chloe looked on with amusement.

'Nothing wrong in holding onto your knight in shining armour,' she said.

Dee laughed. 'More like Sleeping Beauty than a knight. He spent more time unconscious during my rescue than awake.'

She went to give him a playful dig in the ribs, remembering just in time before she made contact with his wound.

'Aye, well.' Teàrlach finished his drink.

Dee met his eyes. His father was dead, his side was still giving him pain, but he'd never looked so happy as he did there in that brief moment in a quiet Glasgow pub.

A LETTER FROM THE AUTHOR

Thanks so much for reading *Silent Ritual*. If you want to join other readers in hearing all about my new releases, you can sign up for my newsletter here.

www.stormpublishing.co/andrew-james-greig

Please consider leaving a review. This can help new readers discover a book you've enjoyed and gives us all a big boost!

I decided to set this book in the gritty urban city of Glasgow. A serial killer is always a fascinating character to deal with, and it's the motivation behind such crimes that Teàrlach has to understand to have any chance of saving the victims. Is this essentially a story about love or the absence of love? Can anyone commit unspeakable acts if the reward is sufficient?

I very much look forward to sharing my next book with you. You can peer under this author's bonnet at:

andrewjgreig.wordpress.com

facebook.com/andrewjamesgreig
x.com/AndrewJamesGre3
instagram.com/andrew_james_greig
tiktok.com/@andrewjamesgreig
mastodon.scot/@ajg

ACKNOWLEDGEMENTS

My thanks to Claire Bord and the team at Storm Publishing for their hard work, expertise and enthusiasm; my family and friends for their support and encouragement, especially Shona. Special thanks to the reviewers, bloggers and everyone who makes the publishing industry work and most important of all to you, the reader.

Printed in Great Britain
by Amazon

54647097R00189